SINNERS
NEVER SLEEP

SINNERS
NEVER SLEEP

Leigh McKnight

URBAN BOOKS
www.urbanbooks.net

This is a work of fiction. Any references or similarities to actual events, real people, living or dead, or to real locales are intended to give the novel a sense of reality. Any similarity in other names, characters, places, and incidents is entirely coincidental.

URBAN SOUL is published by

Urban Books
1199 Straight Path
West Babylon, NY 11704

ISBN-13: 978-1-59983-065-0
ISBN-10: 1-59983-065-5

First Printing: October 2009
10 9 8 7 6 5 4 3 2 1

Printed in the United States of America

SINNERS
NEVER SLEEP

1

"God, when did it all happen? When did my life change so much?"

On her front porch, in an old rocking chair, with her long legs stretched out in front of her, Rayanne Wilson sat and contemplated the last few years of her life. It was strange how things turned out. One day, she was living in New York, the city that never sleeps, enjoying a life few could only dream of—a young, successful, and wealthy playwright, with most of her plays performed on Broadway to sold-out crowds. A celebrity and a socialite, she found her life and her exploits not only chronicled in well-known black publications, but in the national and international mainstream press as well. In her private life, she was deeply in love with Ralph, the handsome, sophisticated man of her dreams, even though he was ten years her senior. And then, she was caring for her elderly parents back home in Sumter, a small South Carolina city where most of the residents were in bed by midnight. The comparison was stark. She hadn't realized giving up her life in New York, at the peak of her writing career, to move back into the family home after her father's second heart attack meant that she would be taking on the responsibility for everyone living there, putting their needs before her own.

Absentmindedly, she sighed and ran her fingers through her thick sable hair while staring across the lush, deep forest green lawn, illuminated by the quickly approaching twilight.

In the eight years since returning to South Carolina, after witnessing the death of both parents, she had taken up the role of caretaker for the remaining family members, filling her parents' shoes, left empty by their deaths. The youngest of six siblings, Rayanne had become many things to many people. To her brother Josh, two years her senior, who still refused to admit or accept he was an alcoholic, even though he'd been in and out of more substance abuse centers and programs than she cared to remember, she was an unlicensed nurse. Each time she was forced to have Josh involuntarily committed for treatment, her mother had piled on the guilt. Adding more fuel to the already unbearable emotional fire that Rayanne was saddled with, when her mother died, she never forgave Rayanne for Josh's alcoholism.

To Jeremy, her eldest sister Lila's son, and his daughter, Charlotte, nicknamed "Swan" because of her gracefulness, she became their mother when Lila directed her bitterness for Jeremy's father to her son and grandchild.

For a while, Rayanne felt she was victim to horrible, uncontrollable circumstances that had turned her life inside out. So much so, in fact, she found herself spending an hour on a therapist's couch once, sometimes twice, a month, trying to get a handle on all the complex emotions that assaulted her. She felt anger at Josh and her deceased mother, sadness for her sister's illness, hope for Jeremy and Swan, grief for her parents' passing, and a mixture of depression and grief for her former life. She battled with feelings of being overwhelmed while caring for others and resentment of not getting her own needs met. Her therapist, her family, a lot of prayer, and the love of a good man helped her work through her feelings and enabled her to build a life that encompassed all the good things from her glory days in New York and home in South Carolina. As she sat rocking back and forth on her front porch, she continued reflecting on her incredible journey.

2

It was the first autumn since Rayanne's return home. She'd almost forgotten how beautiful South Carolina was during the fall. She passed the time by taking long walks, driving through the country and marveling at the wonders of nature's majesty. The leaves on the trees in the woods glowed in bursts of red, gold, and green in the late-afternoon sun, and those leaves falling to the ground showered the earth after each gentle breeze passed through them. Looking out over the fields, she enjoyed the beauty and the accompanying tranquility. She took a breath of crisp, clean country air, and New York seemed so far away.

Rayanne enjoyed the way people at home greeted one another with a smile, a nod, or a friendly wave of the hand, while New Yorkers concentrated more on what they were doing and where they were going. Being home again made Rayanne really appreciate Southern hospitality.

Rayanne was now in her early thirties, living back home with her parents, and although unmarried and childless, she was deeply in love. She couldn't stop thinking about Ralph, her New York love, and she was excited about his upcoming trip to Sumter. It'd been nearly two months since she'd seen him and she missed him terribly.

* * *

"You've been on my mind constantly, honey," Rayanne said when Ralph called to say he'd be in Sumter on Friday. One of the things Rayanne missed most when she moved back to South Carolina was not seeing Ralph almost daily. "And I can't wait to see you."

"You sure I can't persuade you to come back to New York with me? It's a different world here without you," Ralph said.

"It's not easy for me, either, baby, but you do understand that I need to be here, don't you?"

"Call me selfish, but I'm a man in love and I need my woman here with me," Ralph answered, still not pleased that Rayanne hadn't accepted his marriage proposal and had left him behind.

"Honey, we went through all of this before I left. Besides, we can see each other often. You can fly here, or me there."

Ralph arrived on Friday. Rayanne picked him up at the Columbia Airport and their first stop was at a hotel, where they spent the night, making love and catching up. The following day, Rayanne took him to Swan Lake, one of Sumter's premier recreational spots. The garden was beautiful, the air laced with the scent of magnolias and yellow jasmine. As they walked, circling around the lake, they took advantage of every secluded place they came across to duck into and make out like lovestruck teenagers. Every time Rayanne looked into Ralph's eyes, she saw the love he had for her. As he held her, touched her, she marveled at the fire he ignited in her.

During his visit, Ralph met Aunt Bessie. She liked him but told Rayanne later that he was a rascal. He had that look in his eyes, she'd said. Rayanne was struck by her aunt's remark, because it was the same warning others who had met Ralph had said.

At the end of Ralph's visit, he and Rayanne stood facing each other at the airport as sadness overwhelmed her. "I don't want you to go," she said.

"And I don't want to leave you," he said. "I know you love your family and want to be here for them, but do you really believe that after the excitement of New York, this will be enough? I love you, Rayanne, and I miss holding you in my arms every night, but I want you to be happy."

"I'm missing you already," Rayanne said, resting her head on his chest.

After one last kiss and one last embrace, he was gone. They'd crammed a lot into Ralph's short stay and it had been an enjoyable visit, but a much too short one.

The following months, Rayanne and Ralph visited often and experienced sad good-byes. After driving back home after one of Ralph's trips to see her, Rayanne stood on her front porch and looked at her watch. Ralph should be home in New York by now. She wandered across the yard, lost in the memory of Ralph's kisses.

"Rayanne, telephone," her mother called out to her from the side door.

Rayanne rushed across the yard and raced into the house. It must be Ralph! She took the phone from her mother, kissing her on the cheek.

"Hello!"

"Girl, I'm getting married!"

She swallowed her disappointment—it was her good friend Ivory, from New York. "Hey, Ivory, girl, what's up?"

"I just told you," Ivory said with mock sarcasm. "I'm getting married," she repeated with laughter filling her voice.

"You're lying," Rayanne said, happiness for her friend overriding her yearning for Ralph.

"No, Desmond and I are getting married in June, and, of course, you and Dorian are going to help me plan my wedding."

"You better believe we are. You go get married without consulting us, and Desmond will be spending his honeymoon by your bedside in ICU, Ms. Thang," Rayanne joked.

"Oh, putting me in ICU because I didn't consult you about my wedding," Ivory chuckled. "I'm the bride-to-be and you're the one most likely to become the prima donna. Well, I've got lots to do, but I'll get back to you later. Desmond just asked me and I just had to tell you first."

Rayanne hung up, wishing for one crazy moment that it were she and Ralph getting married. But when she thought of Ralph settling down in the madness that was her life, filled with endless family members, her heart broke. That definitely wasn't Ralph's scene. He loved her, would come to her on countless visits, but she couldn't see him giving up New York City for the slow pace of country life in South Carolina.

Time passed quickly with Ivory and Dorian making frequent trips to South Carolina, as well as Rayanne going to New York where they spent numerous hours working out the details of Ivory's wedding back in South Carolina. On the day of the blessed event, Ivory was an exquisite bride in her white Dior gown, with its twenty-foot train. Dorian and Rayanne were maids of honor, and as Ivory repeated her vows, Rayanne looked over at Ralph. Although his hair was graying at the temples, and his hairline receding a little, he was still the most handsome man there. She tried to catch his eye, to smile at him. Was it her imagination or was Ralph avoiding eye contact with her? As a matter of fact, for most of the wedding, he looked a little uncomfortable. Later, though, when he came up to her and whispered, "I love you," her apprehension melted as he kissed her, and then led her away from the others.

Ralph's kiss had been magical the first night they'd kissed, and it still was.

Within a year, Ivory gave birth to a beautiful baby girl, Stephanie Lynn, who was christened and blessed with two godmothers, Rayanne and Dorian, but the year that followed didn't produce a husband or child for Rayanne. Let alone an engagement ring.

The distance between Rayanne and Ralph had increased not only geographically, but in their relationship. After he didn't make the trip to her parents Helen and Raymond's fiftieth wedding anniversary celebration, it was a sign of the first of many disappointments to come, due to her choice to move back to Sumter.

In the ten years that Rayanne and Ralph had been together, he'd been devoted to her. He'd always been dependable, now that was changing. She'd hoped the old adage "Absence makes the heart grow fonder" would hold true in her case. But absence certainly wasn't making Ralph's heart grow fonder. In fact, he'd missed his last two promised visits, and Rayanne wanted answers. She decided that if Mohammed wouldn't come to the mountain, the mountain would be on the next flight to see Mohammed.

Her plane arrived at LaGuardia Airport late in the afternoon. She took a taxi to Ralph's apartment, and let herself in with her key. Just as she finished her shower, she heard his key in the lock.

"Hello," Ralph called out. He'd obviously seen her jacket hanging over the back of the couch.

"Hello," she replied.

"Who's there?" he teased.

"Why don't you come and find out."

Ralph entered his bedroom and rushed over to embrace Rayanne, but not before she caught him quickly scanning the room. She pushed what she saw out of her mind once she felt the heat of his hand caressing her body and the passion of his hot kisses trailing down her throat. Oh, she had some questions for Ralph and she wanted answers, but tomorrow was another day and those questions could wait. Tonight would belong only to them.

Rayanne woke up alone the next morning. She got out of bed, pulling off the well-used sheets, dropping them on the floor as she replaced them with fresh sheets. While picking up the soiled sheets, she noticed a dusty condom wrapper on the floor slightly hidden by the dresser. Rayanne was stunned. After the initial shock, everything that happened that past year now made sense. Ralph was seeing another woman. No wonder he made fewer trips to South Carolina. His needs were being met in New York. In the very bed where they'd spent the night. Only, she hadn't expected to find out this way, if at all.

Rayanne finished making the bed and then went to retrieve a blouse that she'd hung in his closet the night before. As she reached to pull it out, something else caught her eye. It was the scarf that she'd misplaced, the one she didn't like very much, but she didn't remember wearing that scarf to Ralph's home. And why hadn't he returned it to her?

Ralph returned with groceries and poked his head into the bedroom, looking for Rayanne, but she wasn't there.

Moments later, she returned, wearing running clothes, sweat glistening over her body.

"There you are." He walked over and kissed her.

"Miss me?" She eased out of his arms.

"Where did you go?" he asked.

"I went for a run."

"I wasn't sure what to think when I came back and found you gone."

"I'm here now," she said. "I need to get cleaned up. I'll be out in a few minutes." She headed toward the bathroom.

"May I join you?" He reached out and caught her hand.

"Why don't you finish up here?" She nodded to the food he was about to prepare for breakfast. "The sooner I get back, the sooner we can eat."

She left the room with a stunned Ralph staring after her.

As she undressed, she had to admit she was experiencing an emotion that she hadn't dealt with much in the past. Jealousy. She was feeling jealousy toward some woman who was screwing her man, and she didn't like it.

She showered and changed. When she returned, Ralph was sitting at the table waiting for her.

"Something smells good," she said.

"Was it something I said?" he asked, looking at her.

"What?" Rayanne sat down across from him.

"Did I do or say something to upset you?"

"Why would you say that?"

"Well, something has changed since last night."

"I'm just a little tired, I suppose," she lied.

"Are you sure that's all it is?"

She smiled, stood up, and leaned over the table. "What else could it be? Now come here, you." She caught him by his ears and pulled him to her until their lips met.

Ralph had slept with another woman. It had happened and there wasn't a thing she could do about it. She wasn't going to return to New York City permanently. Maybe it was best this way. Just enjoy their moments, be glad he used protection with the other woman, and stop investing in him emotionally. As easily as she'd fallen in love with Ralph, she planned to fall out of love with Ralph.

Right.

They spent the next couple of days in each other's arms, shutting out the rest of the world, and they were ecstatic. When it was time for them to part, Rayanne wondered who Ralph would be sleeping with that night and the nights afterward. Her flight back home was anything but a happy one.

Rayanne picked up her car from the long-term parking lot at the airport and was driving home when she saw several police cars, lights flashing and sirens wailing. As she passed by, she saw three young black males, handcuffed, and being herded toward the police cars. She wondered what had happened. Whatever it was, it was serious.

Rayanne arrived home and carried her bags inside. She was tired; her shoulders were knotted and tense. She looked out the kitchen window and saw her father unloading firewood from the back of his truck.

"How are you, Mama?" Rayanne put her bags down and hugged her mother as she entered the kitchen.

"You're home," Helen said, releasing Rayanne. "How was your trip?"

"It was good. Is that Josh in there?" Rayanne asked, looking into the den.

"Yeah, Beverly kicked him out again," Helen said, taking a pan of biscuits from the oven. "We gon' let him stay here till he gets hisself straight."

"Oh, Mama," Rayanne said.

The last time that happened, Josh stayed more than six months, and when he left, Rayanne had to replace the mattresses and the carpet in that bedroom because Josh urinated all over the place.

"Honey, it won't be long," Helen said, seeming to read Rayanne's mind.

"Whatever, Mama."

Rayanne picked up her bags and began walking toward her room. She just didn't have the energy to deal with her mother's denial of Josh and his drinking problem today. Knowledge of Ralph's infidelity was already negatively monopolizing her life.

3

Two years after returning to South Carolina, Rayanne had decided to go back to school. She enrolled, and not only did she find the courses challenging and stimulating, but she met two women, Brenda and Hilary, who were close to her age. Brenda, who was separated from her husband, Cardell, had two teenage sons. Hilary and her husband, Ben, had a ten-year-old adopted daughter. The three women quickly struck up a friendship. Rayanne felt as though they'd always been friends.

After classes one day, Rayanne shared with Brenda and Hilary what occurred on her last visit with Ralph.

"At least the son of a bitch is playing it safe," Brenda said, reminding Rayanne of Ivory. "But you need to drop his ass. He is just going to continue cheating on you while the two of you are apart, and screwing you when you come to visit. I know you love him, but if he loved you, he wouldn't be screwing another woman."

Rayanne politely listened to Brenda and Hilary's advice, but she was still torn. Before they went their separate ways, Rayanne pulled tickets from her purse. "My brother's base-ball club is having their annual banquet the last Saturday night in the month. I've got tickets, if you can make it," she offered.

"I'm up for it," Brenda said. "I don't have anything else going on."

"I'll have to pass. My daughter Jessica has her dance recital that night," Hilary said.

"No problem," Rayanne said, handing a ticket to Brenda.

The drive home gave Rayanne time to think about Brenda's advice. Then she pushed it aside to focus on some exercises that were covered in class and she made mental notes of questions she'd ask in the next class. On her arrival home, she found her father in the yard, working. He looked tired.

"Hey, Daddy," she said.

Raymond looked up from the paint can. "How you doing, daughter?"

"I'm well, but what about you? What are you doing?"

"I'm mixing up some paint. Old Miss Jamison had a grease fire in her kitchen yesterday and the walls got messed up some, mostly behind the stove. I done replaced all the bad wood, but now I wanna get that painting done or she'll worry herself to death." Raymond looked at Rayanne. "How are your classes going?"

"The classes are fine, but I'm worried about you, Daddy. Why are you doing all of this yourself?"

"You know what they say. If you want somethin' done right, you gotta do it yourself."

"Where is Josh?" she asked, and Raymond pointed toward the house.

Josh had an engineering degree, and Rayanne knew he could do a little carpentry and painting work, but it didn't take long for her to know why Josh couldn't do that job, or any other job at that time.

Rayanne entered the house and found her mother folding

clothes in the den, but Josh was nowhere in sight. "You're home early," Helen said.

"The instructor left sick and they canceled my last class."

"It's good to see you home early for a change."

"Mama, where is Josh?" Rayanne asked.

"He's in his room, drunk. I'm telling you, Rayanne, somethin' gotta be done," she said, shaking her head.

Rayanne couldn't agree more. Before class the next morning, she obtained information from a local rehab center on their AA program, which she reviewed with Josh once she got home. He agreed it was the best course of action for him and he promised he'd go every day. They both knew AA had astounding success turning alcoholics' lives around, and Josh hoped that with the treatment he could put his life back together.

Four days before the winter school break began, Rayanne came in from class and found several messages: Aunt Bessie needed to see her, and her agent, Greg, couldn't get a buyer for her last play. And there was a message from Ivory. She always brightened when she heard Ivory's voice. She was the one person who could always cheer her up. She dialed Ivory's number, expecting to have her mood lifted.

"Rayanne, it's Dorian," Ivory said, sounding tired.

"Dorian? What's wrong with her?" Rayanne asked, alarmed.

"She's doing coke again, and I can't seem to reach her anymore," Ivory said, frustrated.

"I'll be on the first flight out tomorrow," Rayanne vowed. "And get some rest. You sound tired."

"Don't you have classes?"

"One class tomorrow, but I can make that up later."

"Okay. I'll see you tomorrow then. Thanks, Rayanne."

"No problem. I love her, too."

"You'd better let Ralph know you're coming, so there won't be any more surprises waiting for you." Ivory chuckled.

"Forget you." Rayanne laughed.

"Aren't you planning to see him?"

"I will if I have time. If I don't, it won't make that much difference, will it?"

"I'm scareda you," Ivory said, and they chuckled.

Rayanne returned her Aunt Bessie's call, and on her drive over to Bessie's house, the dark sky and low-hanging clouds foretold of a major storm threatening to unleash its ugly fury. It was mild in comparison, though, to what Rayanne felt when she saw her aunt Bessie and learned that Bessie's son, Stevie, had not only stole from her, but had attacked her as well. Aunt Bessie must've put up a struggle, because her fair complexion was splashed with dark bruises. She was seventy-four, and though she shouldn't have to suffer abuse of any kind, she *certainly* shouldn't have to suffer at the hands of her own son.

Rayanne went into the bathroom and returned with a warm, wet towel that she gently rubbed over Aunt Bessie's face. "I'm going to take you to the emergency room to have these bruises checked out," Rayanne said.

Aunt Bessie waved her right hand, as if to silence Rayanne for talking nonsense. "I don't need to see no doctor. I'm all right, but I was afraid Stevie Junior woulda hurt me for real if I didn't give him the money he wanted. That was the first time that boy ever scared me."

"Where is he now?" Rayanne demanded.

"I ain't seen him since this morning. Said he was gon' go back up the road," Aunt Bessie said. "That boy took money from me and things out of my house. I don't want him back in here till he learns to behave like a man."

Aunt Bessie objected to going to the emergency room all

the way there, but Rayanne was relieved when they learned that her aunt didn't suffer any serious injuries. It was a lot easier persuading Aunt Bessie to spend a couple of days with Raymond and Helen. Violence was becoming a major concern. Even in small Southern cities, people were attacking one another every day, but when mothers were being attacked by their own sons—that was despicable.

Rayanne got Aunt Bessie settled in one of her parents' spare bedrooms and began packing a few clothes in an overnight bag for her trip to New York. Just as she finished, she heard Josh coming in through the back door. The past couple of months, he'd come a long way. If he was still drinking, it wasn't noticeable. He had now returned to the land of the living, holding down a steady job and helping Raymond with necessary repairs. It reminded her of old times when she and Josh sat in the kitchen and talked.

In the early morning, Rayanne was on a flight to New York. There was a sense of déjà vu when she met Ivory at the airport. On the ride to the loft, where they all had roomed once upon a time, Ivory talked excitedly about decorating the home on Long Island that she and Desmond bought.

Dorian had continued to live in the loft, sharing it with two other girls. Upon entering the loft, Rayanne and Ivory were shocked by its condition. Once so beautiful, the place was now in shambles. Dirty. Old newspapers and clothes were strewn over the couch, the table, and the floor. The appearance of the loft was bad enough, but seeing Dorian left them speechless. She looked and smelled as though she hadn't bathed or washed her hair in days, perhaps weeks. Black circles ringed her eyes. She probably hadn't slept much. The gorgeous girl who'd once been filled with vitality was now reduced to someone who appeared to have just walked out of skid row. After cleaning Dorian up, they packed a suitcase for her, and the three of them went to Ivory's house for the night.

Desmond, with Stephanie Lynn in his arms, met them at the door. He greeted Rayanne and Dorian and kissed his wife affectionately as she took the baby from his arms.

"How is my little girl? Was Daddy mean to Mama's baby?" Ivory teased Stephanie Lynn, who nodded in agreement. "Bad Daddy," Ivory said, and kissed Desmond again, as they went into the den.

Ivory had a great four-bedroom, split-level home, tastefully furnished and carpeted throughout. The walls were either wallpapered or painted in a lovely soft yellow or blue pastels. Rayanne and Dorian each took a bedroom, and after dinner, they talked into the night.

Rayanne and Ivory quickly got Dorian admitted to a fine rehabilitation center. Dorian understood she needed help, yet she couldn't help feeling being abandoned by them. Rayanne and Ivory tried to reassure her that they loved her and they weren't abandoning her, just doing what was necessary.

The counselor at the center explained to Rayanne and Ivory what Dorian's treatment would entail and that she wasn't allowed to have any contact from outsiders for two weeks. Ivory and Rayanne were grateful to be allowed to spend the day with Dorian at the center, but they were told not to expect changes overnight.

Rayanne spent her last night in New York with Ralph and insisted that he use a condom. When he questioned her, she said, "I just think it's best."

Seeing him, being with him, was as good as it had ever been. She pushed the knowledge of his infidelity out of her mind while they were together. At the airport, they promised they wouldn't allow as much time between their visits—a promise they vowed to keep.

On the plane trip back home, Rayanne was haunted by the dark circles that surrounded Dorian's eyes. She'd lost a lot of weight and she looked awful. Rayanne didn't realize she'd been crying until the passenger in the next seat handed her a Kleenex and asked whether something was wrong.

"No," Rayanne said.

"There are tears on your cheeks," the passenger replied.

"Thanks." Rayanne accepted the tissue and wiped the tears away.

Ralph called Rayanne that evening, and later, she called the center and was assured that Dorian was settling in. She'd eaten a little lunch and a good portion of her dinner. Rayanne felt some relief, and when she called Ivory later, they talked at length between tears.

Sometime later that evening, Rayanne received a call from Brenda reminding her of Thursday's psychology exam and wanting to know would she be able to make it.

"You bet. Thanks, Brenda," Rayanne said.

Rayanne called the center daily to check on Dorian, and on her visit to Dorian with Ivory that weekend, they were encouraged with her progress.

4

Saturday night, Rayanne arrived at the Sumter Recreational Center, meeting Brenda at the door. They entered the grand banquet hall, which was decorated with bright streamers, balloons, and a wide colorful banner suspended from the ceiling congratulating all the teams. Long rows of tables draped by fancy white tablecloths, and a lavish floral centerpiece with a large card written with each table's number on it, were arranged throughout the hall to accommodate the seven-hundred-plus guests.

Rayanne introduced Brenda to her brother, John, several years older than she, and his wife, Christen. John made Brenda feel so at home, so fast, that by the time they parted, she was referring to him as her big brother also. Both women looked around the hall, noticing it was filled with mostly baseball players and their dates, whose body language shouted, "Hands off my man." Neither Rayanne nor Brenda had any intention of invading those ladies' territory and setting off World War III.

Rayanne and Brenda made their way to their table just as the servers were setting out plates and silverware before the buffet dinner began. They helped themselves, along with the other guests, to fried chicken, barbeque ribs, beer-battered fish, and an array of vegetables and desserts. Although the hall provided the food, each player brought their own bottle. After dinner, trophies were awarded to both teams and individuals for their perform-ances. The party got in full swing when the DJ took his place on the podium and began cranking up the volume.

The dancing started and both Rayanne and Brenda danced a couple of times with a few fellows who showed up alone. Returning to her seat after working up quite a sweat on the dance floor, Rayanne noticed Brenda watch-ing two men who were sitting across the table. One man was paying a lot of attention to Brenda, whose light com-plexion, large dark eyes, and attractive dimples never failed to catch most men's notice. Everything about her from her chic silk dress to her curly, tapered salon cut showed that she had class and style. Plus, it didn't hurt she was outgoing and a lot of fun to be around.

Brenda pushed her plate away, lit up a cigarette, and smiled, her eyes nearly closed. "So what's up?" Rayanne asked. Rayanne knew Brenda had something devious in mind. She reminded Rayanne so much of Ivory when it came to mischief, but she couldn't help taking the bait.

"You see that old fart over there?" Brenda asked.

Rayanne looked across the table to a couple of men. "Which one?"

"The one on the left in the hideous lime green suit. He's been sitting over there, drinking *our* brother's liquor all night."

"So?"

"Hell, liquor is expensive. Besides, he's got a flask that he's only touched once and he hasn't offered anyone a drink," Brenda said with a smirk on her face.

"Well, he can only drink a stomach full." Rayanne laughed.

Brenda put out her cigarette, still smirking. "You wanna have some fun?"

"What do you have in mind?" she asked apprehensively.

"Pass me that flask."

"What?"

"Pass me the flask," Brenda repeated.

"What are you gonna do?" Rayanne glanced at the men across the table and slowly reached for the flask.

Brenda smiled broadly at the men. "Not yet," she whispered.

"Oops." Rayanne slowly withdrew her hand and took a sip of her rum and Coke. The man returned his attention to the dance floor.

"Quick, grab it," Brenda hissed.

Rayanne grabbed the flask and handed it to Brenda. She emptied it and replaced its contents with iced tea.

Brenda acting so much like Ivory caused Rayanne to remember once when Ivory had started a new job and wanted to go out of town. Knowing she wouldn't be given leave so soon, Ivory concocted a story about a death in the family, with Rayanne typing up a funeral program, complete with Ivory and her family listed as surviving relatives. After her vacation, Ivory returned to work with the fraudulent funeral program and found a beautiful pot of yellow mums and a sympathy card waiting on her desk. Rayanne hadn't liked participating in the deception, but Ivory had asked and she'd done it.

As the liquor supplies dwindled, the man across the table held his flask under the table, poured a shot into his cup, and looked around. Rayanne and Brenda pretended to not notice. He took a sip and then looked oddly into his cup. Rayanne and Brenda snickered hard after catching a glimpse of his face.

"Fixed him," Brenda said, and they snickered again.

* * *

Rayanne flew to New York that Friday, meeting Ivory at the rehab center, where they spent the day with Dorian. Rehabilitation was making a big difference in Dorian's life. She looked healthier, both her eyes and skin were clearing up, and she said she was feeling so much better, but they all knew she still had a long way to go. Yet, it was a start.

Rayanne left Ivory later that night to be with Ralph. They went to a popular night club, dancing cheek to cheek. She told him about Dorian's progress, but kept the rest of the conversation light and nonintimate. Rayanne still cared about Ralph and enjoyed spending time with him, but she knew she'd never get past his infidelity.

Rayanne traveled to New York twice a month while Dorian was being treated. She even attended one of the sessions, along with Ivory. They'd learned more in that session about Dorian's past. Before her parents' fatal car accident, Dorian had been a happy child, secure in her parents' love and their promise that they'd always be together. She was devastated after her parents were killed. Since there was no other family available, friends of Dorian's parents took her in. Shortly after, the couple divorced and Dorian suffered the trauma of another loss. From that point on, she went from one foster home to another, finally running away to New York at the tender age of sixteen. She'd never forgiven her parents for dying and carried the pain and insecurity of loss with her every day. However, the therapy was helping her work through her feelings of betrayal and abandonment.

Dorian had taken odd jobs that enabled her to put herself through high school. Shortly after arriving in New York, she'd met Henry, an older man who had looked so much like her father that she'd transferred her feelings for her father to him. Henry, though, was a playa, taking advantage of Dorian's vulnerabilities to have a sexual relationship with her. Dorian realized that she was never in love with Henry. She saw him as a father figure, confusing the love for her father with sex with him.

After Rayanne and Ivory moved out of the loft, she felt as if she were losing her family all over again. To compound things, Henry never divorced his wife, Olympia, but he dropped Dorian for another woman. It was just too much for Dorian to handle and pushed her over the edge.

While she continued to be supportive of Dorian, Rayanne was afraid to get too happy for Josh. He continued to attend daily Alcoholics Anonymous meetings, and though it appeared he was making good on his promise, she couldn't help but feel cautious. She wondered how many more people that she loved would cross over to the dark side of drugs and alcohol.

5

Rayanne met Scott by accident.

Literally.

One rainy morning she was running late for her eight forty-five class. Rain fell in a constant drizzle, but she had made the forty-mile drive to Columbia in good time, despite the wet highway. Once in town, she seemed to be stopped by every red light on her route. At every red light, she would grab her notes off the passenger seat and review them.

Someone once said that something always seemed to go wrong when you were already late. Sure enough, while engrossed in her notes, she took her foot off the brakes and pressed down on the accelerator, unaware that the vehicle ahead of her was not moving. She ran into it.

She looked up upon hearing the sound of crunching metal and broken glass. "Oh no!" She tossed her notes back on the seat and got out of the car.

The young man she'd hit approached her as she looked at the damage. "Are you all right? I'm so sorry," she blurted out. "I can't believe I was that careless."

"I'm fine." He held out his hand. "I accept your apology, and, yes, you were careless," he said. "I'm Scott Christopher. Are you all right?"

"I'm fine," she said. "I'm Rayanne Wilson. Are you sure you're all right?"

"I'm fine now, but I'm certain that by Friday, I'll need a good neck rub," Scott Christopher said as they checked out the damage to their vehicles.

"Excuse me?" She looked questioningly at him.

"I said I'm fine now, but I probably could use a neck rub by Friday." His eyes held hers deliberately.

Rayanne looked at her watch. "It doesn't appear we have a lot of damages, so if it's all right with you, can I give you my insurance information so you can have your repairs done? I'm scheduled to take an exam in about twenty minutes and I need to get to class, if that's all right with you, of course."

"Just give me your phone number, Rayanne Wilson, and I'll call you."

"I really appreciate this," she said, calling out her phone number as she got back into her car.

He wrote the number down and smiled. "Drive carefully, Rayanne Wilson."

She nodded, her gaze going over his six-foot-something broad-shouldered frame. His pecan tan face was stamped with intelligence, and his dark brown eyes were downright hypnotizing. To say that he was handsome would be an understatement.

Rayanne arrived for class exactly two minutes before her professor closed the door and began to administer the exam. Brenda and Hilary were there and they appeared eager to get started and have the exam behind them.

An aide collected the first part of their exam and the students were given a twenty-minute break before the second part of the exam was given. At twelve o'clock, the test was over. On the way to lunch, Rayanne told Hilary and Brenda about the accident and the handsome hunk she'd met. They fussed over her, but she assured them she was just fine.

"I hope I passed, because I don't want to have to take that test again."

"You got that right," Rayanne agreed.

"If I get the full ten points on that classical conditioning question and five for the question on the three main forces in a man's life, then I think I'll get an A on the test," Hilary said, her gray eyes appearing large behind her horn-rimmed glasses. She was attractive, but not beautiful. Slender and well-groomed, her intelligence often hid the fact that she was somewhat naïve.

Brenda said, "Well, I'm not gonna sweat it. We're gonna know the results soon enough."

After sipping her tea and wiping her mouth, Hilary asked, "What are y'all doing while on break?"

"I'll be volunteering at the retirement home for a couple of days, and I may go to New York for a few days," Rayanne said. "What about you two?"

"Working." Brenda signaled a waitress. "I can't afford to do anything else right now."

"Jessica will be visiting Mama, and Ben and I are going to take care of some things around the house," Hilary said, glancing over at Brenda. "How are the boys?"

"They're fine. I just want them to grow the hell up and get out of my house," Brenda teased, but Hilary's expression revealed she didn't think Brenda was joking.

"They are your children, Brenda. You should want them around forever," Hilary said.

"Get real, Hilary," Brenda responded. "Shit, no one wants their kids around forever."

Rayanne could've challenged her on that point, because if her parents had their way, they'd have all six of their children living under their roof until they all died.

"I can't believe you said that," Hilary said. "I want Jessica to always be with Ben and me. I know that's not going to happen, but I can wish, can't I?"

"I don't give a damn how anyone else feels, Hilary," Brenda began. "Hell, you've got one child and a husband who takes care of both of you. I've got two boys and no husband. You do the math. You walk in my shoes a year or two and see if you don't change your damn mind."

"Have you thought about getting back with your husband?" Hilary asked.

Brenda had told them she still loved Cardell, but since they'd been separated, she'd started dating again, and she liked it. And even though they'd been apart nearly two years, they still maintained a close relationship, seeing each other and even sleeping together occasionally.

"What can I say? Cardell has a weakness for good-looking women, and I like a lot of money. I look good and he makes good money, so it works for both of us—as long as we don't have to live together," Brenda said.

"And you use your beauty like a shovel digging for gold," Hilary said.

"Honestly, I adored Cardell, and I thought he was crazy about me. It turned out that the man was just damn crazy. He cheated on me," Brenda huffed. "On our anniversary, I was returning from dropping off the boys at my mom's and I saw Cardell pulling into a hotel parking lot. I called a girlfriend and asked her to get a cab to the hotel. She drove my car and followed as I drove Cardell's car to a grocery store parking lot and left it. After driving my friend home, I went home and waited to see what kind of lie he'd invent. It was our eighth anniversary. I had an expensive teddy laid out on the bed, a great dinner in the oven, and a bottle of Dom chilling for our celebration. Obviously, he had other plans. After what I saw, I threw the food in the garbage, put on a pair of flannel pajamas, and drank champagne until my nose bled all over the place. That was supposed to be my night, not hers, whoever the hell she was."

"What happened?" Hilary asked, really getting into Brenda's story.

"When Cardell finally got home at three o'clock in the morning, he told me some lame story about stopping at the mall to pick up my gift, and when he came out, his car was gone," Brenda replied.

"Did he have a gift?" Hilary asked, and Brenda and Rayanne rolled their eyes toward the ceiling.

"Hello," Brenda said, tapping the side of her head with a finger. "He had to add credibility to his story, and besides, it was our anniversary, remember?"

"What did he get you?" Hilary asked.

Brenda shook her head. "What the hell difference does that make? The point is that *knee-gro* was cheating and lying and trying to cover his tracks."

"Men," Rayanne said, eating some salad. "We can't live with them and we can't live without them."

"Oh, I forgot," Hilary said apologetically. "Your man is cheating on you, too."

"No need to apologize," Rayanne said, putting her tea glass down on the table, patting Hilary's hand. "Men just seem to have that cheating gene."

"Not all of them," Hilary said, finishing her lunch and wiping her mouth.

"Yeah, right," Brenda said with disbelief.

"If you think Ben cheats on me, you're wrong," Hilary said, hurt.

"Relax, Hilary. The important thing is that you two love and respect each other and treat each other well," Rayanne said.

"You're not also saying Ben is fooling around?" Hilary asked Rayanne.

"I didn't say that," Rayanne said. "I don't know what

Ben is doing. I don't even know Ben. I just think it's important that people know how they feel about their situation, no matter what anyone else thinks. Yours and Ben's relationship seems to work and that is what's important."

"Ben makes me very happy," Hilary said.

"I heard that," Rayanne said.

"Give this woman a round of applause," Brenda said, then added in a more serious tone, "I've never had anyone who's made me feel secure to the point where I thought he only wanted me."

"Don't you feel any better about yourself than that?" Hilary asked.

Brenda stared at her. "It's not even about that. I've been involved—I've trusted, loved, tried to be loved. Hell, I've tried it all. I wanted it all—a husband, kids, a nice home, a car, money in the bank. I've tried to have those things, but I've failed miserably. The only good things about my life are my children, Chris and Devin. They're my successes." Brenda laughed. "And, hell yeah, they can stay in my house until they are old and gray."

"I knew that all along." Hilary smiled.

"It seemed you and Cardell loved each other a lot, at one time," Rayanne said.

"Can't you two work through this and put your lives back together?" Hilary asked.

"I've given Cardell more chances than he deserved. When he cheated, I sent his ass packing, and I'm happy," Brenda said, but her eyes told a different story. "You know Cardell and I never talked about that night. He thought I was angry because he pulled an all-nighter on our anniversary. Don't ask me why I didn't tell him." Brenda put down her drink and shrugged. "Maybe because I was embarrassed, hurt, or just too much in love. Crazy, huh?" she asked, sadness filling her beautiful eyes.

"I suppose you did what you felt you had to do," Rayanne said.

"I should've gotten up close and personal with his ass," Brenda said. Turning to Rayanne, she asked, "What would you have done?"

"Gotten up close and personal with him," Rayanne joked, only it wasn't so funny when she'd learned of Ralph's indiscretions. After a thoughtful pause, she said, "I told you guys what happened between Ralph and me, but I really don't think anyone knows how they would respond until they're in that situation."

"I don't speculate, and I'm not one to tempt fate," Hilary said. "But I don't ever want to be in that position."

"I was young and foolish at the time, but I don't know if I would handle that situation differently today. When I'm in love, I'm a fool in love," Brenda said.

"Why do you still see Cardell?" Hilary asked.

"What can I say? The man is good in bed." Brenda laughed.

"I always viewed love and commitment as prerequisites for sex," Hilary said.

"You must be one boring bitch," Brenda retorted.

Brenda was so like Ivory—independent, strong, very opinionated.

"That may be true, but I'm the one with the husband, and I'm happy," Hilary replied.

"You have no sense of adventure. You want all of life's little uncertainties to be clear. I like living on the edge, having a good time," Brenda said.

"But if you live your life taking chances just for the sake of a good time—excitement without any real meaning—you could suffer some unpleasant consequences," Hilary said.

"What else is new?" Brenda said. "I will settle down one day, but it won't be today."

Rayanne thought that her sister Lila and Brenda had the same philosophies about life.

"Everything is already fucked up," Brenda said sadly. "I've been through hell trying to deal with one man. I used to walk around so engrossed in my own dilemma that I didn't know what was going on around me. I've been fucked, fucked with, and fucked over, and I don't need any more of that. I'm doing what it takes to make Brenda happy. Besides, Cardell is not out there playing dead. He wasn't when we were together, so you know he ain't now." Then she smiled and asked, "Anyone up for a trip to Atlanta this weekend?"

"What's happening in Atlanta?" Rayanne asked.

"Us," Brenda replied simply. "We could leave early Saturday morning, do a little shopping, hit a few clubs, and drive back Sunday afternoon. You girls in?"

"Sounds like fun," Rayanne said.

"I don't have any real plans. Ben's got some things he wants to get done, and Jessica and my mom can't get enough of each other," Hilary said.

"Oh hell, I'm practically packed and ready to go, but I don't have any money. Damn, I'll be glad when school is over. Then I can sell some houses and make some real money," Brenda said.

"All these great plans and no money." Hilary laughed.

"I can let you have some money," Rayanne offered, and chuckled softly remembering all the times Brenda had insisted on supporting their outings with her credit cards.

Brenda waved away Rayanne's offer. "When has not having money ever stopped me? I've got plastic," Brenda said. "One day, I hope to have your kind of money, Rayanne."

They laughed.

Rayanne looked at her watch. "I guess we're going to Atlanta. Now I've gotta get home."

"So do I," Hilary said. "Jessica will be home soon. And Brenda, you are a good person. You're very pretty, and you could have a monogamous relationship with any man you want, so I'm not gonna give up on you. You deserve so much better."

Brenda stood up and that gleam was back in her eyes. "Don't worry about me. If you were half as happy as I am, you'd go into cardiac arrest," she said, laughing. "I may want the lifestyle that you have, but believe me, I don't want it now. Hell, I'm good to go."

"Well, it's your life," Hilary said, lifting her hands.

"That's what I've been trying to tell ya." Brenda chuckled and they paid their checks and left the restaurant.

Rayanne arrived at the Central Seniors' Retirement Home at a quarter to four. Just as she was about to enter, she remembered that Mrs. Shapiro, one of the people assigned to her since she began to volunteer at the center, was low on her sinus tablets. Rayanne rushed down to the grocery store and purchased two boxes, not thinking to check the contents before leaving the store. She entered the home and Mrs. Shapiro's eyes lit up.

"How are you, Mrs. Shapiro?" Rayanne greeted.

"Fine, but this sinus is driving me crazy," she said.

Rayanne opened a box and discovered it was empty. She opened the second box, got a glass of water, and gave two tablets to Mrs. Shapiro.

"I'll be back," Rayanne said.

Rayanne returned to the store, walked up to the assistant manager, who was doubling as a cashier, and explained what happened. The assistant manager looked at the box in Rayanne's hand, but he continued to wait on other customers as though she hadn't said anything. After repeating her story, he continued to ring up customers, saying, "I'll be with you in a minute."

Rayanne waited while he rang up another customer. She looked at her watch, thinking of all the things she had to do that afternoon. She looked at the man as he began ringing up yet another customer. Irritated, she slapped the empty container on the counter, went to the shelf, and took another package of tablets, making sure to check out its contents. Leaving the store, she called over her shoulder, "Don't worry, you don't owe me anything."

She returned to the home, giving the box of pills to Mrs. Shapiro. After reading for an hour to her and Mrs. Gordon, Rayanne assisted Mrs. Hunter in getting started on her new puzzle, and after praising Mrs. James on her progress crocheting an afghan, she left the home.

Arriving at her house, she found her father in the backyard working too hard, as usual. Rayanne quickly got out of the car, dropping her things on the porch to help him push a concrete-filled wheelbarrow onto the back of his truck.

"Daddy, what are you trying to do to yourself?" she asked.

There were times her father made her angrier than anyone else. Parents always said their children had hard heads, but that was kind compared to what she was thinking about her father.

"You gon' get dirt in them nice clothes you got on there," he said, avoiding her question.

Rayanne was wearing the pale yellow pants suit she bought while on their trip to Atlanta. "You doing okay today?" She used the back of her hand to wipe perspiration from her forehead.

"Doing fine. You had a good day?" Raymond asked, pulling a clean handkerchief from his pocket to hand to Rayanne.

After wiping her face, Rayanne returned the handkerchief to her father, giving him another look. She headed toward the porch to retrieve her belongings before going inside the house. Helen was mending socks in front of the TV and watching the seven o'clock news. She looked up upon hearing Rayanne enter. "Hey, honey," she said.

"Hey, Mama," Rayanne replied.

"I baked a couple of your favorite pies today," Helen said.

Rayanne had definitely caught a whiff of apples and cinnamon wafting from the kitchen. "Good old pumpkin pies," Rayanne teased, hating pumpkin pies.

"Bite your tongue. I also baked a couple pans of that yeast bread you like so much."

"I'll have a piece," Rayanne said, putting her things down and looking over at Josh, who was sound asleep in a chair in front of the TV. "Why isn't Josh helping Daddy?"

"He just got in here. Said he been looking for work. Josh, Josh," Helen called out to him. He opened one eye and looked over at Helen. "Go on outside and help your daddy."

"I'll go out later, Mama. I don't feel like it right now." Josh stirred in his chair.

Internally, Rayanne had had enough. She walked over to Josh, and standing a foot away from where he was sprawled back in the chair, she placed both hands on her hips, bent down to face him, and said, "You ought to be ashamed of yourself. Get your sorry behind up out of that chair and go help Daddy." The smell of alcohol emanating from Josh signaled he was drinking again, and it was a disgusting sight. Josh opened his eyes halfway, then focused. Rayanne yelled, "Get your butt out of that chair and find your way outside and see what Daddy needs you to do."

"All right. All right. You don't have to yell." Josh got up on unsteady legs and staggered outside.

"You don't seem to understand anything else," Rayanne yelled after him. When she turned to find her mother looking at her, she was slightly embarrassed about the scene between Josh and her. "I'm sorry, Mama."

"Come on in here and sample this bread." Her mother smiled. "And tell me about your day."

Rayanne told her mother about her day, and Helen shared with her the happenings on the soap operas, all while enjoying yeast bread and iced tea. Rayanne admired her mother, and they were as close as any mother and daughter could be. It was a relationship they cherished. Rayanne thought of Josh, wondering what was it about mothers that made them want to protect their young, when, as in Josh's case, the young was old enough to be a grandparent.

6

Maxine turned into the driveway and waved to Rayanne and her father, who were sitting on the front porch. She drove around to the back of the house, parked her car, and came up to the kitchen door.

"Hey, Maxine," Helen said, holding the door open. "Come on in and have something cold to drink." Helen embraced her daughter. "How's Marcus and my grand-children?" She released Maxine, filling glasses with ice, and took a pitcher of lemonade from the refrigerator.

"They're fine. Bobby got two A's and Bruce got B's. Let me help you with that," Maxine said, taking the pitcher from her mother's hand.

"That's not too shabby, but remind them that Grandma pays for A's only," Helen said, setting the glasses on a tray. She and Maxine joined Rayanne and Raymond on the porch.

"Marcus took the boys to a softball game," Maxine said.

"You got yourself a good man, him spending so much time with the boys and all," Helen said.

"I know, Mama," Maxine said, feeling blessed in so many ways.

Raymond pulled a crumpled envelope from his back

pocket and handed it to Maxine. "Thanks, Daddy," Maxine said, still a little embarrassed about accepting the $300 a month from her parents to help support her boys, since Fred, her first husband, ran off, leaving them and never looking back. However, Marcus had vowed to accept responsibility for them all from the day he fell in love with Maxine and married her.

Rayanne shopped for the boys and gave them spending money all the time; however, Maxine always refused her numerous offers to help financially.

Rayanne laid down her pen and pad and accepted a glass of lemonade from Maxine. "Thanks," Rayanne said, and looked to her.

"Don't go there, Rayanne. We are not going to have that conversation again," Maxine said, knowing Rayanne wanted to offer her money again. "The only reason I'm taking money from Mama and Daddy is because they intend for each of us to own one of those rented houses one day."

"I know that, Max," Rayanne said, but she knew from the look on Maxine's face that she would be fighting a losing battle to try to persuade her otherwise.

"Bruce was accepted at Clemson." Maxine changed the subject as she sat on the porch steps.

"That's great," Rayanne said.

"He'll enroll in their engineering program this fall." Maxine was beaming with pride.

"My, how time flies," Helen said. "Seems like it was just yesterday when that boy was running 'round in diapers, and now he's almost a man."

"He is still in diapers," Raymond teased.

"Daddy!" Rayanne laughed.

"Raymond, don't be so hard on the boy," Helen said.

"You gotta be hard on them if they're gonna 'mount to anything," Raymond said.

"You weren't hard on yours and they turned out all right," Helen said.

"Wonder what happened to Josh." Raymond avoided his wife's eyes, knowing she didn't like him speaking badly about any of their children.

"Raymond, we're talking about Bruce, not Josh," Helen said.

"I was only joking 'bout that 'cause Bruce is gonna do real good," Raymond said.

"Yeah," Helen agreed. "That young man got a good head on his shoulders."

"I was hoping he would've picked one of the schools that offered him a full scholarship." Maxine sipped her lemonade.

"If you're worried about money, Maxine, and you don't want to accept help from the family, there's a lot of financial aid out there," Rayanne said.

"We're looking into that. Clemson will give him a partial scholarship. He visited several good schools, some with full scholarships, but Clemson was his choice. And if that's where he wants to go, then that's where he should go."

"They have a wonderful engineering program," Rayanne said. "And I agree it's important for the young adult to be able to go to the school he really wants to, instead of where he has to."

"Something else bothering you, Maxine?" Raymond drained his glass and held it up for his wife to refill.

"No, not really," Maxine lied.

"You may as well come on out with it. Anybody can see you got something on your mind," Helen said.

Maxine remained quiet, looking out across the yard. "Bruce has been asking about his daddy a lot lately, and I don't really know what to tell him."

"Tell him the truth. Fred Duncan been living here all his

life, and if the boys don't learn the truth from you, they're gonna hear it from somebody else," Helen said.

"What does he want to know about that jackleg anyhow?" her father asked.

Rayanne got up to go and sit beside her sister on the steps. "All kinds of things," Maxine said. "Why he left? Was it their fault? Did he love them? Things like that. I always told them that he went away because he didn't want to live here anymore. I don't want my kids blaming themselves for something that butthole did. Anyway, after a while, they stopped asking, but now that they're getting older, they're curious again. Fred has never loved anyone but himself, but do you tell that to your children?"

"'Course not," Helen said sympathetically.

"You just tell them the truth about that bastard," Raymond said.

Helen used a hand to swat her husband on the knee. "Hush up, Raymond. Can't you see that this thing is troubling the girl?' she said.

"Yeah, but those kids don't need to be thinking their daddy's some saint," Raymond said. "Them boys are old enough to know the kind of man Fred is. He sure was a nasty one when he was married to you, Maxine. And he run off like some coward and ain't never looked back. I don't believe he's gonna change. Just tell 'em their daddy wasn't perfect and that they don't wanna be nothin' like him. Them boys ain't stupid. They'll understand."

Maxine looked at her watch. She got up, took another sip from her glass, and said, "I gotta pick up Marcia Raylyn from her dance class. You know how that child gets when I'm late."

"Tell that little lady she's getting slack," Helen said. "She hasn't called me all week."

"She is getting slack, but I'll tell her what you said.

Do you want me to take this tray back to the kitchen?" Maxine offered.

"No. You go on, and don't keep my granddaughter waiting." Helen chuckled. Then she became serious. "Don't you worry. It'll all work itself out."

Maxine kissed her parents. "I love you both."

Rayanne and Maxine set their glasses on the porch steps and walked around the house to Maxine's car.

"What's really going on with you, Maxine?" Rayanne asked.

"You know me so well," Maxine said, getting into her car. "Come ride to the store with me."

"What about Marcia Raylyn?"

"This won't take long."

Rayanne got into the car. "You heard from Fred, haven't you? Only Fred could upset you this much."

"You know he's a minister in Florida, right? Well, I heard he's going to be the guest minister at our church in a couple of months, and get this—he's bringing his new wife. Can you believe that?"

"Fred's coming here?" Rayanne asked, and Maxine nodded. "Apparently, Mama and Daddy don't know. Well, they're gonna hear about this sooner or later." Maxine nodded her head up and down. "You're gonna tell them, aren't you?"

Maxine didn't answer. She stopped her car in front of a neighborhood grocery store. Without turning off the engine, she opened the car door and said, "I'll be right back."

Moments later, Maxine exited the store and got back into the car, carrying a single bag. She unscrewed the cap off a bottle of beer, and Rayanne gasped when Maxine turned up the bottle and took several large swallows from it before replacing the cap.

"Good God!" Rayanne exclaimed. "Do you want me to drive?"

"I'm fine." Maxine sprayed her mouth with breath spray.

On the way home, Maxine explained that Althea came over to her house and gave her the details after she was told to book Fred Duncan to speak at the church. Althea was the church's program coordinator and one of Maxine's best friends. When they pulled back into Rayanne's yard, they got out of the car. Maxine deposited the near-full bottle of beer into the trash can that sat in the backyard before getting back into the car. As she was about to drive off, they noticed a car stopped in the middle of the street, near the house. The driver was talking with a young man who was walking along the street.

"Look at that. Dealing drugs in the middle of the street, in broad daylight," Maxine said to Rayanne, who was shaking her head. The driver handed something to the man when he approached the car. He drove away after they noticed they had the attention of the two women. Maxine said, "I've got to go. I'll call you later."

"Get home safely," Rayanne said as Maxine drove away.

Rayanne walked around to the front of her house and watched the young man who was talking to the drug dealer, until he was out of sight.

Maxine called at nine forty-five that night. "Sorry I'm just getting back to you, but I had lots to do."

"I just got home myself. I was visiting Aunt Bessie," Rayanne said.

"It's a damn shame how Stevie treats her."

"He needs his behind whipped."

"I never thought Stevie would've turned out this way. I know it's mostly because of the drugs. Still, that's no excuse."

"So you want to talk about it?"

"Where do I begin," Maxine said with a shaky laugh.

"Anywhere you like."

"Rayanne, it pisses me off that Fred has these kids and he ain't doing shit for them. I feel guilty as hell using Marcus's money to do things for Fred's kids. Marcus doesn't mind, but it's the principle. How can anyone be so uncaring about his own flesh and blood? And they're great kids, but he doesn't care."

"When he comes here, tell him how you feel. Let him know the kids have questions."

"He's always had that happy-go-lucky, carefree life. I think it's time that he pays the piper."

"Don't let it get to you like this. You keep this up and you'll end up as bitter as that sister of yours," Rayanne teased, referencing Lila.

"She's your sister, too."

"That's not my fault," Rayanne retorted, and they laughed.

"I think I'll call Mrs. Duncan." Maxine was referring to her former mother-in-law.

"Why not go see her and talk to her. How bad can it be?"

"Let's just say, like mother, like son," Maxine joked, but she agreed to go and see Mrs. Duncan.

"Do your part, Maxine. And if Fred doesn't want to be involved in his children's lives, then it's his loss."

"Enough about me," Maxine said. "What about the guy you ran into?"

"I haven't heard from him, but I think he's okay. Fine too," Rayanne said, and they giggled.

"Marcus is pulling into the driveway. Let me put his dinner on the table. I'll talk with you tomorrow."

Rayanne picked up the mail from the table. When she saw the letter from Maggie, she smiled as she reminisced of her old neighbor from New York. She was glad they still kept in touch.

7

It was eight o'clock Friday night. Rayanne was sitting on the front porch, sipping from a glass of rum and Coke, enjoying the fragrance of the roses, yellow jessamine, dogwoods, and magnolias floating by in the early-evening breeze. Although the yard was picture-perfect, Helen was always doing something to improve it.

The CD player in the living room sent popular tunes through the open windows as Rayanne searched the sky for the Big Dipper. The phone rang, interrupting her search, and she got up to answer it.

"Hello?" she said.

"May I speak with Rayanne Wilson, please?" the caller asked.

"This is she."

"How are you?"

"I'm fine. Who is this?" Rayanne didn't recognize the voice.

"How quickly she forgets."

"Who is this?" she repeated.

"Well, it's Friday, and I believe I'm due a neck rub. May I collect?"

"Mr. Christopher," she said, remembering he was the man she'd hit on her way to class that rainy morning.

"No. Mr. Christopher is my daddy. I'm Scott," he teased.

"Okay, Scott, how are you?"

"I'm fine. Just need that neck rub."

"What?"

"The neck rub. We talked about it the day we met."

"Oh . . . yes."

"How about it?"

"I have to warn you. I haven't had a lot of practice, but I'll do my best."

"That's good enough for me. Can I come over?"

"Do you know where I live?"

"No, but I follow directions pretty well."

Rayanne gave Scott directions, and within thirty minutes, Scott's dark green truck pulled into her driveway. Rayanne invited him in and offered him a drink.

"No thanks. I don't drink," he said, taking a seat beside her, thinking she was even prettier than he remembered.

"Water or iced tea?"

"I'm fine," he said, staring at her hair. He wanted to reach over and touch it. "I want to share a secret with you. I'm a hair freak and you've got really pretty hair."

"Thanks."

"I love a woman with a head of pretty hair." Then he asked, "So what you been up to?"

"School mostly," she replied.

"What are you studying?"

"I'm just taking some courses right now, psychology, dabbling a little in real estate."

"You're gonna sell me a house?"

"That would be nice, but lately I've been thinking about selling something important to kids," Rayanne said, concerned about the violence that was on the rise across the country.

"What do you mean?"

"It's a long story."

"I'd like to hear it sometime," he said, looking into her eyes. "You're very pretty. Is there a Mister around?" He pretended to peek around her.

"You waited a fine time to ask, don't you think?"

"Better late than never."

Rayanne laughed softly. "So, Scott, tell me about yourself."

"I'm in the construction business. I build houses."

"That ends my career as a Realtor. Doesn't appear I'll be selling you a house."

"You never know. I also like cars, fast cars. I work on them in my spare time and I do a little racing."

"That must be exciting."

"Yeah. All that speed, all that power. It gives me such a rush. I also coach a Little League softball team." He smiled, and Rayanne knew this man enjoyed what he did. Scott was intelligent and interesting. Rayanne wanted to get to know him better.

"I can tell you enjoy what you do."

"I never do anything I don't enjoy."

"Never?"

"Well, almost never," he said, and they laughed as Helen appeared at the door.

"Oh, I didn't know we had a visitor," she said. Rayanne made the introductions.

"Do you live around here, young man?" Helen asked.

"Yes, ma'am, across town on Manchester," he answered.

Before Helen left the porch, she'd learned all about Scott—what he did for a living, the church he attended, and that he'd never been married. "It was nice meeting you, Scott. You must come and go to church with us some Sunday." Helen extended her hand at the end of their conversation.

Scott accepted it. "Yes, ma'am, I will. It was nice meeting you, too, Mrs. Wilson, and I hope to see you again soon," he said as she left to go back inside the house.

Scott remained on the front porch with Rayanne talking into the night. Their conversation covered everything, including her relationship with Ralph. Scott talked about his son, Donnie, and his son's mother, Frannie. He mentioned he'd lived with them before the relationship went bad. Rayanne listened as Scott shared that Frannie often told him that he wasn't the boy's father.

"I've never been one hundred percent sure that Donnie is my son. I want him to be with all my heart, and I'm the only daddy the boy knows."

"If you want to be sure, get a paternity test."

"What's the use? I love the kid."

Rayanne smiled. "How old is he?"

"He's two and he's a great kid." Scott smiled.

"You have pictures?"

"Sure do." Scott quickly removed his wallet from his pocket and opened it to the photo section.

Rayanne leaned over to get a closer look. "He's a cutie."

"I wish his mother thought so," he said, and Rayanne caught a glimpse of sadness crossed his face. Then just as quickly, he was all smiles again. "Am I gonna be able to collect on my back rub?"

"I thought it was a neck rub," Rayanne reminded.

"Okay, a neck rub, then."

"Where would you like to sit?"

"Right there between your legs is fine with me." He grinned.

"In your dreams." she smiled and patted the floor beside her feet.

When he was seated, she began massaging his neck. As she did, Scott thought how easy she was to talk to. He hadn't felt that comfortable with anyone he'd just met as he did with her.

"You have great hands. You sure you haven't done this before?"

"I said I didn't have a lot of practice."

"So what are you doing here when that man of yours is a thousand miles away?"

"I came back home to help take care of my parents."

"And he didn't follow you back here? He's a fool."

"You're not suggesting he give up his life, his home, his career, and come live in the South because I did?"

"I would have."

Rayanne's hands became still. She felt a little uneasy from that comment, yet strangely exhilarated at the same time. She had to admit that she would've done exactly what Ralph wanted also. And, as if Scott had read her mind, he asked, "You love this Ralph guy, don't you?"

"What kind of question is that?"

"Just a question. Am I being too personal or too nosy?" He smiled. Nosy, she thought, tightening her hands around his throat, pretending to choke him. "I get the message." He laughed. After a moment's silence, he said, "I think we are having a tremendous bonding experience." He turned his head to look up at her. "It's like we're old friends."

Rayanne had liked him also, and it seemed as if they'd known each other much longer.

At ten after one, Saturday morning, Scott said good night, but before he left, he got Rayanne to agree to have dinner with him Sunday evening. She went to bed, about to doze off just as the phone rang. She answered it.

"Hey, girlfriend," Ivory said.

Rayanne's mind leaped to Dorian. "Ivory, what's going on?"

"Everything's fine. Dorian's doing well, but I've been thinking about you."

"I tried to get Dorian earlier but got her machine."

"She went out to dinner and a show with friends," Ivory explained.

"I got all B's in my classes."

"B's are great. Congrats, girlfriend. Well, I've heard your voice. Now I'm going back to sleep."

"Good night, Ivory," Rayanne said, breathing a sigh of relief that Dorian was okay.

Rayanne was studying in the den when she heard a contestant being introduced on a television show. The young girl began to sing, and soon she had Rayanne's full attention. The performer was no more than eleven or twelve, but what a talent. Her competitor was good, but Rayanne knew who'd win, and within minutes, the young performer received one of the highest scores the show had ever seen.

At three-thirty, Rayanne put her books away and was about to get on the treadmill when Maxine called. She'd met with Fred's mother. "He doesn't want to see me or the boys. He's a different person now, Mrs. Duncan said. He has a new life, a new wife, and he was moving on, completely forgetting about his children," Maxine said angrily.

Rayanne knew how Maxine felt. She also knew that Maxine wouldn't stop at that. The one thing Fred didn't realize was that Maxine didn't just get even, that woman got ahead—no matter how long it took.

That must've been the day for her sisters to call, because as soon as Maxine hung up, Lila called. Jeremy's girlfriend, April, was pregnant, and Lila had no intention of supporting that girl or her baby. Lila sometimes put the cart before the horse, and this was one time when Rayanne hoped that was the case.

8

Late that afternoon, Ralph called.

"I won't be coming next weekend as planned. I'm going on a fishing trip with some of the guys."

"I was so looking forward to spending some time with you. I'm disappointed, but I understand. I'll just look forward to seeing you the next weekend," Rayanne said.

Scott arrived at exactly eight-thirty that evening. They went to Logan's Steak House for dinner, then a movie. On their way home late that evening, a beautiful ballad began to play on the car radio.

"I love that song," Rayanne said.

There was hardly any traffic on the street. Scott stopped his car, got out, and walked around to her side. Rayanne was baffled when he opened the door and reached for her hand. She got out and followed him to the front of the car. What happened next was one of the most romantic things she'd ever done. In the headlights of Scott's car, they danced in the middle of the street. Rayanne wasn't happy about Ralph canceling his trip, but she had to admit, she was enjoying the evening with Scott.

After arriving home, they sat on the front porch, and Rayanne realized that not only was Scott very romantic, he was a great conversationalist. It was a lovely night and they enjoyed the quiet.

When Scott spoke again, he said, "I thought about you a lot today."

"What?"

"Where did you disappear to? I'm not boring you, am I?"

"Absolutely not. I'm enjoying your company," she said, thinking he must've sensed her trepidation. "I was looking forward to Ralph's visit next weekend, but he's going on a fishing trip instead."

"A fishing trip?" Scott said, with raised eyebrows. "That joker is a bigger fool than I thought. He can go fishing anytime. I can see you're upset, so if you wanna talk about it, I'm here. And if you'll let me, I'll stay until you feel better."

"It's not that important." Rayanne tried to mask her disappointment. "If he can't make it, he can't."

"But it doesn't work like that. Anytime two people are in love, nothing is impossible. If you wanna see that joker next week, call him and tell him. It sounds to me like he made up his mind—then he called and told you. Don't let him call the shots. You two are in this thing together and you should decide together." Scott scratched his head. "If I had a lady like you, she'd never feel second best to anything. Especially no damn fishing trip."

Rayanne looked at Scott and she was really glad they'd met, however unfortunate the circumstances. "What is Frannie like?"

"Frannie?" He looked up questioningly.

"You're so sweet and caring. I wonder why she would ever let you go."

"The usual story, I guess. Our goals changed, we drifted apart."

"That simple, huh?"

"That simple."

"Do you miss her?"

"I did."

"And now?"

"Well, you know what they say. Some people come into our lives and leave quietly, while others leave an imprint on our souls."

"Has anyone ever left an imprint on your soul?"

Scott answered, looking up at the stars. "She was the most beautiful woman I'd ever seen, and I fell hopelessly in love with her at first sight. Would you believe sometime later I took a sewing class because she was the teacher?"

Rayanne had a puzzled expression on her face.

"Oh, didn't I tell you. I was in the fifth grade." Scott laughed softly.

"You are too much," she said, pushing on his shoulder.

"You should've seen some of those little stuffed animals that I made. They were so cute," he said, and they laughed out loud.

"That's adorable." When Rayanne turned her head to look at Scott, she was shocked to see that he'd stopped laughing and was staring at her. "What's wrong?"

"I just love your hair. I told you I'm a hair man, didn't I?"

"Yes, you did."

"I enjoy women. They are beautiful and special, and they should be treated that way. They should know they're appreciated, but"—he held up a finger—"I think women are most beautiful with a head of pretty hair."

"You're such a romantic."

"I've been called worse. Besides, what's wrong with being romantic?"

Days ago, Rayanne and Scott had been strangers, but that night, their friendship blossomed.

Scott studied her face, toying with the idea of kissing her, but he quickly tossed that idea aside. He liked the way their friendship was progressing, and he wasn't going to do anything to jeopardize it. However, those thoughts belonged to him, and he knew if he could hold her in his arms just once, it would stay with him a lifetime. As they continued to talk, they were surprised as the moon and stars began to vanish and the sun prepared to wake up the sky.

9

The rain fell softly the morning Scott drove Rayanne to the airport. As the drizzle settled and glistened on the highway, it reminded her of the day they met. Scott seemed moody when he arrived that morning. She tried to drag out of him what was wrong. He said there was a problem at one of the sites and had left it at that, and they rode the rest of the way in silence.

"When will you be back?" Scott asked as he drove into the parking lot at the airport.

"In a few days," she replied.

"Will you be seeing what's his name?" When Rayanne looked at him, he said, "Of course, you will. What a stupid question."

"I'm gonna miss you, Scott."

"I'll miss you, too. As a matter of fact, I already do."

They got out of the car, Scott removed Rayanne's suitcase, and they entered the airport. He saw Rayanne board the plane and watched until the silvery glimmer disappeared in the sky.

The trip to New York was quick, and that evening, Rayanne, Ivory, and Dorian had dinner at Rachelle's, one of New York's upscale restaurants. It was semicrowded. Dorian ate very little and talked even less.

"Dorian, you're quiet," Rayanne said.

"Yeah," Ivory said, sipping from her wineglass. "Are you all right?"

Dorian began to cry. "You are too good to me," she said, looking from Ivory to Rayanne. "I don't deserve your friendship."

Ivory and Rayanne looked at each other. "We are family," Ivory said, reaching across the table and taking one of Dorian's hands in hers. "We're supposed to be here for each other."

"And both of you have been terrific." Dorian continued to cry.

"Dorian, you're terrific as well." Rayanne wiped her mouth with her cloth napkin.

"I haven't been a good friend. I've betrayed you in the worst way," Dorian said, her gaze darted to Rayanne, then to her plate.

"What are you talking about?" Rayanne asked. "You've been like a sister."

"It's Ralph," Dorian blurted out.

"Ralph?" Rayanne frowned. Something about the look on Dorian's face made her uneasy.

Rayanne wasn't sure she wanted to know what it was about Ralph; yet she had to ask. "What about Ralph?"

Dorian's lips quivered. "Ralph and I have been sleeping together."

"What the fuck . . . ?" Ivory began, but fell silent.

As Dorian's words sank in, Rayanne became speechless.

Recovering, Ivory looked from Rayanne back to Dorian. "Honey, you're not feeling well. Is that it?"

Rayanne, still unable to speak or think, could only give Dorian a look of disbelief.

"I'm sorry, Rayanne." Dorian dabbed at her eyes. "We didn't mean for it to happen."

Rayanne's expression changed from disbelief to horror.

Ivory signaled the waitress and paid the check. "Come on. Let's get out of here," she said, and they went back to the loft.

Rayanne was silent. Dorian's words had hit her like a hurricane, jolting her. One moment Rayanne felt like her mind was caught in a maze; then the next, it raced like a fire out of control.

"Henry's divorce never happened. All the property I thought he owned really belongs to Olympia—the apartment complex, the magazine. Olympia owned everything, including Henry—" Dorian began.

But Rayanne interrupted, asking, "When did you start sleeping with Ralph?"

Dorian looked at Rayanne, then Ivory, then back to her hands which she was wringing in her lap. "It happened quite innocently one night," she said.

"How does one friend fuck another friend's man, innocently?" Rayanne yelled, and not only did she shock Dorian and Ivory with that outburst, she shocked herself. Rayanne got up and walked around the room. Then she turned back to Dorian. "How does that happen?"

Dorian did not respond.

"Answer me!" Rayanne screamed.

Dorian took a deep breath to steady herself. "I was feeling really low. All of my friends had left me, I'd lost Henry, I had no money. I was all alone. I called Ralph and told him what happened with Henry and me. He knew I was feeling bad, so he invited me over. We had a couple of drinks and talked. It got late, Ralph told me I could stay over. He didn't want me to be alone. I stayed. We drank some more, one thing led to another, and oh God," Dorian said as the sordid picture came back to her, and the tears started all over again. "We made love. Ralph was so kind to me. I haven't had anyone who treated me that way in a long time."

"Oh shit," Ivory mumbled, her eyes rolled toward the ceiling.

Rayanne composed herself as much as she could before asking, "Of all the men that you know, why did you have to fuck Ralph? Why would you do that to me? Why?" Dorian hung her head in silence. "Why Ralph?" Rayanne shrieked.

"Rayanne, I'm sorry. I was at a low point, trying to stay clear of the drugs."

"Why does it always have to be about you?" Rayanne said as tears rolled down her cheeks. Then she said, "Did you even stop to think what this would do to our friend-ship? Or my relationship with Ralph? Did you think what this would do to me? I trusted you, Dorian."

Ivory went to Rayanne and embraced her. "I'm sorry, baby," she whispered.

Rayanne freed herself from Ivory and walked back over to Dorian. "Are you two still sleeping together?" Rayanne screamed.

The sound of Dorian's deep, racking sobs filled the room, but Rayanne ignored the tears. "Am I going to have to repeat myself all damn night? How long has this been going on?"

"Can we talk about this a little later?" Ivory stated, seeing the effect the argument was having on both girls.

"No, Ivory, I want to know how long my supposedly good friend and my man have been fucking each other and playing me for the fool," Rayanne said.

"A couple of years," Dorian admitted, sobbing.

"What?" The simple word escaped Rayanne's mouth in a whisper. Then the room became silent. Ivory looked per-plexed, Dorian looked lost, and Rayanne looked as though

her world was coming to an end. Ralph's behavior now made sense. So many things did now. Then something else came to Rayanne's mind. "My blue scarf," she said, "the one you loved so much. Where is it, Dorian?"

Dorian was baffled, and Ivory looked even more perplexed.

"Your blue scarf?" Dorian looked confused. "I don't know where it is. I have looked everywhere for it."

"Try Ralph's closet," Rayanne spat out.

Rayanne had seen the scarf in Ralph's closet when she'd visited him, but because she wasn't that fond of it, she'd left it there.

"Rayanne, I'm so sorry," Dorian said as fresh tears rolled down her cheeks. "I know what you must think of me."

"No, you don't. You have no idea." Rayanne glared at her. "You're a sinner, and sinners never sleep."

"What are we gonna do?" Ivory sat on the couch, her head in her hands.

"I'm taking the first flight back home," Rayanne said. "That's what I'm gonna do."

"Rayanne"—Ivory went over to her—"please don't leave like this. There's so much at stake."

"It's a little late to try to salvage a friendship," Rayanne said.

"You can't leave like this," Ivory said.

"Watch me," Rayanne said. She got up, walked over and took her cell phone from her purse, and made a call. Ivory went and sat beside Dorian. Rayanne snapped her phone shut and walked through the French doors onto the terrace. It was cold outside, which was exactly what she was feeling inside. She was in so much pain that she didn't notice the chill in the air.

"I thought you might need this," Ivory said, coming up behind Rayanne, placing a coat around her shoulders.

Rayanne shivered, but it wasn't from the cold. "I'm sorry, Rayanne, and for the record, I didn't know. I had no idea Dorian had reached that point." Ivory looked out over the city. "Something awful has happened and it can't be undone, so we've got to deal with it. It's not gonna be easy." Ivory shook her head. "But we can get past it. I know we can." She looked at Rayanne. "What can I do to help? Desmond and I are here for you."

Rayanne was wading through the pain that had reached down and touched her soul, consuming her. "Damn, Ivory, why did they have to do this to me? I can't believe it," Rayanne said, and began to cry again.

"I know you're hurting, you're angry, and you will be for some time, but the answer is time," Ivory said.

Rayanne turned and faced Ivory. "What do you suggest I do until enough time has passed when I can breathe without my heart coming apart a little piece at a time? Am I supposed to act like nothing's happened?" Rayanne said, wiping her nose with the back of her hand. "What I should do is go back in there and kick that bitch's ass into next year."

"You could do that, but what good would it do?" Ivory held back her own tears.

"It would make me feel a hell of a lot better. Ivory, you have no real sense of how I'm feeling because this didn't happen to you."

After a moment's silence, Ivory asked, "What are you thinking?"

Rayanne took a deep breath. "I was just thinking that I can't stop this from happening. I can't stop it from being true, can I?"

Ivory sighed, wrapping her arms around herself. "No, none of us can. It might help to remember what Dorian was going through. She isn't innocent in this—I know that—but I understand how something like this could happen. I just didn't think it could happen to us. This is horrible. We're broken, torn apart by this," Ivory said, and her voice cracked. "But we've got to find a way to put it back together again. We've got to try."

"Honestly, what would you do if this happened to you?"

"I'd kick both of their asses until they belched leather, but that's me, not you. You're the sensible one," Ivory said, then added, "Ralph is not the innocent party, you know."

"It's not fair putting all the blame on Dorian, because she had plenty of help. Ralph was in the middle of it all. He knows about Dorian's fragile condition and he took terrible advantage. He shouldn't have allowed this to happen." Rayanne exhaled loudly. "He's disappointed me before, but this splits my heart into a million pieces. Will it ever be whole again?" Ivory remained quiet while Rayanne talked. "You know something like this had to happen. For so long, what we had was so good. One of us was bound to screw up."

"It was good, and we can fix it, but how can we fix where we are now?"

"I don't know." Rayanne sighed.

"Please don't leave tonight."

"I can't get a flight out until tomorrow, so it looks like I'm stuck here for tonight."

"Good," Ivory said. "It gives us more time to talk." After a moment, Ivory said, "You know, Rayanne, we all have our secrets."

"You didn't sleep with Ralph, too?" Rayanne looked at her incredulously.

Ivory gave her a dark look. "You know better than that, but I did sleep with Mr. Isaacs."

"Ivory, I knew that way back then."

"Did you know that I got pregnant?"

The familiar crease formed on Rayanne's brow. "You? Pregnant?"

"Yep. Remember that Friday when you couldn't find me at school?"

Rayanne knew exactly when she was talking about, because she'd looked for Ivory all day. When she reached her at home later that night, Ivory gave her some vague excuse for not being at school and dropped it.

"Well, I didn't want a baby, so Mr. Isaacs—my high school teacher—took me out of town and I had an abortion."

"You never said a word to me."

"We're human. We make mistakes." Ivory looked at Rayanne.

Rayanne and Dorian spent the night in separate rooms at the loft, with Rayanne refusing to speak to Dorian. Rayanne went to bed with Dorian's words "Ralph and I have been sleeping together" echoing in her brain. Family and friends were important, but trust was also high on the list of things that were important to her. She knew she would never be able to forgive Dorian or Ralph.

The flight back to South Carolina seemed long. Rayanne adjusted her seat, closed her eyes, and tried to sleep. She was tired, emotionally drained, and consumed with pain—literally sick with misery and pain. When she arrived at home, she found a message from Ralph, but she didn't return his call.

At first, everything seemed to stand still. Rayanne got up, got dressed, and went to class, although unable to concentrate. She returned home at the end of the day and repeated the cycle. After a while, the days began to go by quickly, but the pain was still fresh. And since she refused to take Ralph's calls, his letters came and began to stack up on the dresser in her bedroom, along with Dorian's.

One day, Rayanne left the house, running blindly behind her house toward the lake, with tears rolling down her face. She'd cried so often after her New York trip that she was surprised she had tears left to cry. It was there at the lake as the sun began to fade, and night was coming fast, that she realized that although she was hurting, she had to pick herself up and move past her misery. And she forced herself to do just that. She kept busy, started doing things with her friends again, and on occasion, she was able to smile.

Another day, Rayanne entered the house as the phone was ringing. Her parents were nowhere around. She dropped her books on the table and snatched up the phone. "Hello?" she said.

"Rayanne, thank God you answered. I miss you, baby. Please let me come to see you. Please. I can be there in a few hours," Ralph pleaded, but his request was met with a resounding no before Rayanne hung up.

The one positive thing that had happened since that awful night in New York was that Dorian fell in love with a Frenchman, married him, and moved to France. She'd sent Rayanne an invitation and a note with more apologies through Helen, knowing Rayanne wouldn't read any mail from her.

Dorian was disappointed but not surprised that Rayanne wouldn't be a guest for that special event. Rayanne did send a gift.

Trouble never seemed to come alone. Raymond had given them another scare when he had another heart attack. Josh had gone into yet another detoxification center. He stayed sober for several weeks, but as usual, he'd started drinking again. When Beverly kicked him out that time, along with a promise that she was through with him, Josh moved back into the family house once more.

10

Rayanne and her parents left church that Sunday, and after dinner, her parents and Aunt Bessie visited Abigail, a friend, who was in the hospital. Abigail had been mugged and beaten in the neighborhood, and Helen and other neighbors took care of her until she came down with pneumonia and was hospitalized. There was talk of Abigail's daughter moving her back to D.C. with her when she was well.

When the house was quiet, Rayanne sat in her bedroom and stared aimlessly out the window. Lila called and the conversation was based on one major question: Can Jeremy and "Little Charlotte" live with you for a while?

"I can't believe April just dropped off a three-month-old baby with a teenage boy and left, expecting him to take care of her. Shows the kind of mother she is," Lila huffed, then said, "It won't be long. Just until I can decide what to do about this situation. I wouldn't be calling if I didn't need this favor."

"That's some way to ask for a favor," Rayanne said. "If that's the reason for your call, you could have saved your dime."

Lila went on as though Rayanne hadn't spoken. "Jeremy

will take care of himself and the baby, and he can help out around the house."

"Lila, Jeremy isn't going to want to be tied down with a baby. My schedule is pretty full and Mama isn't able to look after a teenager *and* a three-month-old baby."

"I think they would bring some life to the house, and Mama would love it."

Rayanne tried going through it once more, but before she finished, Lila hung up. The phone rang again. It was Ralph. He'd been laid off at work. He was afraid he might even be terminated. Downsizing, he told her, but she didn't believe him. Ralph had been with that Wall Street firm for many years and had done well. If the firm really had laid Ralph off, then it was something other than downsizing involved—more than likely he was back on drugs again.

After she hung up from Ralph, she turned the radio to a station that played slow, soulful ballads. She switched on her computer and wrote while the tunes played softly in the background. As the music played, Rayanne could never remember feeling as lonely as she did at that moment. She'd spent time alone before, but now, she was lonely and there was a difference.

Rayanne was still writing when Scott called. He was coming over at six-thirty. Rayanne showered and slipped into a shorts set. She left the house through the back door, wandered around the yard. It was hot and muggy and the look of the storm clouds promised rain as they passed across the sky. She walked to the end of the backyard, where the trees began, and took the path, which they'd cut as children, to the lake. She loved the way the trees and wildflowers cast reflections on the water. With a little work, Rayanne knew, that would be the ideal setting for writing.

The lake was special for each of the Wilson children. When Rayanne was a young girl, she'd go to the lake, sometimes she'd take her favorite doll with her. Growing up in a home with five siblings caused her to seek refuge frequently, and the lake was perfect, where she could be quiet, talk to her doll, reflect as well as plan. At that lake, she'd decided the college she'd go to and what she wanted to do with her life. She even thought about the kind of man she wanted to marry and the number of children she would have.

There were other times when she and Ivory sneaked off there to read love letters from some boy from school. They'd read the letters and sigh, their hearts filled with love. Together they composed responses and slipped them into the waiting hands of the intended boys.

Rayanne sat on a small clearing near the lake and thought about her conversations with Lila and Ralph, and how her life had changed since returning to South Carolina. She smiled, though, when she thought of the effect her oldest brother, Samuel, had on her life. Sam had encouraged all the siblings to always be true to themselves, do their best, and to take risks. She remembered once when Sam had tied an old tire to the end of a rope, climbed out on a thick limb of a large tree that extended over the lake, and tied the other end of the rope to it, allowing the tire to swing back and forth over the water. At first, no one was brave enough to use it. However, after Sam's encouragement, they were soon swinging over the water, enjoying their new toy, although taking many spills before managing to glide over the water and return safely to land. Soon the swing became their favorite summer sport, and not only did Sam gain the respect and trust of his younger siblings, he was their hero. Sam had a way of making everything right. But that was then, and this was now, and Rayanne knew life would never be that simple again.

Rayanne got up, turned to leave, and saw Scott coming down the path.

"Hey there," he said, reaching her and looking around. "I didn't know you had your own private lake down here. This is nice."

Rayanne replied, "It's a great place to think."

"I'm sure it is," he said as they walked slowly back toward the house.

"What've you been up to?"

"Working mostly, but where've you been? I've been trying to get you all week."

"I've been kind of busy. School, the center, writing," she said as they rounded the house and mounted the steps. "You want to go inside or sit on the porch?"

"The porch is fine," he replied. "I just met your dad."

"He didn't offer you a drink, did he?" Rayanne asked, smiling at him.

"As a matter of fact, he did."

"You didn't accept?"

"You know I don't drink," Scott replied.

Rayanne smiled. Her father had offered Ralph, he accepted and drank a beer, and although her father never did say, his opinion of Ralph changed. Raymond did that with any man his daughters brought home. He didn't approve of anyone drinking. He'd tried but failed to discourage Josh, but when any of his children drank, they'd kept it hidden from him. Their mother knew. She knew everything.

Rayanne and Scott sat on the porch and it wasn't long before Helen appeared, carrying a tray with a pitcher of lemonade and two glasses filled with ice.

"How is Mrs. Abigail, Mama?" Rayanne inquired.

"Abbie ain't much today. She's still scared half to death after being robbed and hurt like that," Helen said. "Tangy was there. She asked about you."

"Okay. I'll give her a call," Rayanne said.

"She's doing real good, expecting her second baby." Helen gave Rayanne a smile she understood only too well.

Rayanne returned the look, wishing her mother would let her get a husband before she started having babies, and had told her so on many occasions.

"I didn't say anything," Helen said, reading her daughter's mind.

"But you were thinking."

"Well, you can't blame a mama for thinking," Helen said, with raised eyebrows. Then she turned to Scott. "How was service at your church today?"

"Very nice service," he said, and went on to tell her what the sermon was about.

Helen smiled. "Good. It was so nice seeing you again, Scott," she said, and disappeared back into the house.

Scott and Rayanne talked as the day faded into night, and as it did, there was a change in the temperature. It became a cool night for such a warm day. After a while, Rayanne became quiet, and Scott asked, "What's going on inside that head of yours tonight?"

"Oh, nothing much," she said, and when Scott looked directly into her eyes, she responded, "I'm all right."

"This is Scott. You can talk to me." He'd gotten to know her, her likes, her dislikes, her moods. "You never did tell me about your trip to New York," he explored.

"That was a while ago. Why are you asking about that now?" she asked, not wanting to think about New York, let alone talk about it. There were too many unhappy memories of New York.

"Something happened there?" he pressed. Although he knew she wouldn't say, he had to try.

"Why do you think something happened?"

"Because you haven't been the same since you came back."

"I really don't care to dig up ancient history," she said, and looked away, but not before Scott saw the pain in her eyes.

"It hasn't been that long. Besides, it might help to talk about it," he coaxed, ignoring the strange sensation in his stomach as he watched the crease deepen in her brow. "It's usually you who gets me to talk. When I do, I always feel better."

"I appreciate that you want to help, but it's a little embarrassing for me to discuss that trip with you."

"You don't have to be embarrassed about anything with me."

"Leave it alone," she begged.

Scott hated the way she was shutting him out, but he thought he'd better not push. He didn't want to run the risk of killing off the friendship before it had a chance to grow. But she just looked so sad. "We have a relationship here. We're supposed to talk about what's bothering us."

"We do not have a relationship. We've had a few dinners and a couple of movies, but that doesn't constitute a relationship," Rayanne corrected.

"Well, excuse me," Scott said, and slapped his arm, then quickly added, "Hold that thought. Can we go inside? These mosquitoes are eating me alive."

They went into the living room, and sat in front of the TV set. He looked at his watch. "Why don't you put it on Channel 7. *Wild Kingdom* will be on in a few minutes." She obeyed and sat beside him. "So you don't think we have a relationship?"

"We have a friendship," she said flatly.

"Friendship." Scott said the word slowly. He'd hoped they'd move their friendship to the next level, but since that wasn't what she'd wanted, he was willing to accept what she was willing to give. "I like the sound of that. Now that we've established that we're friends, let this friend help. Let's talk about what's bothering you."

"Look." She pointed to the TV, trying to divert his attention. *"Wild Kingdom* is coming on."

"Nice try."

She got up and left the room. She returned with a rum and Coke in her hand and sat back down beside him.

During a break in the program, Rayanne asked, "How old are you, Scott?"

Scott looked at her. "Where's that coming from?" he asked.

"I'm just curious. And you've never said."

"You've never asked."

"I'm asking now."

"Okay, I'm twenty-seven."

Rayanne knew Scott was young, but she was surprised that he wasn't as young as she'd thought. She asked, "You want to know how old I am?"

"Only if you want to tell me."

"I'm thirty-six."

"Okay."

"I just thought you might want to know." She sipped her drink.

"Age doesn't matter to me. I hope it doesn't matter to you. I'm a man, and the last time I checked, man was spelled M-A-N, not, A-G-E."

They watched the program, and when the last segment was over, Scott looked at his watch. "May I have a neck rub before I leave?" Rayanne didn't respond. "Hey!" He nudged her shoulder with his. "Where are you?" Rayanne looked at him. "How about a neck rub, please?" he said, lifting his hands as a dog would his paws. Rayanne looked at him and smiled. He sat on the floor beside her legs and she began to massage his neck, his shoulders, and his temples. "God, you've got the best hands. Have you ever thought of getting into the business?" he teased. "You sure got the right touch." Rayanne remained quiet. "You think you can control yourself just a little." He continued to tease her, she continued the massage. "Hey, you, the silence is killing me." Scott tried to turn his head to look at her, but she held his head, preventing it. Then they heard the key in the back door's lock, and she knew it was Josh—and the way he was fumbling with the lock, she also knew he was drunk. She stared at the glass of rum and Coke that sat on the coffee table. Scott twisted his neck from the pressure that she was suddenly applying.

Rayanne was certain that Josh was too drunk to open the door. She got up and opened it. Josh staggered inside. She helped him to a chair and draped a blanket across him, hoping he'd sleep the alcohol off before trying to move around. She'd been bailing Josh out of one situation after another for some time, and here she was, helping him in yet another situation. Her patience was wearing thin.

The last episode that had landed Josh in jail was three weeks ago when one of his buddies had gotten into a fight and the other party ran away. Josh thought the only way he could help his buddy was by blocking the highway so that his friend could catch the man. Well, when the authorities learned what Josh had done, not only did he lose his license, he was put in jail. It was Rayanne who'd posted bond and gotten him out, with him promising all the way home that he'd never touch another drop of alcohol. Josh had kept that promise the entire fifteen minutes it took them to get home. Then he was off again, only to return later—drunk.

When Rayanne heard Josh in the bathroom, she picked up her drink and poured it down the kitchen sink. At that moment, she decided never to drink anything alcoholic again.

Rayanne found herself feeling responsible for Josh's

drinking. Why was it that she felt responsible for things of which she had no control? What kind of personality allowed that kind of thinking? "I really should see someone about that," she mumbled, returning to join Scott.

"Is everything all right?" Scott asked.

"I wish Josh wouldn't drink so much," she said, resuming Scott's massage.

"I know that bothers you. He's family and you love him. We wish we could help them so they don't hurt themselves or anyone else, but we can't always. Just keep talking to him. Sometimes the more we talk and deal with a situation, the quicker the healing can begin," Scott said, and Rayanne wondered whether Scott was wrestling with demons of his own. The look on his face made her think that they weren't just talking about Josh's drinking. He continued, "Some people come by hurt and disappointment firsthand that cause a change in their behavior, and some a little further along, but it doesn't make it any easier if it involves people we love. It's not always easy, but you don't have to handle any situation alone. You've got family, you've got friends, and you've got me. You've always got me."

"We're talking about Josh, aren't we?" Rayanne asked, looking at him.

Scott looked at her, a weak smile on his face. "Yeah."

Although Rayanne had shared many things with Scott, there were still things she kept to herself, burdens she'd suffered alone. Now she asked herself why. Scott had always been supportive and understanding, and hadn't he always offered to help? That night as she looked at him, she decided it was time to share her misery with him, her worries about her dad, Josh, and the situation involving Dorian and Ralph.

"I knew this long-distance romance between Ralph and me would have its challenges, and as much as I hate to admit it, I've even accepted the fact that he's been involved with someone else, but he's done something I never thought he'd do. I'd alway trusted his love for me, but all that's changed." Her voice was just above a whisper, and the look on her face made Scott believe that she was remembering better times. "Ralph and Dorian have been sleeping together."

Scott shook his head. "Unbelievable," he said. "What can I do to make you feel better?" he asked, unconcerned about the pain that cut deep in his own heart at the look in Rayanne's eyes when she was thinking of Ralph. That look told Scott that despite all Ralph had done, she still loved him, and because she did, she'd forgive him. "You've got a lot on your plate, but you are handling it really well," he said.

"It may look that way on the outside, but underneath I'm struggling to hold it together," she said. "Please be patient with me. I'll get past this."

"Whatever you need, baby," he said, and sat on the coffee table to face her. "Hey, I've got an idea. Patti and Bobby are coming to the Township next week. Wanna go?"

"That would be great." Then she said, "You're a great friend."

There was another pause. Then Scott said, "You can, you know."

"What?" She frowned.

He looked into her eyes. "Trust me, count on me, love me. It's safe," he said. Scott seemed to have turned his full attention to the dismantling of her life, and he promised to stand by her while she put it back together. Rayanne remembered a prior conversation she'd discussed with Scott. She valued his opinion and couldn't help feeling fortunate to have him in her life. She'd said, "Life has a way of throwing us lemons."

"Then you make lemonade."

"Does the same principle apply when life throws you a curve?"

"Then you hit it out of the ballpark." She'd laughed about that situation then, only she didn't feel like laughing now.

"You're a bright lady. If you get knocked off your feet, you're the type to get back up and walk away wiser," he said. "Always remember that people come in and out of our lives like Grand Central Station. Some leave a moment in the soul that can last forever, and then there are those who just quietly go away."

A wave of tenderness swept through her. Not only was Scott young, the man was wise.

"Get over here, you, and let me finish that neck rub before I change my mind," she said, and laughed.

"I love you," he said softly.

"Yeah, right," she said, but she did appreciate the gesture.

"I do love you."

"You just think I need to hear it."

"You want to hear it, too, because I know you've got love hiding around in there for me," he said, pointing a finger toward her heart.

Scott was like a candle in the darkness. "You make me feel grateful for today and eager beyond anything I can imagine about tomorrow. You give me hope," she said jokingly, but her words were truer than she realized.

"Spoken like a true poet," he said.

"You're the poet in this family. Now get on over here," she ordered. He obeyed, and they sat and listened to the sounds of the night—cars honking, crickets chirping, and dogs barking, adding to the melody.

11

When you have good health and happiness, you should count your blessings, because all that can change in an instant. In her thirties, Rayanne was the only one of the trio of best friends who hadn't yet married, and Josh was in rehabilitation centers more than he was out. Nothing, though, had prepared her for the shock and the incredible sense of loss that overwhelmed her when her father died.

Rayanne had accompanied Tiffany, who'd co-owned a typing service with Rayanne in New York, to a meeting in San Francisco, where she was being recognized as an enterprising young businesswoman. Rayanne had sold her share in the partnership, but the business still bore the name RayTiff, and Tiffany had wanted Rayanne to be there with her.

Rayanne returned three days later on a hot summer day to find her father alone in the yard, working as usual. When she returned home, Rayanne had persuaded her father to hire a handyman to do the upkeep on the rental houses, which her father had built and leased to tenants who couldn't afford to pay much rent, as well as do work around their house. Although the handyman did an excellent job, it wasn't long before her father was doing most of the work again. Rayanne did notice his health improving, but she also knew that if he wasn't careful, Raymond Wilson would run into trouble again and end up back in the hospital. He looked tired. Perspiration stained his long-sleeved shirt, which he wore rolled up, and Rayanne wished once again that he wouldn't work so hard.

Rayanne hugged her father, and he tried not to soil her clothes.

"Daddy, come inside and rest awhile. It's a very warm day," Rayanne said.

"I'll be in there in a little while. You go on in and tell your mama to have a cold drink waiting for me," he said just as Helen was coming out of the house with a pitcher of lemonade and two glasses. Rayanne knew from the expression on her mother's face that she, too, had tried but failed to get her husband to quit work—at least, until it was cooler.

"Where is Josh?" Rayanne asked.

"I thought he was out here with your daddy," Helen said, looking around for Josh. "That boy's got such a good head on his shoulders, but he's just throwing it all away." Then she said to her husband, "Come on over here, Raymond and sit with me awhile." He climbed down from the back of his truck. "Here," she said, first handing him a wad of paper towels, which he took and wiped the sweat from his face as he sat on a bench with his wife. Then she handed him a glass of lemonade. "This is nice and cold."

Raymond took a sip of lemonade, closed his eyes, and said, "Next to you, woman, this is the closest thing to heaven." Helen blushed and fanned her hand at him. "This really hits the spot."

"I thought it would," she said, and leaning closer, she whispered, "Who knows? You might get a notion to make it up to me later."

"You better believe it." He winked at her.

Rayanne snickered as she observed her parents from the kitchen window. How lucky they were to be so much in love for more than fifty years. She turned away, smiling, and checked her messages. As she was going to her room to change, she heard a noise. Someone was snoring.

"That'd better not be Josh in there sleeping with Daddy working outside," she said, and walked toward the sound. She entered his room and saw Josh sitting in a chair behind the door, his head thrown back, sleeping. She approached him. "Josh!" she screamed his name. The air surrounding him reeked of alcohol. She shook him and he opened one eye just a slit.

"Rayanne. Hey, what's going on?" His words slurred as he focused on her.

"What are you doing in here?" she asked.

"I just came in a little while ago. I'm gonna go back out in a minute." He squinted up at her.

"Daddy's out there working alone in all that heat."

"Let me just pull myself together. I'm hurting so bad right now."

Josh was only two years older than Rayanne, but he'd wallowed in self-pity, drank, and fooled around with so many women that he could have passed easily for forty-five, even fifty.

As Rayanne moved closer to him, she saw an ugly scar on the side of his head, his jaw was swollen, and there was blood on his clothes.

"What happened to your face?"

"It's nothing to worry about." He tried to get up. "Phew. This thing hurts like hell." He rubbed his jaw.

Rayanne kneeled down, took Josh's face in her hands, and said, "Josh, your jaw may be broken. You need to see a doctor. Go and clean yourself up, and let's go to the emergency room."

"I'll be all right. I just need a couple of aspirins."

"You need to see a doctor." She eyed his face. "I'm glad the folks didn't see you like this."

"I don't think they even know that I'm here."

"Yes, they do," Rayanne said, and Josh looked at her.

After Josh had cleaned himself up, he waited at the front of the house for Rayanne. Once in the car, she asked, "So what happened to you?"

"I was fooling around with some old gal, and her husband found out. That sucker popped me a couple of times."

"That woman you were hanging around with last week?"

"Oh, hell no. This is someone else."

"Sinners never sleep," Rayanne said, and they chuckled, heading to the hospital.

Josh's jaw was fractured. He got several stitches on his head and they left the hospital. When they returned home around nine o'clock, they were surprised to see so many cars when they pulled into their driveway.

Josh growled.

"Looks like everyone's here," Rayanne said, and chuckled as she parked the car. They sat a moment.

"Someone must've seen us at the hospital and called Mama and Daddy, and it looks like they done told everybody else," Josh said, rubbing the side of his face.

"We may as well go on in and face the gang." Rayanne chuckled again as Josh complained. "If you choose to live your life this way, you have to face the music."

"Let's go in through the side door and avoid the questions," he pleaded. "You better get your butt on in here."

As Rayanne put her key into the lock, the door suddenly opened, and there stood Maxine, with tears in her eye and a tissue in her hand.

"Maxine, what's wrong?" Rayanne asked, startled.

Tears rolling down Maxine's face, she replied, "It's Daddy."

"What's wrong with Daddy? Is he sick?" Rayanne

asked, walking quickly past Maxine, going toward her parents' bedroom. "He's been doing too much. I keep telling him that, but he won't listen," Rayanne said over her shoulder to her sister.

Maxine rushed after Rayanne, caught her arm, and turned her around to face her. "Rayanne, Daddy's dead."

The words slammed into Rayanne's brain. She felt dizzy, her head began to spin, and the last thing she remembered was a scream tearing its way out of her throat.

She awoke in the middle of the night in her own bed, not knowing how she'd gotten there. She tried to recall the events of the evening. When she tried to move, pain shot through her head, disabling her.

"You lie back down and rest, child," Aunt Bessie said from the chair beside Rayanne's bed.

"Aunt Bessie, is that you?" Rayanne tried to focus in the dim light. "What are you doing here?" She eased up on an elbow, meeting the tormented expression on Aunt Bessie's face. Then she remembered. It was like a kick in her stomach. "Daddy's dead," Rayanne said.

"Yes," Aunt Bessie answered.

Rayanne couldn't talk anymore. She could only lie back and cry softly into her pillow, with Aunt Bessie seldom leaving her side.

"How are Mama and the others?" Rayanne asked.

"They are holding up as best as they can," Aunt Bessie replied. "Your daddy fell in the backyard, had another heart attack, and by the time your mama could get help, it was too late."

"Oh, my God. It's my fault," Rayanne said, shaking her head.

"No, child," Aunt Bessie answered. "Ain't nobody's fault."

"If I had been here, I could've helped, and Daddy might still be alive," Rayanne said.

"Now, child, you listen to me. You had no control over what happened here today. It was the will of the Lord, and you gotta get that in your head. This is the Lord's doing. It hurts us, but we gotta accept it."

"I've got to check on Mama," Rayanne said, trying to get out of bed.

"You lie down. Helen is okay. Your mama is a strong woman," Aunt Bessie said.

"Aunt Bessie, my daddy is gone. He is dead." Rayanne sobbed. "What am I gonna do without my daddy? What are we gonna do? Daddy is gone. Daddy is gone."

Aunt Bessie sat on the side of the bed and wrapped her arms around Rayanne and held her until she stopped crying. Then Rayanne lay back down and was silent. Aunt Bessie talked with her during the night, rubbed her hands, comforting her as best she could. Although dazed, Rayanne heard the door to the house opening and closing throughout the night.

As the sun began to wake up the morning, Aunt Bessie left the room and returned with a glass of warm milk and two pills, which she pushed into Rayanne's mouth. When Rayanne woke in the early afternoon, Aunt Bessie was still there. Rayanne closed her eyes, a vision of her father in her mind, and fresh tears rolled down her cheeks. She looked at Aunt Bessie, sitting with her, strong and brave, and it was at that moment that she realized that through her own sorrow, she hadn't thought how the death of her father had affected her aunt.

"My God, Aunt Bessie, I'm sorry. You were my daddy's only sister. How traumatic this must be for you. I am so sorry," Rayanne said, reaching for her aunt.

"I know, my child. I know," Aunt Bessie replied, and this time, they wept together.

* * *

The days that followed were almost unbearable. Rayanne had never experienced such a sense of loss. Her father was gone, and she'd never see him again. That thought was too much to handle. Rayanne found that the only thing she could do for days was cry, but as time passed and she observed her mother or Aunt Bessie, her faith and strength were renewed.

The day of the funeral, there were so many in attendance that it was impossible to fit them all in the church. There were more mourners in the fellowship hall and outside the church than inside, and there were numerous plants, flowers, and wreaths. There were so many that the family decided that some of them should go to patients in the hospital, which would have pleased Raymond.

Ivory, her family, and Dorian and her husband, attended the funeral. Although Rayanne didn't expect Ralph to make the trip, and he didn't, he did call. Rayanne and Dorian hadn't spoken since that horrible night in New York, and even though their visit started out strained, Rayanne, Ivory, and Dorian spent some time catching up. Before Dorian and her husband left South Carolina, Rayanne expressed appreciation for Dorian being there.

Dorian knew that was true, but she also knew that Rayanne wasn't anywhere close to welcoming her back into her life.

12

Scott was angry at Ralph. He saw how Rayanne agonized over the loss of her father. Although a lot had happened to put distance between Ralph and Rayanne, Scott knew that Rayanne needed Ralph at that time, more than ever. Rayanne's vulnerability had quite an effect on Scott the night after the funeral. She'd cried like a lost, frightened child, and Scott wanted to comfort her in any way that he could. He would've done anything to make her world right again.

Most of the family left a couple of days after the funeral. Lila stayed a little longer, but when she returned to New York, Jeremy and Charlotte were left behind, with a promise that she'd return within two weeks for them. But the weeks grew into a much longer period, Lila seldom called, and when she did, she kept putting off picking up the children. Rayanne felt really bad for Jeremy. Since Rayanne had come from a home of loving supportive parents, she could only imagine what he must be feeling. Lila had never shown him any real love, she constantly put him down, and there were times when she assured him that he'd never have been born if she'd learned of her pregnancy sooner.

The weeks that followed, Rayanne and Jeremy talked a lot. She introduced him to young people at church, she helped him get his permit, taught him to drive, and he got his license the first time he took the test. It'd been quite an adjustment: listening to music so loud that the walls seemed to vibrate, the sound of a baby crying in the middle of the night, and teenagers parading in and out of the house day and night.

Initially it wasn't bad. They kept reasonable hours and it was tolerable. Rayanne and Helen made snacks for the kids, they enjoyed the renewed life in the house, and it was reminiscent of times when Rayanne was a teenager and her friends came and made themselves at home.

When September came, and it looked as though Jeremy and Little Charlotte were there to stay, Rayanne knew it'd been no accident, but a calculated, well-orchestrated plan of Lila's. She'd worked on Helen and had gotten her wish.

Jeremy enrolled at Sumter High School to complete his senior year. Rayanne knew that not many teenage boys could be relied upon to care for an infant, and Jeremy was no exception. As it turned out, Little Charlotte would wake up in the middle of the night, wet and crying, and there was no way to know how long this would've gone on if Helen or Rayanne hadn't intervened and taken care of the baby. By that time, Rayanne was counseling teenage girls three times a week, helping to build their self-esteem. She was putting in a number of hours at the adult center, and she was still going to school. She served on several committees at church and she was writing every chance she got. She loved the children, but her hands were full.

Some evenings, Rayanne arrived home so tired that all she could do was shower and go straight to bed. One of those nights, the baby began to cry. Rayanne opened her eyes but lay there, thinking maybe Charlotte would go back to sleep or Jeremy would take care of her. Instead, the baby continued to cry. Rayanne threw back the covers and went into the room that they'd set up for Jeremy and the baby. She picked up the baby and found her soaking wet—there was no sign of Jeremy and his bed was still made. Rayanne wondered where he was. She changed the baby, gave her a bottle, and put her back to bed, where she slept through the remainder of the night. Jeremy still hadn't made it home when she checked on the baby at three in the morning.

Rayanne made breakfast and waited for Jeremy to come into the kitchen. She wanted to talk to him before he went to school. She looked at her watch, thinking he should be up by now. Rayanne got up from the table, went to his room, and knocked on his door.

"Jeremy," she called out. When she didn't get a response, she entered the room and turned on the light. She approached his bed. "Jeremy, get up or you're going to be late for school."

"I don't think I can make school today, Aunt Rayanne," Jeremy said, shielding his eyes from the light that flooded the room.

"Why? What's wrong?" she asked.

"I don't feel so good."

"Does something hurt?" She leaned over and touched his forehead. "I don't think you have a temperature." She left the room and returned in minutes with the thermometer, but Jeremy was asleep again.

Rayanne got dressed, and after giving instructions to Madeline, the young lady whom she'd hired to look after the baby and keep her mother company, she drove to the university. She called home midday to check on everything and learned that Jeremy had gone out shortly after she left and hadn't returned.

* * *

As Rayanne drove home that afternoon, she thought of her mother. The woman who once had enormous strength and insight had changed. The changes occurred shortly after Raymond had died. She'd never seen her mother cry. Helen had mourned and grieved, but she didn't cry, not when Raymond died or at his funeral.

Rayanne didn't witness tears from her mother until about a month after her father died. She'd just checked on the baby and was returning to her room. As she was passing her mother's door, she heard her say, "Damn you, Raymond. Why did you have to die and leave me? What am I gonna do without you? I miss you so. Oh, Raymond. Why? Why? Why?"

Not only was Rayanne surprised by her mother's cries, she felt completely helpless. She didn't know what to do to help her mother with her grief. She knew she couldn't go in at that moment. Her mother had been keeping all her grief inside, and Rayanne had watched the pressure build up in her daily. Once when Rayanne had tried to get her mother to talk about her father's death, she'd said that death was a part of life and that they had to accept it. Only Helen *hadn't* accepted it. She'd kept it inside and had suffered as a result.

As Rayanne stood with her face against the door, she knew her mother needed to cry. More than anything else at that time, she needed to cry. Rayanne kept watch on her mother during the night, and she appeared to sleep peacefully, but to Rayanne's amazement, she awoke the next morning to the smell of breakfast. Her mother had gotten up and cooked breakfast and was folding a bunch of towels she took from the dryer.

"Wow," Rayanne said, entering the kitchen. "What's all this?"

"Breakfast. What do ya think it is?" Helen said with her usual quickness that Rayanne admired so much.

"You must've gotten up at the crack of dawn."

"You know it don't take me long to put a little breakfast on the table," Helen said, continuing her chores.

"You certainly have been busy this morning. Breakfast. Laundry. My goodness," Rayanne said, piling her plate high with grits, eggs, bacon, and a piece of toast. She ate heartily, and as she did, she watched her mother. "So how are you this morning, Mama?"

"I'm fine, honey," Helen replied, but Rayanne noticed her actions contradicted her reply. She was doing everything twice the normal pace.

"Mama, are you sure you are okay?" Rayanne was feeling uneasy.

"Your mama is fine. Just got a lot to do today."

"Mama, Madeline will help," Rayanne said; then to Madeline, "Right, Madeline?"

"Right," Madeline replied.

Helen gave Madeline a dark look before she picked up a stack of towels and left the room. Although her mother appeared to be her old self, before Rayanne left home that morning, she asked Madeline to keep a close eye on her.

In the weeks that passed, Rayanne and Helen visited Raymond's grave, and she watched her mother become a different person. One morning in late November, when Rayanne didn't have any classes, a call came in from a doctor's office reminding Helen of her appointment the following day. When Rayanne hung up, she wondered what was wrong with her mother. Why was she seeing a psychiatrist? And why wasn't she told?

Rayanne called Maxine about that phone call and was surprised that Maxine knew about the doctor visits. Helen had been going through periods of depression after Raymond died, and to add to her dilemma, her best friend, Abigail, was moving out of town.

"Rayanne, I didn't tell you because I didn't want you

to worry," Maxine said, and it was true, but Rayanne would've preferred being told up front.

Rayanne arrived home late one night after she and Brenda had gone out to dinner at a jazz lounge restaurant. She got into bed and it seemed she had just closed her eyes when Little Charlotte began to cry. She waited a moment, thinking Jeremy would take care of her. Not so. The baby cried out again. Rayanne got out of bed, and when she checked Charlotte, the infant had a slight temperature. Rayanne took some Infants' Tylenol from the medicine cabinet, gave some to the baby, and shortly afterward, Little Charlotte was smiling, kicking her tiny feet and waving her hands. What annoyed Rayanne was that Jeremy was nowhere around.

Within an hour, the baby was back in bed, and Rayanne called Lila. As she suspected, her call went to Lila's voice mail. Rayanne left a message.

Lila returned the call the next morning.

"Lila, I'm concerned about the hours Jeremy is keeping," Rayanne began. "There's a lot going on in the streets in South Carolina, as well as New York, and I think it would be best if you made some other arrangements for Jeremy and the baby."

"Rayanne, I've been tied down with Jeremy most of my life, and I need a break. Besides," she said, "I don't see what harm it would be for them to stay on, especially since Jeremy will graduate soon, not to mention he is helping out around the house."

Rayanne didn't mention the fact that Jeremy was hardly ever at the house. "Lila, Mama isn't doing well, and I don't have time to look after the children and do the things I need to do."

Rayanne was in for yet another surprise when Lila told her that she'd talked with Helen and had convinced her that if Jeremy stayed in New York, something awful would happen to him. Of course, Helen, feeling the way she did about family, assured Lila it wouldn't be a problem for Jeremy and the baby to stay on as long as they liked. Well, it was settled.

Early the following morning, Rayanne heard Jeremy go into his room. She got up, went to his door, and paused a moment before she knocked and entered. "Jeremy, it's nearly four o'clock. Where've you been?" she asked.

"Just hanging out," he said, pulling his oversized sweatshirt over his head. He sat on the side of the bed and kicked his shoes off, allowing them to drop to the floor with a thud.

"Your little girl was sick tonight." Rayanne tried not to show her anger.

"What's wrong with her?"

"She's all right now, but she had a temperature."

"I'm glad she's okay," he said, almost nonchalant. "I'm gonna turn in now, Aunt Rayanne. Good night."

"Don't try dismissing me, Jeremy. Your daughter was sick. I'd like to think that you'd be a little more concerned," Rayanne said. "What's going on with you? This is not the first time that you've disappeared during the night, returning in the wee hours." Rayanne sat on the foot of the bed and looked at Jeremy. "You're young and I know it's difficult being a parent, but you've got to take some responsibility. If the baby had been seriously ill and I had not been here, I don't know what would have happened to her, and that frightens me. Mama isn't able to take care of the baby." Rayanne paused as Jeremy appeared not to be paying any attention. "Jeremy, are you listening to me?"

"Yes, Aunt Rayanne."

Rayanne looked at him and sighed. "You go on to sleep, but we're going to talk about this." She left the room, closing the door behind her.

For some time she'd wanted to talk with Jeremy about his strange comings and goings. There were times when he'd come in, wander around in his room, and she'd hear him leave again and get into a waiting car.

One evening after Helen had gone to bed, Jeremy was sitting at the kitchen table doing homework and Rayanne was sitting in the den, rocking the baby to sleep. When she put Little Charlotte to bed and returned to the den, she sat on the couch and began thumbing through vehicle magazines.

"What are you gonna do with the car you have, Aunt Rayanne?" Jeremy asked, looking up from his work.

"I'm not sure. With the baby, I don't think I need a Corvette," Rayanne replied, leafing through the book.

"Why don't you let me have it?"

"Jeremy, there are a lot of responsibilities owning a car," Rayanne said, though her intention had always been to give him that car.

"Yeah, I know—insurance, taxes, gasoline, repairs . . . ," Jeremy said.

"Those are some, but I'm more concerned about you behaving responsibly."

"Aunt Rayanne, please let me have the Vette."

"No late-night comings and goings, and help to look after your child."

Rayanne could see the excitement in Jeremy's eyes. "I will, Aunt Rayanne. I promise."

Jeremy got the Corvette, kept his promise, and Rayanne couldn't have been more pleased.

For weeks, it appeared everything was going to be all right until one day Rayanne arrived home to find Jody Brown, a known drug dealer, sitting in the kitchen with

Jeremy. Jody was older than Jeremy, and he was bad news. If Rayanne had her way, a guy like Jody Brown wouldn't be a friend of Jeremy's, and neither would he have been invited into their home.

Jeremy was feeling abandoned, deserted by both parents, and was in search of himself, his own independence, but what he found was something entirely different. Rayanne was afraid that without some intervention, he'd be selling or using drugs himself, or both.

She talked with Jeremy, not as some domineering person, but like someone who cared. Although she didn't condone some of the things she suspected he was doing, she didn't criticize him. Jeremy had a lifetime of hearing negative things about himself, and Rayanne was determined not to treat him that way. She did take a hard line with him, though, letting him know what she expected from him and what he could expect from her. In order that they coexist, it meant working together, and no one said it would be easy.

Rayanne had planned a girls' night with Hilary and Brenda. Rayanne was about to leave the house when Jeremy approached her. He'd made plans and he wanted to know whether she would look after the baby. Rayanne had been accommodating whenever she could, but tonight she needed to get out and shoot the breeze.

"You're out every night, Jeremy. You're gonna have to cancel your plans this evening."

Rayanne knew Jeremy was upset about having to stay in, but she had no idea how desperate he was until she went into the bedroom to kiss the baby good night and caught him attempting to give the baby cold medication to make her sleep.

"What are you doing? Get away from her," Rayanne yelled so loud that Jeremy dropped the bottle, spilling its red liquid on the carpet.

Rayanne canceled her plans for the evening, but told

Jeremy that under no circumstances should a similar situation ever reoccur. Little did she know at that time, that she'd be spending even more evenings at home taking care of the baby. Because, not long after that night when she went to check on the baby, she saw from the bedroom window Jeremy climbing into the Corvette and driving away. Rayanne had wanted a husband and children one day, but she had no idea she'd suddenly have two children thrust upon her without the benefit of having a husband. Her life was coming to a standstill, but Jeremy's was moving on, full speed ahead.

"What you got there?" Helen asked from where she and Madeline were hanging curtains at the kitchen window.

"Just a few things for the baby," Rayanne replied, holding several packages in her hands.

She paid Madeline, and after the caregiver left, Rayanne told Helen that she'd gotten an A and two B's, Brenda got two A's and a B, and Hilary, three B's.

"You girls are doing real good. Won't be long now before y'all will have all that behind ya." Helen was having a good day, and Rayanne was glad.

"A couple of semesters and it will be over," Rayanne said, putting the last tieback in place. "Let me show you what I got."

Rayanne removed the items from the bag.

"Oooh. How pretty. Why, I don't know which one I like best," Helen said, looking at the dresses.

Charlotte was beginning to walk and she was as graceful as a swan. It wasn't long before Little Charlotte lost that nickname and became Swan. She was Swan to everyone, except Lila.

After they had dinner that evening, Jeremy began making phone calls, which wasn't unusual, but what made Helen and Rayanne pay attention was that he'd made three phone calls to three different girls, saying the exact same thing to each of them.

"What's up, baby?" he'd said. "I've been thinking about you all day. Yeah. I'm crazy about you, baby, and I'd like to see you this evening. Are you down with that? I thought we could get together, have a little pizza, something to drink, and chill."

Rayanne and Helen looked at each other, shook their heads, and laughed. Then Rayanne picked up Swan from the floor, where she was playing, and they left the room. Jeremy was eighteen, handsome, and popular. He stood over six feet, his complexion was medium brown, and his jet black wavy hair was cut short. Rayanne was sure that, even at his early age, he'd left some broken hearts behind.

Rayanne was going through the mail the following day and she saw a letter from Sumter High School. Jeremy was missing classes. When he was present, he didn't pay attention, never turned in homework, or was disruptive in class.

Rayanne had thought she was being too tough on Jeremy and had decided to give him a little more freedom, but when he came in that night and went into his room, she followed him. Jeremy sat down hard on the bed. He could barely keep his eyes open.

"Jeremy, we need to talk, but obviously this is not a good time. You get some sleep, but we will talk tomorrow." She left the room, questioning giving him her old car. She'd wanted Jeremy to have things teenagers wanted, she just hoped it wasn't a mistake.

Rayanne returned to her room. Unable to sleep, she opened the newspaper. Crime was running rampant. Not just in this country but in her own backyard. Rayanne knew that something had to be done to make the world a better and safer place to live.

13

"Here comes that lying ass, Brenda," Hilary said.

"Sssh," Rayanne said. "The girl just likes to have fun."

They were having lunch after class. Brenda came through the line, tray in hand, to join Rayanne and Hilary. She saw someone she knew and stopped to speak.

"It's more than that," Hilary replied.

"You're not jealous, are you?" Rayanne teased.

"I'm concerned that she's sexually involved with all those guys," Hilary said.

"Brenda's not stupid. She knows what she's doing."

"I know she's practicing safe sex and all, but it still bothers me that she's falling into bed with every man she meets," Hilary said, clearly disgusted.

"Hilary, I don't think it's like that," Rayanne said in defense of Brenda.

"You don't even have to guess at what she does. She puts it all out there for you."

"Brenda is just trying to have a little fun. She's been through a lot. She hasn't said this, but I think she's still in love with Cardell."

"Really? You think they'll get back together?"

"I don't know, but if that's what she wants, then I hope it happens."

"I like Brenda a lot, but the woman has no morals."

"She's all right," Rayanne said as Brenda approached the table.

Sitting at the table with their salad and iced tea, Brenda said, "So what's up with you two?"

"Things are going okay with me. What's up with you, girlfriend?" Rayanne asked.

Brenda laughed. "My question is, do you really wanna know?"

"Oh heck," Rayanne said, "why not? Let's just live dangerously for five minutes."

"I don't know if I want to hear this," Hilary said, putting a fork of salad into her mouth.

"Well, let me tell you, anyway." Brenda pointed to a hickey on her neck. "This is what Jason gave me last night."

Rayanne said, "I thought you were seeing Matt last night."

"Wait a minute and let me tell you what happened," Brenda said, and the girls were all ears. "Matt, with that big black ass of his, called me yesterday, and I agreed to see him. I asked him to call before coming over. I wanted to take a little nap so I could be fresh for him when he arrived. Well, Jason decided to stop by."

"Is he the nineteen-year-old?" Hilary asked.

"He's older than that now. Do you think I got older, but he didn't?" Brenda asked, looking at Hilary with her mouth hanging open. "Wrong."

Hilary clicked her teeth and said, "He's still just a boy."

Rayanne and Brenda laughed.

"That so-called boy's got his act together. Just look at y'all. A bunch of nosy old women." Brenda chuckled.

"Okay, don't tell us. See if we care," Rayanne said, biting into a piece of dill pickle.

"Oh hell, y'all care. You ain't shitting me?" Brenda chuckled again.

"Go on with your sordid little story," Hilary said. "You know you're dying to, anyway."

"As I was saying"—Brenda dabbed her lips with her napkin—"Jason stopped by just as I was getting out of the shower. He was just sitting there in my living room, looking at me. Then he started licking those sexy lips of his."

"His lips or your lips?" Hilary asked, perched on the edge of her seat.

"His lips, Hilary. Pay attention," Brenda said, rolling her eyes. "Then he poked his tongue out and started wiggling it around."

"Where were the boys?" Hilary asked.

"They spent the night with my mother," Brenda said, winking at Rayanne.

"Hello," Rayanne said, and gave Brenda five.

"Jason got up from his chair, got down on his hands and knees, and he crawled over to me," Brenda said, and paused a moment.

"What happened then?" Hilary lifted a fork of salad to her mouth, but not paying attention to what she was doing, the salad fell off the fork, and she pushed the empty fork into her mouth. Realizing what she'd done, she laid the fork on her plate.

"I didn't do anything. He did it all. He kissed my feet, licked my legs up to my knees, and then . . . ," Brenda said, making the girls wait while she filled her mouth with salad. She chewed slowly on it and washed it down with a couple of sips of tea. Brenda looked at Hilary and burst out laughing.

"Are you going to finish this disgusting story?" Hilary asked, clearly interested.

"Sure," Brenda said, taking another sip of tea. Rayanne chuckled, knowing Brenda was enjoying the mileage she was getting out of her story. "Then he opened that wonderful mouth of his and he began sucking my knees." She paused. "Have either of you ever had your knees sucked?"

"My goodness." Hilary caught her breath and peered over the rim of her glasses. Hilary was usually a little naïve about some things, but she was right there with the others, and the implication of what Brenda was saying spurred her imagination.

"It's not bad," Rayanne answered.

"No, it's fucking good," Brenda said. Then to Hilary, "What about you, old lady?"

"This is your story," Hilary spat out.

"I'm scareda you!" Brenda said, and she and Rayanne chuckled. "Anyway, Jason was turning me on, and he hadn't even laid a hand on me yet. Guess what happened next? The phone rings, and who do you think it is?"

"Matt," Rayanne and Hilary said in unison.

"You got it. I went into the kitchen to take the call, and there I was leaning against the table with my back to the door, talking with Matt, when all of a sudden Jason comes up behind me. He put his arms around me and kissed my neck. Then he rubbed my stomach and sucked on my earlobe," Brenda said, her eyes closed.

"Were you still talking with Matt while all this was going on?" Hilary asked incredulously.

"Yes, Hilary. I was multitasking."

"I asked a simple question." Hilary popped a piece of roll into her mouth.

"Yes, I was still talking with Matt. Then he came around and faced me." Brenda took another sip from her glass and looked at Hilary. "Jason, that is."

"I know who you meant!" Hilary exclaimed.

"Just making sure we're on the same page," Brenda said. "Well, Jason pushed me back on the table, and opened my robe with his mouth. The things that man can do with that mouth of his."

"Couldn't Matt tell something was going on?" Hilary asked.

"Matt was talking dirty to me, so I suppose he thought my moans were meant for him," Brenda answered.

"You didn't allow him to make love to you there on the kitchen table, did you?" Hilary asked.

"No, we didn't make love at all that day." Brenda smiled wickedly at Hilary. "Does that mean my virtue is still in tact?"

"Hardly!" Hilary snorted, and they laughed. Then Hilary said, "Rayanne thinks you're still in love with Cardell."

Brenda's smile faded and she looked at Rayanne. "Why would you think that?"

"Because it's true," Rayanne replied.

Brenda rolled her eyes to the ceiling. Then she looked at Rayanne. "That's water under the bridge now," she said sadly.

"Not if you guys love each other," Rayanne said.

"Believe me, it's over. Why are we talking about Cardell, anyway?" Brenda got up to go to the dessert bar.

Rayanne reached out and caught her arm. "Brenda, wait a minute."

Brenda looked hard at Rayanne, then sat back down and accepted coffee from the waitress. "What now?" she asked, looking at each girl.

"I am concerned about you," Rayanne answered.

"Don't be. Look, ladies, we've been all through this. Cardell and I separated after all possibility of reconciliation had been explored."

"But you never divorced," Rayanne said.

"No. The boys, I guess," Brenda said.

"You probably gave up too quickly, just as you always

do when something doesn't go your way. You—" Hilary began, but Brenda cut her off.

"I hope you're not judging me now about things I did at a time when you didn't even know me. Look, I went through hell back then," Brenda said, and it was obvious she was still feeling the pain of years gone by.

There was a slight lull. Then Hilary reached across the table and took Brenda's hand. "Brenda, I just want you to be happy. That's all."

Brenda stared silently at Hilary. Then she said, "I didn't say anything, but Cardell came by last week and we talked. He did mention getting back together."

"That's wonderful," Hilary said.

"Don't go jumping the gun. We just talked. Cardell would have to change a lot, and I'm not sure he's ready or willing. I'd have to make some adjustments myself." Brenda laughed, then said, "Don't let your imaginations run away with you. It'll just make all of us unhappy if things don't pan out. Anyway, I'm still hungry," she said, about to get up again.

"If there's a chance to put your marriage back together and bring your boys' dad back home, don't you think it's worth a try?" Rayanne waited for a response. None came.

"He wants to get back with you. Doesn't that tell you he still loves you and he's changed?" Hilary suggested.

"No. It tells me he wants to control my life. He knows I'm having a good time, so he wants me back under his thumb, with my head in the sand," Brenda said. "I've always been vulnerable to Cardell, but I've learned to be more cautious. This time, I'm trying to make my decisions with my head, and not my heart. That man has hit me with a hard dose of reality more than once," she said, remembering times when he'd say, "Let's get back together." She'd be all for it, even after what he'd put her through; then he'd change his mind again. Brenda shook her head, not wanting to remember, and said, "Never mind."

"What?" Hilary asked.

Brenda took a deep breath. "One minute, he talks about getting back together, I start to show a little interest, and then he backs away. He does that shit to me all the time. Confuses the hell out of me." She threw her hands in the air. "Anyway, it's no big deal."

"It is a big deal if you love him and want him in your and your kids' lives," Rayanne said.

"I don't want to take the emotional risk," Brenda said.

"Everything involves risk. Find out what he wants. Let him know what you want," Rayanne said. Brenda smiled and shook her head negatively. "Ah, give the man a chance."

"I've given him too many chances," Brenda said.

"Give him another." Rayanne smiled.

"What if it doesn't work out? What if he hurts me again?"

"What if he doesn't? He did make you happy once," Rayanne said.

"He's made me just as unhappy," Brenda came back as Hilary listened to the exchange.

"I know what you're going through." Rayanne was sympathetic.

"Obviously not, or we wouldn't be having this conversation," Brenda replied.

"There aren't any guarantees, but I think it's worth a shot," Rayanne said.

Brenda slid out from behind the table, stood up, lifted both hands, and said, "I can see that the only way I'm gonna be able to get something else to eat is to tell you two what you wanna hear—especially you, Rayanne. I'll think about it. That's all I can say." With that, Brenda left the table.

"Are we still going to New York on that shopping trip?" Hilary asked when Brenda returned.

"I'd like to," Rayanne said. "What about you, Brenda?"

"What?" Brenda said, slightly distracted.

"Are you going to New York on Thursday?" Rayanne asked. "I can go if I get a babysitter. Madeline is off this week."

That was another thing about Rayanne's life that had changed. She couldn't pick up and go as she'd done in the past. She had to get someone to look after her mother and Swan, since Jeremy couldn't be depended upon to do anything.

"How are Jeremy and the baby?" Hilary asked.

"Swan." Rayanne smiled. "She's great. Jeremy? What can I say? He's a teenager."

"Now you know what it's like to be a mother." Brenda chuckled. "And about that New York trip, count me in. I ain't got no money, but my plastic still works."

Brenda still depended on her credit cards. Her motto was "Live and enjoy yourself today and pay later. Always pay later."

"This woman charges everything. Ben lets me have one card, which I use primarily for gas. He cut the others. He's concerned about the ridiculous interest rates, and he's right, but one card is fine as long as I'm going in the direction of Bloomingdale's." Hilary giggled.

"I've always wanted to shop there," Brenda said. "There are lots of great stores in New York. Rayanne, I hope you can make it."

"We'll see," Rayanne said.

"What is the limit on that credit card of yours, Hilary?" Brenda asked.

"Fifteen thousand."

"Good," Brenda said. "Beause mine is only five thousand. If I run short, I know I can hit you up. If I had fifteen thousand on my credit card, I'd spend my ass off. Hell, life's a bitch, but I would have my cake and eat it now, and when I die, I want to owe everyone, even Jesus."

"Mercy," Rayanne said, and laughed.

"Isn't she shameful?" Hilary laughed. Rayanne nodded in agreement.

Brenda looked at her watch. "Girls, I've gotta run. I wanna finish that paper that's due Wednesday, and I wanna see what Victor Newman is up to today."

"Oh, he's gonna stick it to Jack," Rayanne said, dropping her napkin on her plate.

"I don't see how you do it. I don't have the time to watch soap operas," Hilary said.

"It's escapism for me," Brenda said before they departed, and Rayanne thought, that's what they were becoming for her as well.

Rayanne arrived home just as the moving truck pulled away from the curb in front of Abigail Brunson's house. The street in front of her house was crowded with neighbors, who had met there for the sad farewell that angered them. Abigail wouldn't have moved away, had it not been for that brutal attack she suffered, which left her afraid to walk down the street in her own neighborhood.

14

It appeared that Jeremy's life was spiraling out of control. He'd shunned all responsibilities as a father, and Rayanne couldn't help feeling that Jody Brown had more of a negative influence on Jeremy than anyone else. When she first met Jody, she didn't have a good feeling about him. He looked like trouble. Another thing she found disturbing was the way Jody looked at her, and she mentioned it to Jeremy.

"You're a fly lady, Aunt Rayanne. You can't blame Jody if he likes what he sees," he'd said.

"Mercy." Rayanne shook her head.

Jody was only several years older than Jeremy, and it was embarrassing the way the boy's eyes traveled over Rayanne's body. Jody came by one day, wandered into the kitchen, and asked for a drink of water. He was wearing his hat backward, his pants so low that the crack of his behind was exposed, and he wore designer sneakers that were strung up only halfway. Rayanne poured a glass of water for him.

"Why do you wear your pants that way?" she asked.

"That's the nyle," Jody replied.

"What?" Rayanne looked confused.

"It's the nyle," he repeated, and Rayanne was thinking,

There is that word again. "Everybody's wearing 'em like that."

"Are you saying this is the style?" Rayanne asked, thinking the young fart couldn't even pronounce the word.

There were many distasteful things about Jody that sent her mind racing, and she had to wonder why Jeremy would want to associate with someone like that.

Madeline announced that she was getting married and moving out of state with her husband. As a result, Rayanne would have to hire someone else to look after Helen and the baby. Unfortunately, a lot of time had passed and Rayanne still hadn't had that talk with Jeremy. As she entered the house, she was thinking that she'd make that a priority. However, as fate would have it, the talk would still have to wait because when she entered, her mother called out to her. Rayanne picked up the mail from the table and walked into the den, where Helen was mending a pair of Josh's slacks. To her surprise, her mother's hair was completely gray.

Since Raymond died, Helen had worn a scarf on her head, but today she didn't. It became evident the impact Raymond's death had had on her.

"I want us to sit and talk when you have a little time," Helen said.

"Sure, Mama. What do you want to talk about?" Rayanne went over and sat beside her. "Are you okay?"

"I talked with your daddy today," Helen said, a smile curling her lips.

"What?" Rayanne asked as the mail fell from her hands to the floor. Helen had been doing so well lately, but that statement left Rayanne stunned.

"Oh, did you see that letter you got from that agent of yours?" Helen asked.

"Yes," Rayanne replied, trying to get over the shock as

she picked up the mail that had splattered across the floor. She'd also noticed a letter postmarked from France and knew it was from Dorian. She'd put it with the others that were unopened in her dresser drawer.

"Well, go on, open it."

"I will, Mama, but that can wait."

Rayanne knew from the size of the envelope from Greg that he'd shopped her play, was unable to get a buyer, and was returning it. She didn't have to open the envelope to know what the letter said. It'd been the same since she moved back home.

"Mama, you said you talked with Daddy today," Rayanne said.

"What are you talking about, honey? Raymond's dead." Helen had an odd expression on her face.

Rayanne knew that her mother had said and done things in the past that were odd, but she seemed to have come so far from that.

"Don't give up on your dreams," Helen was saying. "You been a good storyteller since you were a little girl. You did good in New York, and you'll do good here. Just wait and see."

Helen had gone through a lot since Raymond had died, but the one thing that had remained constant was her faith in her children. Rayanne turned in her seat to face her mother.

"You sound just like Daddy."

"Your daddy and I been together fifty-some-odd years, and if he didn't go and die, we'd still be together. When you live with someone that long, you become like one. Your ways become that person's ways."

As Rayanne observed her mother, she noticed that Helen's eyes were red and swollen and were surrounded by wrinkles. Helen had never looked her age before, but she did now. Rayanne took her mother's hands in her own.

"It'll be all right, Mama." Then she released her mother's hands and asked, "So what did you want to talk about?"

"Rayanne, you got a lot on your plate, and I wish there was more I could do to help you."

"Mama, you couldn't help me any more than you do already, all the wisdom you provide, and you are here for me and the kids. Nothing could be more important than that."

"I know that's how you feel, but what I want to talk to you about now will be one less burden you'll have to bear later on."

Rayanne was puzzled. "What is that, Mama?"

"I want the two of us to plan my funeral."

15

Scott called at half past nine that night. There had been another robbery in the neighborhood, and he shared the frustrations of his day with Rayanne. Frannie was demanding more money for Donnie. "I don't have a problem taking care of the boy, but I get so tired of Frannie hanging out, leaving Donnie home alone, and she's gotten back to telling me I'm not Donnie's dad. I'm not having a good day, but I hope yours was better," Scott said.

"No such luck. My entire week never left the ground, and to top it off, Madeline is getting married and moving away in less than a month, and not a single person I have interviewed to replace her was suitable. Jeremy punched a boy at school over some little girl and has gotten suspended. I've told him many times that he should keep his possessive tendencies in check, but he doesn't listen. And I don't need to tell you how furious I was at finding marijuana in his room in our home."

Jeremy had changed. He was a man, in that he was eighteen, but he still behaved like a spoiled child. He spent very little time with the baby, he didn't do any chores, but what bothered Rayanne most was that Jeremy had started lying.

"Now," she said after revealing all to Scott, "have I sufficiently ruined your day?"

"Not exactly, but I wanna be with you when you confront Jeremy. Teenagers can be so unpredictable, especially when they're involved with drugs, big money, and they think that lifestyle is being threatened," Scott said.

"I appreciate that, Scott, but I'll handle it."

"All right," Scott said slowly. Then he asked, "What about Peters? Have you given that tired old dude his walking papers yet?"

"Pe-ter-son. The man's name is Peterson," Rayanne said. "And no. I haven't given him any papers yet."

"You better kick that old dude to the curb before you give him a stroke or something." Scott laughed out loud.

She'd run into Billy Peterson after ending her relationship with Ralph, and they'd begun dating again. Billy hadn't changed much from when they dated in high school. Billy and his wife divorced after fifteen years of marriage, and although he didn't satisfy all the things Rayanne craved, he wasn't married, and considering the men that were available, she continued to see him. She knew Billy loved her and she cared for him, but there were no fireworks. She didn't experience any of the things that she did with Ralph. *Ralph.* Speaking of Ralph, she wondered who he was messing over now. Anyway, it didn't matter. He was out of her life, and it would stay that way.

Rayanne received her master's degree in psychology on Friday, and later, Scott took her to see a movie. When he dropped her off afterward, she checked on Swan and her mother, but Jeremy was not around, as usual. Rayanne went into the den and picked up the newspaper. She looked at it, but unable to concentrate, she tossed it aside and looked at her watch.

"Where is Jeremy?" She looked out the window. The street was practically deserted, except for an occasional car passing by. She waited up for Jeremy until midnight. Then she went to bed and drifted into a troubled sleep.

The hour was late when Rayanne heard Jeremy come in. She climbed out of bed and went into the kitchen, where Jeremy was getting the sandwich that she'd left for him. Jeremy's cell phone rang. He pulled the phone from his pocket.

"This is 'J,' speak to me," he said. Rayanne waited and listened while Jeremy carried on a conversation. "Hey, baby, what's up?" He paused. "Getting something to eat before turning in." He listened. "Sounds like a winner. That was a phat outfit you had on today. It was slamming." He listened again. "Look, I'll holla at you tomorrow," he said, and listened again. "Now, see, you didn't even have to go there. Yeah, everything was cool until you went there." He paused. "Oh, so it's like that, huh?" Another pause. "Well, if that's how you feel, that's fine with me." With that, he clicked the caller off. "You still up, Aunt Rayanne?" he said, sitting at the table and beginning to devour the sandwich.

"Did you hear about the robbery that occurred in the neighborhood today?" Rayanne asked.

"I heard about it," Jeremy replied.

"It certainly is not like it used to be," Rayanne said, more to herself than to Jeremy. She looked at him. "It's late for you to be coming in on a school night." Rayanne set the teapot on the stove before she sat across from Jeremy.

"I was just hanging out."

"Jody doesn't go to school. You do."

"I didn't say I was hanging with Jody," Jeremy said, pouring a glass of milk and drinking half of it before returning to the table.

"He is the only person you seem to hang out with

anymore, and he certainly doesn't seem to be doing anything with his life." Rayanne got up to make herself a cup of tea.

"Jody's got it going on. He's got this truck and he makes these runs twice a week, and he makes plenty," Jeremy said, and took a bite out of his sandwich.

"Jeremy, I don't care what Jody is doing. I'm concerned about you, and when did you get a cell phone like that? That phone is not cheap."

Jeremy got up and took a handful of cookies from the jar.

"I know what your mother sends you," she said, and her mental calculations told her that with buying school supplies, clothes, and shoes, there wasn't that much left.

"Sounds like you've been talking with my mother. Why is she all up in my business? She didn't want me, so I wish she would leave me the hell alone," he snapped, getting up to get another glass of milk.

"Does your mother know you talk like this?"

"She would if she talked to me." He sat and placed the glass on the table.

Rayanne sipped her tea. "Have you changed your mind about the prom?" she asked.

Jeremy stopped chewing, looked at Rayanne, resumed chewing, and replied, "No."

"Why don't you want to go?"

Jeremy got up and pulled a couple of towels from the roll that hung over the sink. "I just don't," he answered, nonchalant.

"That kind of event is usually a landmark night in young people's lives. Why would you want to miss it?"

"Proms are for kids." He turned his glass up and drained it. "Besides, you don't want to talk about no prom. So why don't you say what's on your mind," he said, going back to the refrigerator to refill his glass.

"It's difficult to talk to a moving target. Your buzzing around is making me dizzy." She gave a little laugh.

"Cute, but I wish you would cut me some slack. I just want to eat and go to bed. I've got school tomorrow."

"I don't think so."

"Excuse me?"

"Why didn't you tell me you got kicked out of school today?"

Knowing his aunt had her facts right, and that she wasn't one to play with when it came to education, Jeremy decided not to stretch the lie he'd been about to tell. "I didn't think it was important."

"What are you saying? Graduation is less than two months away. Are you even going to graduate?" When he didn't answer, she asked, "Have you given any serious thought to what you're going to do after graduation?"

She'd asked that same question of him since he came to live with them, but she'd never gotten an answer.

"Sure, I'm going to graduate. Then I suppose I'll get a job."

"Doing what?" Again Jeremy didn't respond. "Do you not know how difficult it is to get a decent job even with a college degree? It is tough. The job market is not at its peak right now. It's going to be next to impossible to carve out a place for yourself without a decent education. That's why I always stress staying in school and getting something here." She poked her finger to the side of her head.

"I've got this friend who's going to hook me up," Jeremy said, taking a bite of a cookie and wiping his mouth with the back of his hand.

"Are we talking about Jody Brown again?"

"What's wrong with Jody?" he asked, and struck by a new thought, he said, "I sure hope you don't think Jody had anything to do with those robberies, because he didn't. He's an all right guy." Rayanne didn't agree. She knew that

Jody was trouble with a capital *T*. He didn't have a conscience, and Rayanne wished Jeremy wouldn't spend so much time with him.

"It's common knowledge that Jody is a drug user. He's ruthless and I think he's bad news."

"Aunt Rayanne, you don't really know Jody, so I don't know how you can say that."

"He's been around enough for me to have formed an opinion, and that is what I see." Jeremy did not respond and Rayanne continued. "Let me tell you something else. I found something in the house, specifically in your room, and needless to say, I don't like it, and it's not going to continue."

"What?" He looked at her with a challenging stare, but he felt his heart skip a beat.

"Marijuana."

"No kidding. Uncle Josh don't just hit the bottle, huh?" Jeremy stuck another cookie into his mouth.

"Josh drinks like a fish, but he does not do drugs, and even if he did, he'd never bring it into this house."

"At least you're giving him the benefit of the doubt."

"Jeremy, I've tried to look at things from your point of view and be understanding. I know you're young and have had some tough breaks, but you can't expect everyone to feel sorry for you, and you wallow in self-pity when you've done something wrong and have been caught. I've told you before that you've got to start taking responsibility for yourself and your daughter. You are a father. That was a choice that you made, and you've got to start acting like a responsible parent. That child needs a father. Her mother abandoned her when Swan was an infant, so, in essence, you represent both parents for her. Mama and I don't mind helping out, but from now on, I want you to take an active role in your daughter's life, spend some time and bond with her. Let her get to know you." Rayanne got up and put her teacup in the sink. "What I'm going to say has nothing to do with trust, but fact." She turned to look at Jeremy. "I know you're involved with drugs, and you have brought drugs into the house, our home." When Jeremy tried to protest, she closed her eyes and raised a hand to silence him. "I believe drugs are hidden in this house right now. It's the drugs that are behind the late nights, the odd hours you have been keeping, but you will not—and I repeat, *will not*—do those things here, and I mean it. I love you very much, Jeremy, and I mean that, too, but I have got to do what's best for all of us. I will not allow you to subject this family to any of that."

"That's an interesting monologue, but your little scenario is all wrong. I don't do drugs, I don't sell drugs, nor have I brought any drugs into the house," Jeremy spat out.

Rayanne knew he was lying, but she had no intention of arguing the point.

"That's good to know, because I'm having a crew of cleaning people that are coming in here tomorrow and going through this place from top to bottom, and they've been instructed to destroy anything they find that does not come under the item of household goods. And they will return on a regular basis until further notice from me." Rayanne watched Jeremy's reaction. Although he tried to play it off, it was obvious that he was feeling trapped.

And just as she had thought, Jeremy had been lying. Long after Rayanne checked on Swan and her mother and was back in her own bed, she could hear Jeremy rummaging through his room. She hoped he'd have the good sense to get some sleep, because he would be getting up in the morning and going to school, and she'd be with him. There'd be no more of his hanging out all night and not going to school the next day. No more pretended illnesses, when, in fact, all that was wrong was that he was burning the candle at both ends. She'd see to it that he stayed in school until he graduated.

Rayanne didn't believe in using friendship for gain, but this was one time she was glad that George Thomas, an old classmate, was now the principal at Sumter High School, where Jeremy attended, and she was glad they had kept in touch and remained friends.

Although Jeremy's contention was that Jody was an all right person, what happened two days later confirmed Rayanne's prior suspicions. Jody must've crossed someone, because according to the news, someone had fired several bullets into his house and car. Jeremy looked a little spooked when he found out about it. Rayanne hoped that he'd think about what happened to Jody, what could've happened, and that he would have an attitude adjustment.

Rayanne did follow through with having the house cleaned randomly; to her surprise and joy, nothing out of the ordinary turned up.

Rayanne was teaching a course in psychology and sociology at the university. She was grading papers and watching TV one evening when the phone rang. She answered it, and when she hung up, her hand shook as she dialed John's number. Jeremy had been arrested on drug charges. Maxine was taking Helen and Swan to her house for the night, and John would meet Rayanne at the county jail. Helen didn't have a particularly good day, and Rayanne didn't want to leave her and the baby home alone. Mrs. Marshall, the retired nurse, who cared for Swan and her mother, despite Helen's objections, hadn't returned from Atlanta, where her daughter was having a baby.

As Maxine was taking Helen and Swan with her, Josh

came up the driveway, staggering. Maxine looked at Rayanne and shook her head. Josh caught one of Marcia Raylyn's ponytails and tried to play with it, but the child pulled away. She loved her uncle Josh, but like the others, she didn't like to be around him when he was drinking. Rayanne stood aside and allowed Josh to enter and heard him bump into something, making his way to wherever he was going.

"I think I oughta stay here with Josh," Helen said, looking nervously toward the house.

"He'll be all right." Rayanne was hoping that was true, but she couldn't worry about that now. She knew if he didn't burn the house down, he'd be all right.

"You sure he'll be all right by hisself?" Helen asked.

"Yes, Mama. As soon as we check on Jeremy, I'll come back home and check on Josh," Rayanne said. Helen appeared satisfied and went willingly with Maxine.

The county jail was filled with people of all ages, and the majority of them were young black men. After waiting an hour, John and Rayanne were met by Nathan Woods, their attorney. They couldn't do anything for Jeremy that night, but he'd be released in the morning. It was difficult leaving Jeremy locked in a cell overnight, but it couldn't be helped. Rayanne debated calling Lila that night or waiting until morning. She decided to call and left a voice mail knowing from past experiences Lila wouldn't answer her phone.

Rayanne was exhausted as she approached her street, but instead of turning into her own driveway, she passed her house, heading in another direction. Scott had been working out of town on construction sites a lot and was surprised when he opened his door and saw her standing there. He stood aside, allowing her to enter. She sat.

"Scott, I'm so sick and tired of all this. I'm fed up to here," Rayanne said, marking herself at the throat. "I think

I have been dependable, but I'm so tired of being everything for everyone." She got up and paced back and forth. "I know I'm wallowing in self-pity, but tonight I don't care." Scott was silent and listened. "I have been there for my family, haven't I?" She looked questioningly at him.

Scott was thinking there should be a limit. At some point, she'd have to let others accept responsibility for themselves, but he said, "You still are."

Rayanne sat next to Scott on the couch and said, "I don't know what's wrong with Jeremy."

"I know, baby," Scott said.

Rayanne mentioned the state Josh was in when he arrived home that evening. She ran her fingers through her hair. "But I can't even think about Josh right now," she said. "I hate the thought of Jeremy being in that place all night. I feel I need to be doing something." Feeling helpless, Rayanne got up and began to pace the floor again.

"There's nothing we can do tonight."

"I know. Thanks for letting me cry on your shoulders." She laughed a little. "I'm gonna get out of here and let you get some sleep. Thanks again." She turned to go to the door.

"Why don't you stay here tonight?"

"You're a sweetheart, and I appreciate the offer, but I'd better get on home."

"Why? Your mother and Swan are at your sister's house. We can't do anything to help Jeremy until the morning. So why do you think you need to go home?" Scott asked, going over to her.

"Josh is there."

"And Josh can take care of himself, but tonight you need someone to take care of you. Let me take care of you tonight."

"Are you sure about this?"

"Absolutely. I want you to stay."

She allowed her head to drop against his chest. "Why are you so good to me?"

"I don't know. Maybe 'cause I sorta like ya."

"You do?"

"Yeah."

"Just sorta?"

"Maybe a little more than sorta."

"How much more?" she teased.

"A lot more." He put his arms around her. She looked up into his eyes. "Thank you," she said. He walked with her to the bedroom.

She climbed onto his bed. "Stay here with me awhile," she said, and he obeyed. She awoke sometime during the night and turned over in bed to find Scott still there. She reached over and touched his face with her hands and he opened his eyes. Then she put her arms around his neck and she pressed her lips to his, forcing her tongue into his mouth. Scott held her and kissed her back. "Make love to me, Scott," she whispered. "Please make love to me now."

She began unbuttoning his shirt and placed little kisses on his chest. Scott didn't encourage her, but he continued to hold her. She began tearing at his clothes and he only held her tighter, restricting her movement. When she realized she couldn't break free, she began to cry, and he could only lay there and listen to her sobs. It wasn't that he didn't want to make love to her. There was nothing Scott wanted more than to take her in his arms and make passionate love to her, but not like this. He wanted her when she could come to him with the offer of her love. He respected her too much to have it any other way.

For a long time, they lay together, and although their bodies touched, a deep silence lay between them. The following morning, Scott turned over in bed to find Rayanne putting on her shoes.

"When I reached for you and you were gone, I began to think that last night was a dream."

"Maybe it was," Rayanne sneered.

"If it was, it was some dream. I thought I'd died and gone to heaven," he said, trying to ease the tension that filled the room. Rayanne didn't respond. She continued to tie her shoelaces. "About last night," Scott said, sitting up in bed, "you don't know how much I wanted you." Rayanne looked sideways at him. "Are you doubting that? Rayanne, I wanted you more than I've ever wanted anything in my life."

"You could've fooled me."

"If I thought that was what you really wanted—"

"Look, Scott, let's not analyze last night to death. I was tired, slightly emotional, and I needed someone, and you were there, or you weren't there. Whatever the case, I can assure you, it won't happen again."

The words were like a slap in his face. Was she upset that he *didn't* take advantage of her vulnerabilities? Wouldn't she have been even more upset if he had? There was no way he would've taken advantage of her—no matter how much he'd wanted her or needed her.

"Are you telling me you were just going to use me?"

"Isn't that what you guys do to us all the time?"

"Not all of us, and not all the time."

"Whatever."

Scott was upset, and he didn't try to hide it. "If that's how you feel about what didn't happen last night, then I agree. I'm glad things didn't go any further, and it shouldn't happen again." He reclined in bed with his arms folded under his head.

Rayanne sprang up from the bed. "I've gotta go." She turned at the door and said, "Thanks for last night. I don't know what I would've done without you."

"No problem," he said, and without another word, she was gone. Scott sat up on the side of the bed and lit a cigarette.

* * *

When she returned home, Rayanne entered the house through the kitchen door. Josh was sitting at the table, smoking.

"Morning, Josh," she said, looking tired, going to the phone, and dialing a number.

"Where did you spend your night? Looks like the sinners didn't sleep," he said.

"It wasn't that kinda night," she replied, hanging up the phone after receiving a busy signal. She looked at him. Not only was his alcoholism killing him, he was worrying the rest of them to death. He'd been going to the daily program more times than she could count and it hadn't helped. Although Josh insisted he could quit drinking anytime he wanted, Rayanne knew he was deluding himself, because alcoholism was an illness and required treatment. She redialed the number. This time, it rang.

"Maxine, how is it going?"

"Everything's fine here. John told us what happened with Jeremy. I called you last night, but I didn't get an answer. I figured you took a pill and crashed," Maxine said. "Swan is fine, Mama had a restful night, and I decided to take the day off, so there is no reason for you to worry about them."

"Thanks, Maxine. I am meeting John downtown at eight-twenty."

"John just walked through the door," Maxine said. "He said he can pick you up."

"Tell him I'll meet him there."

When Rayanne hung up, she made breakfast. "Did Lila call this morning?" she asked. She'd called Lila last night and left a message on her voice mail.

"I don't think so," Josh said. "I sure miss Mama this morning."

"Let's just eat before the food gets cold," Rayanne said, extending her hands across the table to Josh. "Dear Lord, we thank Thee for this food that we're about to receive. Bless us, Father, and strengthen us here on earth each day in Your name and the name of Your Son, Jesus. Amen."

"Amen," Josh echoed.

Rayanne had taken one bite of eggs when the phone rang. "Hello," she answered.

It was Lila. "What happened to Jeremy?" she demanded to know.

"He was arrested. Didn't you get my message?" Rayanne asked.

"That's why I'm calling. You let my son run the streets and now he's been arrested," Lila said. Rayanne tried to interrupt, but Lila continued. "Why didn't you call back this morning?"

"What good would that have done? Maybe if you start answering your phone at night, you'd know what's going on in other parts of the world."

"You know I don't answer my phone late at night," Lila screamed.

"Bet this is one time when you wished you had." Rayanne knew that comment stung, but she didn't care. She was tired of Lila always getting her way. It was time that she squirmed, if only for a short while. There was silence, which was rare for Lila. "Look, I know you're upset. We all are, but John and I are going back downtown this morning to see what we can do."

"My son is still in jail?" Lila screeched. "Jeremy spent the night in jail?"

"There was nothing we could do last night, but I told you John and I will do what we can this morning."

"Don't you have an attorney?"

"Of course."

"And he wasn't able to do any better than that?" Lila

asked, and since Rayanne saw that as a rhetorical question, she didn't reply. "Rayanne, do I need to be there?"

"Lila, it is now seven-twenty. John and I plan to be downtown within the hour. There's nothing anyone can do between now and then. I'll call you as soon as I know more."

"Are you sure you can handle this mess without me?"

"We are going to do our best." Rayanne snapped.

"What's wrong with you?" Lila replied at Rayanne's snide remark.

"Look, Lila, we will call you later."

"What's happening to my son?"

"We have been through this already."

"And we're going to go over it again. I want to know what my son is getting himself into down there."

"You're asking me?"

"Yes, I'm asking you."

"Well, don't, because I tried talking with you about Jeremy's conduct and you didn't do one thing about it, so don't start pretending you care now."

"I do care, but you're supposed to be looking after him."

"By your choosing."

"Only because I didn't want him to live in the city and get into trouble. Doesn't look like he's doing any better down there," Lila complained. "You can say what you want about me, but Jeremy was never arrested while he was with me. If you were as responsible as you claim—" Lila started again, but she was interrupted by a pissed-off Rayanne.

"Lila, I'm in no mood to hear this shit from you. The best thing for you to do is let John and me do what we can for your son, or you can put that fat ass of yours on a plane, get down here, and take care of this mess, as you put it, yourself," Rayanne yelled into the phone.

"Don't think I won't come if I need to," Lila said.

"Don't think I would try to stop you," Rayanne mumbled.

"I can get a flight out of here and be there this afternoon," Lila said.

"I don't give a damn what you do. Do you want someone to meet you at the airport?"

Lila was silent. "Well?" Rayanne raised her voice.

"Don't bother," Lila said. "Just let me know what happened, if you don't mind." With that, Lila hung up.

"Just as I thought, bitch," Rayanne said, looking into the mouthpiece of the phone before she hung up. She sat back at the table to eat her breakfast. "Now my food is cold," she said, dumping a fork of eggs back onto her plate.

Josh was somewhat startled by that outburst, since Rayanne seldom used profanity. "Is she coming?" he asked.

"What do you think?" Rayanne got up and scraped the cold food into the garbage.

Rayanne got dressed and drove to the detention center, where John was waiting. After posting bond, Jeremy was released, and Rayanne and Jeremy headed home. She asked, "You want to tell me what happened?"

"Aunt Rayanne, I think you know the deal."

"I'm asking you."

"Where's my daughter? Is she all right?"

"She's fine. She's with Maxine. What about you?"

"I'm okay."

"What's going on with you?"

"I don't know."

"Jeremy, you have got to feel better about yourself. Don't you want the absolute best that life has to offer for you and your child?" He didn't respond. "You know something. I am literally in love with myself, and I try to do what is best for me. I have to have a positive attitude to love myself, and that empowers me to do the things I want to do. I learned early in life that I am allergic to poverty. Seriously, I get a rash just thinking about being poor." She laughed a little, looking over at Jeremy. "So, with that in mind, I have to always put my best foot forward." They were quiet a moment. "Do you think you need this kind of mess in your life? You will soon be nineteen years old. You're a black male, and now with a record—" Rayanne started.

"Go on," Jeremy interrupted. "Tell me you told me so."

"I'm not going to tell you that. Do you think I'm happy about this? We are not playing games to see who can say I told you so. Can't you see that no one wins in a situation like this? We're family, and when there's a breakdown in the family, we all lose. You need to be thinking about the kind of future you want for yourself and your daughter. You don't want to start off your life by getting into this kind of trouble. You're bright and capable of doing so much. The future is ahead of you and it's up to you to make the best of it." Rayanne looked at Jeremy, and he was staring at her. "Talk to me. Tell me what you're thinking," she said.

Jeremy hesitated a moment before saying, "I was just thinking that you're so different from my mother. You are sisters, but you're nothing alike. She's a good lady and I love her, but I've heard so much that I'm nothing, never going to amount to anything. I was beginning to believe it."

"Jeremy, you can't allow anyone else's opinion to guide your life, especially when that opinion is negative. We all make mistakes, but mistakes force us to grow up, and if we're smart, we learn from our mistakes."

"Aunt Rayanne, I've never completed anything or made good on anything in my life," Jeremy said, "so don't expect any big miracles from me."

"Your life is really just beginning and you're about to graduate. I don't know about you, but I think that's a major accomplishment. Don't set your reality by your failures, but rather build on them. This world is full of opportunities, but we've got to prepare. You'll be taking a big step soon, so build on that. Anyone can turn his life around if he tries. I heard someone once say that opportunities will come our way that we wouldn't believe, but when they come, be prepared to grab them even if we don't know what to do with them at the time. Grab them and figure it out later, but grab them, because they may never come again. The fascinating thing about life is that we don't have to live where we are right now. There's always tomorrow. We are living in difficult times and it is not going to be easy, but we have to do our very best. You can do anything you want. You know why?" she asked. He looked questioningly at her. "Because you're special. You have God-given talents and God intends for you to use them. You're here for a purpose, and you'll soon realize it," Rayanne said. As they drove past Mrs. Abigail's house, they saw a black BMW parked in the driveway and the FOR SALE sign posted previously was now gone.

"Looks like we got some new neighbors," Jeremy said, looking over his shoulder at the car. "Grandma and Aunt Bessie miss Mrs. Abigail. They were talking about her yesterday."

"I know. I miss her also. Mrs. Abigail has always been a part of this community and our lives. It's a shame what happened to her."

A rap song began to play on the car radio and Jeremy began to sing along. He was surprised when Rayanne joined in and didn't miss a beat as they rode, singing and snapping their fingers to the music that poured from the radio.

When they arrived home, they called Lila. Before the conversation ended, she gave both, Rayanne and Jeremy, a piece of her mind.

Afterward, Rayanne placed some fresh flowers on her father's grave, and when she drove back home, she and Josh had a heart-to-heart.

16

The sun had long since closed its doors and the moon was high. There appeared to be a million and one things going on in Rayanne's life, and her head was filled equally with as many thoughts, especially of Jeremy. It seemed he was always getting into something.

As Rayanne stood on the porch, the wind gently touched her face and lifted her long brown hair. When the gusts became stronger, causing the cotton robe to swirl about her ankles, she pulled her robe close and held it against her throat. There were things Jeremy had to work through, but she was reminded of something her mother used to say. You raise your children the best way you can, but they grow up to be who they are. How true was that? Jeremy had made some mistakes, but he'd learn from them, hopefully, and would grow as a result of them.

In her mind, Rayanne went over the conversations she and Jeremy had on their way home from the detention center. He'd heard so much in his young life that he was nothing, and would never amount to anything, that he'd begun to believe it. Rayanne and Helen tried to impress upon Jeremy that it didn't matter what anyone told him or what they believed about him. It was how he felt about himself that mattered.

Rayanne told Jeremy he would face adversities in his life, but he had to believe in himself and move past those obstacles. She made sure he knew he'd succeed because he was special. Her desire was to affect his life in a positive way, and in that, she'd try to be supportive of him and his endeavors, without being judgmental.

Her thoughts moved further, to the little bundle of joy lying in the crib in one of the spare bedrooms that had been turned into a nursery. Swan was special. She'd brought immense joy to Rayanne, causing her life to go in a new direction, a new path.

She heard the side door open and close. Josh had arrived in his usual state now. He was drunk—again.

Rayanne went to bed. Lying there, she thought about Scott. She missed him. She hadn't seen or heard from him since the night of Jeremy's arrest. He was one of her closest friends. When four days had passed, and still no word from him, Rayanne put aside her pride and she called him, but got his voice mail. She didn't leave a message.

17

The Prozac that Helen was taking appeared to alter her personality. If Rayanne had known that the drug had been prescribed for her mother, she would have looked for other alternatives. She'd read everything she could find on the drug when she discovered her mother taking it. Although Prozac was considered a wonder drug by some, like other medications, there were side effects, one being bouts of depression.

Rayanne called home to check on her mother and Maxine answered.

"I stopped by to see Mama. She wasn't having a very good day," Maxine began. "I think it's the medication—she takes it, forgets, and takes it again, or perhaps she's trying to harm herself."

"You think Mama is trying to hurt herself?" Rayanne asked, shocked.

"I don't know. She has terrible mood swings. She's depressed. She's not been the same really since Daddy died, and the situation with Josh can't be good for her," Maxine said, and Rayanne silently agreed. "Well, let me tell you what happened today. Josh came in so drunk, he could hardly stand up. He pissed all over the kitchen floor right in front of Mama and the kids."

"What?"

"He couldn't even clean up after himself."

Rayanne rubbed her forehead with her fingertips, trying to take her mind off Josh for a moment. "Do you think Mama needs to see a doctor?"

"She seems to be okay now, but a little down."

Rayanne arrived home, and after checking the medication, she was satisfied that Helen hadn't taken more than the normal dosage. Rayanne wasn't sure why she hadn't added that to Mrs. Marshall's duties, but it would be included from now on.

Helen was watching TV; Josh was sitting in a chair, clean, but asleep. Rayanne put her things down and picked up the baby, who reached her hands up to meet Rayanne's. Mrs. Marshall came out of the kitchen.

"How is that handsome grandson, Mrs. Marshall?" Rayanne asked, holding Swan in her lap.

"He's just fine. Growing like a weed," Mrs. Marshall replied, her eyes beaming with pride. "They're coming in a couple of weeks."

"I know how much you miss them," Rayanne said, playing with Swan's fingers.

"I sure do, but we talk often, so that helps."

Later that evening, Rayanne gave Swan a bath and fed her. After playing with her awhile, Swan was put to bed. Helen set the table, woke Josh, and they ate the meal that Mrs. Marshall prepared. It'd been a while since Jeremy had eaten any meals with the family, and it was nice having him, plus Josh had joined them for a change. The meal was enjoyable, the conversation was more stimulating and meaningful than it'd been in months. Rayanne put off talking to Josh about his drinking or the mess he made earlier. She was tired, and was happy to be able to go to bed without having an argument.

Good luck had a way of not lasting, and within a week, Josh had a repeat performance. When Helen and Swan were in bed, Rayanne switched off the TV and she turned to Josh.

"What's going on, Rayanne?" he asked.

"I heard about what happened here today."

"What?"

"Let's not start this conversation by lying, Josh. I know about you pissing up the house today, and that's not the first time. Enough is enough."

"You mean that little accident I had," Josh said, more nonchalant than Rayanne had ever seen him, and that was enough to motivate her to insist he get help. Once again, Josh signed up at the center. He continued the program daily, he was released, and just when it seemed he was getting his life back together for the hundredth time, Rayanne came home one day to find him kneeling over the commode, puking. Helen was bending over him with a wet towel.

"What's wrong with Josh now?" Rayanne asked stupidly, because the sight of him gave her an answer. She took the towel from her mother's hand. "Go back to the den, Mama. I'll take care of this."

"All right, but if you need me, you call me now, you hear?" Helen said, and walked slowly out of the room.

It was painful seeing Josh like that, but it broke her heart watching the impact the family crisis was having on her mother. Raymond and the children were Helen's entire life, and when the family began to fall apart, it left a void in her life that made it difficult for her to go on.

Rayanne opened the bathroom window to allow the

stench to dissipate. She sat on the side of the bathtub, holding the towel out to Josh.

"I know I fell off the wagon again, sis," he said.

"Did you even try?"

Rayanne and Josh had talked extensively about his drinking and he'd promised he'd try harder.

"I did, but it got the best of me."

"Don't you see what this is doing to Mama? Don't you care?"

"Are you blaming me for Mama's condition?"

"I am not blaming anyone, but Mama is suffering, Josh. She's not the same person. Her will is gone, and her strength. She is suffering, and when someone you love is suffering, you don't ask who's to blame. You just try to help. Mama needs our support"—Rayanne paused—"before it's too late."

"Don't talk like that," Josh said, and began to cry. "I lost my daddy. I'm not gonna lose Mama, too." He was acting like a child, and Rayanne didn't have the patience to pacify him.

Josh wasn't stupid. Why couldn't he understand that alcohol twisted everything around, played tricks on the mind? It magnified some situations, while others appeared softer around the edges. Throughout their verbal exchanges, Rayanne had never talked to Josh bluntly or harshly. Now she used words that she didn't know were a part of her vocabulary.

"I'm going to make this as simple as I can. Either you get it together or get the hell out. You can have it either way you want, but you won't have both."

Rayanne walked out of the bathroom and closed the door behind her. She was surprised to see her mother standing in the hallway, staring at her.

Rayanne took her mother's hand and led her back to the den, where they sat.

"Is Josh all right?" Helen's eyes darted toward the bathroom.

"He's fine, just drunk."

"He can't help it, you know, and he ain't hurting nobody."

"He's hurting us all, himself most of all. Mama," Rayanne said after a moment. "There's so much that is wrong here. I'm not going to give up until I've done everything I can, but I need your help and I need it from Josh. I think that Josh should be put into that intensive program in Florence."

"You can't send Josh away. We'll get help for him right here."

"It's not working that way, Mama."

"Then we have to do something else."

"If you have a solution, please let me hear it, because I'm fresh out of ideas."

"Just don't you send my boy away," Helen said, tears in her eyes. With determination in her voice, she added, "I'll never forgive you if you send Josh away."

"Mama, please don't fight me on this," Rayanne said. She saw something in her mother's eyes that wasn't present before, and she was hoping that her action wouldn't affect the way they had always bonded as mother and daughter. "Josh is doing things that are a threat to all of us, including the baby. I'm angry at myself for letting this situation get so far out of control. There have been times when Josh has come in drunk and left cigarettes burning in ashtrays that sometime fell on the floor and burned the carpet. He leaves water running in the sink and it runs over onto the floors. I just happened to wake up one night and heard the water running. Josh was back in bed. He's urinated in bed so often that we had to replace the mattress twice, not to mention the carpet in that room." Helen had no idea the situation had gotten that bad. "I can't tell you how many times Jeremy and

I have had to pick him up from outside, bring him in, and put him to bed. There are lots of things, Mama, but that doesn't matter now. I just want it to stop, and Josh isn't in any position to help himself."

"I know this is hard on you. You're too young to have all these burdens," Helen said. "We're gonna do something about it. We're a family and we gotta help each other. We can't pick our relatives, like we can't clean germs, but we can help each other. And please take that buckle out of your brow."

Rayanne hadn't heard that expression in a long time, but she welcomed it, and she felt everything was going to be all right.

Rayanne and Maxine signed Josh up and everything was fine until it was time to drive him to Florence. Helen had changed her mind, reacting violently, and she swore again she'd never forgive Rayanne if she took Josh away. Rayanne knew Helen would change her mind when she saw the difference the intensive treatment would make in Josh's life. But as it turned out, Josh didn't keep the appointment for admission to the Florence center. He signed up for the daily program, once again.

18

Maxine entered Mt. Carmel Baptist Church. It was filled to its capacity. The crystal chandelier sparkled, the pews were red plush cushions, and the woodwork shined as though it had been polished with oil. Maxine and Fred had married right out of college, in that church. They had two sons, and although they had spent some happy years together, two years after Bobby was born, Fred split, leaving Maxine to raise the boys alone, with no child support. They later divorced, and Maxine hadn't laid eyes on him until he returned, sporting a new wife.

Maxine found a seat in the fifth row from the front. She sat down, and when she lifted her head, her eyes met Fred's. Their eyes held only a brief moment before he closed his and laid his head back against the seat, where he sat in the pulpit, next to the minister. The years had been kind to Fred. His hair was short, his rich dark skin was clean shaven, except for a neatly trimmed mustache adding to his good looks. He was even more handsome than Maxine remembered. His six-foot frame was well-built.

Maxine had told Fred's mother that she was very happily married, but the boys had questions about their father. Mrs. Duncan assured Maxine that Fred would get the message. She was quick to mention that Fred was happy in his new marriage as well, and he was sorry for any grief he might've caused her and the boys.

All through the service, Fred avoided any further eye contact with Maxine. He delivered a powerful message. "It's good you've turned to the Lord," Maxine whispered. "Maybe you've grown up, after all."

Fred's new bride was a pretty girl. She was slender, well-groomed, and was at least ten years younger than he was. When she played the piano and sang, it sounded as sweet as a songbird.

Marcus and the children didn't go to church that Sunday. That was how Maxine wanted it. She wasn't sure how Fred would react to the boys, and she didn't want them hurt.

After services, Maxine approached. "How are you, Fred?" she said, extending her hand.

"I'm fine, thanks." He shook her hand briefly and released it.

"You're looking good."

"Thank you."

"The boys have been asking for you," she informed him.

"I'll call later today," he said without emotion.

"That's fine," Maxine said, and smiled. "I'll let them know."

Fred quickly moved to another church member. Maxine observed him for a moment and she wondered how a man who was once so sweet and caring could turn so cold. She turned to walk away and she looked up in time to catch a glimpse of Fred's wife leaving the sanctuary.

Maxine caught up to her. "I enjoyed listening to you in there. I'm Maxine Richards," she said, extending her hand.

"Thank you. I'm Irene Duncan, Mrs. Fred Duncan," she said, extending a graceful hand to accept Maxine's.

"I'm very glad to meet you. This is a wonderful church, with warm, kind people."

"I agree," Maxine said, and saw Fred coming out of the sanctuary. "So how long have you and Fred . . . I mean, Rev. Duncan been married?"

"It's been four months now," Irene said, and paused. "I take it you know my husband?"

Maxine was surprised that Fred didn't tell his new wife that she and Fred were married. Since he didn't tell her, Maxine didn't either.

"Yes, he's a homeboy. How long will you two be in town?"

"We'll be here a couple of days," Irene answered as they walked over and stood under a large oak tree to shield themselves from the midday sun.

It was late May and the temperatures already ranged from high eighties to low nineties.

"Fred and I met when he visited my church as a guest speaker eight months ago. My parents invited him to dinner, and he and I got to know each other. The rest, as they say, is history. He's the kindest, most understanding, and honest person that I've ever known."

The person Irene described didn't sound at all like the old Fred that Maxine knew, but she said, "Certainly sounds like a whirlwind romance to me."

"Oh, it was. Fred makes me so happy." Irene stopped herself suddenly and said, "I suppose you think that I'm a silly schoolgirl, but I do get excited talking about Fred. What about you? Are you married?"

"Yes. I've been married twice, as a matter of fact. It didn't work out the first time, but I'm very happy with my second husband. He's a wonderful man, and we have three beautiful children. Maybe I should clarify that. I had two boys by my first husband. Marcus and I have a little girl. They are great kids."

"That's wonderful." Irene smiled. "I hope Fred and I won't have to walk this road again. Hopefully, once will be enough for both of us."

"Neither of you have been married?"

"Oh no. Fred said he's never been in love until he met me, and he's the only man that I've ever loved. I can only say that I'm very glad he waited for me." Irene was acting like a junior high schoolgirl.

"Do you plan to have a family?" Maxine asked.

"Yes. Fred loves children. He wants to start a family right away. He tells me that's the one thing that will make our family complete."

Members from the congregation approached them and shook their hands. When Maxine and Irene were alone again, Irene continued. "The past eight months have been the happiest in my life. Fred and I share everything. He's a good, honest man."

Maxine wondered how many times Irene was going to say how good and honest Fred was. "Nothing like having a good, honest man around." Maxine wasn't sure how much longer she could listen to Irene babble about a man whom she obviously knew very little about.

"Let me tell you what Fred said to me when we were coming here yesterday," Irene said. Maxine smiled, but she felt a little nervous about what might come next. "He said he feels unfortunate never having had children."

"Really," Maxine said, feeling pain somewhere deep inside.

"Yes. When we talk about children, he always looks so sad, but that changes when I remind him that we're still young newlyweds and that there's plenty of time for children."

Maxine struggled to stay calm. It was one thing for Fred to deny her, but to deny the children was unforgivable.

"Tell me about your children," Irene said.

Maxine took a deep breath to steady her voice. "Bruce is sixteen. He'll graduate high school this year, very smart boy. He skipped a grade one year," Maxine said with obvious pride.

"That's wonderful," Irene said, and Maxine could tell she meant it. Maxine believed Irene Duncan was a good person, and Fred was fortunate to have her, but Maxine felt Irene was the unfortunate one.

"Bobby's fourteen and smart as well. I think the boys compete for the best grades. One semester Bobby gets better grades—then the next, it's Bruce." Maxine smiled.

"You must be so proud."

"Our daughter, Marcia Raylyn, is the apple of her daddy's eye." The women laughed.

"I suppose most little girls take that position with their fathers."

"Now, Bobby, my youngest, he's a rascal, cunning, but a real charmer, every bit like his father." Maxine wondered what Irene would think of Fred when she learned that he deserted his own flesh and blood. "They don't know much about their father. They haven't seen him in twelve years," she said.

"That's unfortunate, but it is understandable why you divorced him. Just keep the faith."

Maxine looked at her watch. "I'd better be on my way. My family will be wondering what happened to me." Maxine extended a hand to Irene again. "It was very nice meeting you. Hope you and the reverend will visit us again."

"Thank you."

Maxine released Irene's hand and walked away.

Maxine was too upset to go home, so she drove directly to her mother's home and recapped her story for Rayanne.

"The man acted like he didn't know me, and get this. He never even asked about the boys, but that's okay, because

I plan to take that up with him when we see him later," Maxine fumed.

On her way home, there was no longer a trace of the anger that had overwhelmed her earlier. She was aware that part of her anger was replaced by pity. She had pity for the young woman who'd fallen in love with a man who was less of a man than any other man Maxine had ever known. Irene was innocent and trusting, and she was in for a rude awakening. She fluttered those eyelashes like a silly schoolgirl with her head stuck in a cloud. Well, she had a lot to learn. She had yet to grow up and become a woman.

That afternoon, Bruce and Bobby dressed up and waited for their father. They weren't sure whether he'd call or come, but in any case, they'd be ready. Maxine watched the boys, taking turns, looking out the window or staring at the phone. As it turned out, Fred didn't come, nor did he bother to call.

Maxine didn't go to work on Monday. She got up, made breakfast, and drove over to Mrs. Duncan's house. Fred's car wasn't there. "They're probably at a hotel," Maxine murmured. She didn't get out of her car. She used her cell phone to dial Mrs. Duncan's number. "Mrs. Duncan, this is Maxine. Is Fred around?"

"No, Maxine. Fred and Irene left for Florida this morning."

"He didn't come by to see the boys, nor did he call," Maxine said, disappointed for her sons that Fred had left without a word to them.

"I gave Fred your message, but he said he didn't want to interfere in your and the kids' lives. He doesn't want to confuse them."

"Confuse them? Mrs. Duncan, Bruce and Bobby are big

boys. They know that Marcus isn't their father. They just wanted an opportunity to get to know their real father, talk to him. They were disappointed."

"Fred is married again, to a lovely girl, and I think he wants to move on with his life. There's no need in you all going through all this now," Mrs. Duncan said.

"There is no question about Fred and me forgetting each other, but the children? How can a man who calls himself a preacher forget his children?"

"Maxine, if this is about support for the boys, I'll be glad to help all I can."

"It's not really about money, Mrs. Duncan." Maxine wondered why this woman didn't understand why she was so upset.

"Then what is it?"

Maxine felt if she had to explain it, it wasn't worth it.

"If Fred calls himself a man of God and he behaves this way, then he must be a preacher from hell."

"Don't be ugly," Mrs. Duncan said. "Just let me know what I can do for the boys, but leave Fred alone. Let him be happy."

Maxine knew that Mrs. Duncan was a large part of why Fred was the way he was.

"Mrs. Duncan, these are Fred's kids, and if this is how he wants to treat them, then that's his choice. But don't you worry about them. They'll be just fine." With that, Maxine hung up and began to cry. She cried all the way back home. She didn't cry for herself, or the way Fred had deserted her with two children all those years ago. She didn't even cry because she was so pissed off at him that she could have kicked his ass until he couldn't sit on it. Her tears were for her sons, boys who didn't know their father, but they loved him. And after all this time, they still wanted to get to know him on some level. The boys had looked forward to spending a little time with their father.

And that's exactly what he was, their father. Fred wasn't a daddy, because a daddy would not have treated his children the way Fred had. What would she tell them now? She couldn't tell them their father had cut his trip short because he wanted nothing to do with them.

19

Jeremy and Bruce graduated high school that spring. That was the first time Lila returned since their father's death, when she'd left Jeremy and the baby. She'd called and sent a little money and an occasional dress for Swan, but no visits.

The night before graduation, everyone was at the family house. Bruce and Bobby went to the movies, the men and the other kids were in the den watching TV, and the women were preparing dinner in honor of the graduates. It was a festive time and it would've ended that way, had Lila not gotten into an altercation with Jeremy. The incident could've resulted in a funeral rather than the happy occasion it was meant to be.

Lila had gone out the night before and didn't get home until midday the following day, and she slept the remainder of the day. She joined the others in the kitchen that night. She didn't volunteer to help, but Maxine filled a bowl with white potatoes and pushed the bowl and a knife into her hands and said, "Make yourself useful."

This was one of those times when the women caught up on what was going on with each other. While listening to the radio playing in the background, they talked about their children, their careers, books, movies, and vacations they wanted to take.

"All these hands working in here, I wasn't sure I was needed," Lila said, sitting at the table, where Rayanne and Helen were snapping beans.

"We need all the hands we can get," Maxine said.

"Well, this ain't too bad." Lila rolled her eyes. "I'm just glad I didn't get stuck with cleaning the collards." She laughed.

Eunice and Christen, who were cleaning the greens, each made a face at Lila.

"Lila will do the collards by herself next year," Christen said, and they all laughed.

"Why wait until next year? Let's make her do them at Christmas, or better yet, Thanksgiving," Eunice said, and they laughed some more.

"You girls better not hold your breath for that," Helen said, a twinkle in her eyes.

Maxine and Rayanne, with the help of Mrs. Marshall, had weaned Helen's dosage of Prozac to less than half of what she'd been taking, and she'd bounced back to her witty, wisecracking self. She'd always been a great conversationalist, and everyone she came in contact with was affected by her wisdom.

"Maxine, your skin looks great. Is that a different makeup you're wearing?" Eunice asked.

"I switched to Mary Kay, and I love it. I got the whole kit a few weeks ago—the cleanser, toner, moisturizer, lipstick, all that. I like the way it goes on my skin, and I don't break out," Maxine said.

"Damn, I mean, darn, Maxine," Lila corrected herself, forgetting Helen was in the room. "Sorry, Mama," she said, then back to Maxine. "You sound just like one of those commercials. 'I like the way it goes on my skin.'" She mimicked Maxine. "Are you sure they're not paying you to advertise their products?"

Everyone laughed, except Christen, and since Lila wasn't one of her favorite people, Christen interrupted. "Maxine, your skin has always been beautiful. I don't recall you breaking out that much."

"She doesn't anymore." Lila smiled slyly.

"Lila, honey, do you ever think about anything else?" Helen gave her daughter an equally sly smile.

"Of course, I do, Mama," Lila answered.

"Do we believe that, Mama?" Rayanne continued the joke.

"I don't know. This is Lila we're talking about," Helen teased.

"Can I help it that I got it going on?" Lila said.

"I know that's right," Eunice said, giving Lila five.

Eunice and Lila were friends for years prior to Eunice's marriage to Samuel. Lila had liked Eunice so well, that it was Lila who broke up Samuel's relationship with another girl in order to get him to go out with Eunice. He later proposed, then married her.

Helen and Christen took refreshments into the den for the others.

"Sammie tells me that I act like some machine, and that I expect him to act the same way," Eunice said.

"I know you're not trying to say that my brother is falling down on the job. I knew I shouldn't have allowed my brother to marry a heifer like you, anyway." Lila chuckled.

"I'm not saying that at all, but he'd better keep on eating them oysters," Eunice said, and more laughter followed.

"Sammie is a Wilson, and he'll be a man until the day he dies. Ask Mama." Lila chuckled.

Helen and Christen returned to the kitchen. "Ask Mama what?" Helen asked, going to check the pies in the oven.

"Just a little silly girl talk, Mama." Rayanne laughed.

"Maxine, you have to hook me up with that makeup. I really like the way it looks on you," Eunice said. "My skin is changing. It's getting a little coarse and I need something to revive it."

"Why don't you try mine? We're about the same complexion," Maxine offered.

"Do you have it with you?" Eunice asked.

"I don't lug that stuff around with me, but come to the house tomorrow and try it on."

"Sounds good." Eunice poured several glasses of lemonade and placed them on the table.

"These should be ready in just a few minutes," Maxine said, peeking over her mother's shoulder into the oven.

"Mama, do you think we're baking enough pies?" Rayanne asked.

"I think so. We got two lemon meringue, two pumpkin, four sweet potato pies, and four apple pies. That should be plenty, but if we run out, I got a few more out in the freezer," Helen said.

"What's out in the freezer?" Lila's eyes darted suspiciously from Helen to Rayanne.

"Some pies." Helen tilted her head toward the back porch, where she kept the freezer.

"What kind of pies?" Lila asked.

"Sweet potato." Helen smiled and sipped from her glass of lemonade, which Eunice had placed on the table in front of her.

"As much as I love your sweet potato pies, I can't believe you never said a word until now," Lila grumbled.

Rayanne and Maxine looked at each other and shared a secret snicker.

Helen noticed that look and said, "Maybe there ain't no more pie out in the freezer. Your sisters love my pies, too."

Not only did Rayanne and Maxine sneak pie from the

freezer, but Jeremy would nuke a slice when he felt like it as well.

"I bet you are right, Mama," Lila said, looking from Rayanne to Maxine.

Maxine plugged in the mixer and began blending chocolate cake batter. It was Jeremy's favorite. They'd asked the boys what they wanted for their graduation dinner, and although the list went on and on, the women prepared every item.

Rayanne checked the oven and removed the potato pies and placed the apple pies on the rack.

"Who moved into Mrs. Abigail's house?" Eunice asked.

"I don't know. I've never seen anyone there. Just the car in the driveway, and on occasion, the lights will be on," Rayanne said, putting the dish towel on the sink.

"Me and some of the church members want to go and welcome them to the neighborhood, but we ain't never seen nobody," Helen said.

"Mama misses Mrs. Abigail and she wants another friend," Maxine said.

"I sure do miss Abbie," Helen said.

A song started playing on the radio that had gotten everyone's attention and had provoked a debate among them. The women all joined in—the ones who could sing, as well as the ones who couldn't carry a tune in their hands. Eunice got up and danced around the room as the opinion of the ethnic background of the singer was split.

Lila challenged, "When have you ever heard a white woman sing like that?"

Just then, Jeremy came into the kitchen. He was wearing patchwork jeans, which hung low on his hips, layers of oversized sweaters, and his sneakers were strung only halfway up.

"Who is singing that song, Jeremy?" Lila asked, snapping

her fingers and bobbing her head to the music. "She's black isn't she?"

"No, Ma. That's Lisa Stanfield. Got some pipes on her, too," he said, and the ones who thought the singer was white gave each other five.

Rayanne looked at Jeremy and thought how times and trends had changed. The kids wore their pants so low on their hips, you wondered how they didn't fall off, and you could fit two people in their sweaters, but that was the style, and who was it that brought about change? The young people and the times.

"Where are you going dressed like that?" Lila asked, a frown creasing her pretty face.

"I'm just gon' hang out for a while," Jeremy said, looking down at himself. "What's wrong with the way I'm dressed?"

"Nothing, if you're all right wearing clothes that look like they belong to the Jolly Green Giant. Jeremy, you look like you don't have any behind." Lila walked over to Jeremy and pulled his pants tight, showing the excess fabric. "Look at this. It doesn't make any sense to buy clothes this big."

"This is what guys my age are wearing, Ma. Besides, the girls love the way I look," he said, pouring a glass of lemonade from the pitcher in the refrigerator.

"You look nice, Jeremy," Eunice said, sipping her drink.

"Jeremy, you want a slice of that potato pie?" Helen asked and winked at him.

"Yeah, Grandma." He smiled back at her. Helen got up to cut the pie.

"Listen how he talks to people. No respect at all," Lila said.

"Chill out, Ma. Grandma and I are cool. Right, Grandma?"

"That's right." Helen placed a slice of the still-warm pie on a saucer and handed it to him.

"Mama, there won't be any pie left for tomorrow, if he's going to start eating it tonight," Lila complained.

Jeremy took the saucer, grabbed a hand towel, and slid the pie onto the towel. He was about to leave when Lila said, "And have your behind back here before midnight. Graduation is tomorrow, and I don't want to be up half the night worrying about you. Did you hear me?" Lila raised her voice as Jeremy went toward the sink.

"I hear ya." Jeremy looked defiantly at his mother.

"All right, take your little narrow ass out before you end up staying home. I've already told you, I want to get some sleep tonight."

"Since when have you been up worrying about me?" Jeremy became indignant.

"See how fresh his mouth is," Lila said, and everyone could tell her temper was about to flare.

"At least I don't curse before Grandma."

"Look, young man, I don't think you're gonna be going anywhere tonight. Get your behind in there." Lila pointed toward the den.

"So you're gonna start trying to play Mama to me now. Ma, be for real."

Rayanne knew each of them had a quick temper, and Jeremy was unpredictable, so she hoped they would stop arguing before the situation escalated into something they all might regret. Rayanne wondered why Lila would want to provoke her son unnecessarily on such an important night.

"Jeremy, why don't you go on and try to get back early," Helen said, going over and patting him on his back. "And be careful, son."

"I will, Grandma." Jeremy stuck the last piece of pie into his mouth and drained his glass.

"He's gonna find what he's looking for out there in them streets before long," Lila said.

"Leave the boy alone, Lila," Helen said.

"I'll see you later, Grandma," Jeremy said, putting his empty glass into the sink and kissing Helen on the cheek. Then he walked toward the door.

"If you're not back here by midnight, you shouldn't bother coming back at all," Lila said, slamming the bowl of potatoes and the knife on the table.

"Why doesn't she leave him alone?" Maxine whispered to Rayanne.

Rayanne whispered back, "I don't know. She's your sister."

"Get home soon, Jeremy," Helen said, wanting to cool the brewing situation that was heading toward a fever pitch.

"He makes me sick. He'll just try to spoil the day for me tomorrow. He's no good, just like that old daddy of his. Never going to amount to nothing, no way," Lila said, forgetting her proper way of speaking long ago.

"Lila, for Pete's sake, leave him alone," Rayanne said.

"I will not leave him alone. I'm sick and tired of him walking around here with that arrogant attitude of his." Lila hurled the words at Rayanne. Then back to Jeremy. "Who do you think you are? You are nobody. You hear me? Nobody. You got nothing. You don't want nothing, and you ain't never gonna be nothing."

Jeremy turned at the door. "So what's up, Ma? You can't get wid nobody's husband tonight?"

Samuel entered the kitchen from the den. "What's all the commotion about?" he asked.

"Don't you talk to me like that," Lila said, charging up to Jeremy; then she slapped him hard across his face.

What happened next gave Lila a wake-up call. Jeremy grabbed the knife from the table and lunged toward Lila; everyone screamed. "I told you to leave me alone!" Jeremy shouted.

"No," Maxine screamed, drowning out the other screams in the kitchen.

"Oh, my God," Rayanne said, jumping up with her hands to her mouth.

Samuel reacted with lightning swiftness, managing to get between Lila and Jeremy, and wrestled the knife from Jeremy's hand. "What's wrong with you, boy?" Samuel asked..

"That boy tried to kill me," Lila said, shaken, tears welling up in her eyes. "You all saw it."

"Shut up, Lila," Samuel said to her. Then to Jeremy, "Don't you know this is no way to solve anything, and besides, that is your mother who you were trying to kill. No matter what she says or does, she is the last person you would want to pull a knife on." Samuel tossed the knife in the sink and caught Jeremy by his arm. "Come with me, we need to talk." The two of them walked outside. If Samuel had not been there, Jeremy would've put that blade into Lila's chest.

Later, when everyone had calmed down, Samuel and Jeremy returned to the kitchen. "I'm going out for a little while," Jeremy announced.

"You sure you want to go out tonight, Jeremy?" Rayanne asked, concerned because of the state of mind he was in. She'd often thought about doing public speaking about violence. She was certain now that she'd find some time in her already busy schedule to do just that.

"I won't be long," he said.

Around eleven o'clock, when everyone had left and the house was quiet, Rayanne, Maxine, and Lila sat at the kitchen table and talked over coffee.

"That boy would've killed me tonight if Sam hadn't stopped him," Lila said, shock still lining her face.

"No doubt about that. My God. What is happening to our children? What kind of future do they have to look forward to?" Rayanne asked.

"I have no idea." Lila shook her head and rubbed her hands together. "I don't even know my own son anymore. I don't have a clue what he intends to do with his life. He doesn't talk to me, so I don't know what's going on with him," Lila said sadly.

"Lila, you push too hard," Maxine said, but Lila ignored her.

"I'd hoped that Jeremy would go to school and become a doctor or lawyer, you know, make something of himself," Lila said.

"Most parents have those kinds of dreams for their children. Maybe the kind of life you want for Jeremy isn't as important to him as it is to you."

"That's just it. I don't know what's important to him. Why doesn't he talk to me?"

"Because you don't listen to him," Rayanne said, and waved to Maxine, who left the room quietly, waving good night.

"Good night, Maxine," Lila said nonchalantly, then to Rayanne, "Do you have any idea what his plans are?"

"He's going into the air force."

"The air force?" Lila exploded. Rayanne got up and checked on the baby, who was still asleep. Rayanne closed the door and returned to the kitchen. "Jeremy's going into the air force?" Lila almost whispered when Rayanne sat back at the table.

"Yes, that's his plan."

"He's not going to college?"

"We all would've preferred that, but the air force is his choice, and it isn't a bad choice for now. He can get a handle on his life and an education at the same time." Rayanne hesitated a moment. "Jeremy is very confused right now. You have to know that. He's been dealing with a lot, but he's handling it."

"What is he going to do about Little Charlotte?"

"Swan? We'll take care of her."

"You're going to take care of the baby?"

"Unless you want to," Rayanne teased.

"Oh goodness, no."

"Just kidding. Lila, Swan is no trouble at all. Besides, Jeremy is not going to be able to get himself together while trying to take care of a baby. I'm not saying it can't be done, because single parents do it all the time, but it helps when you've got a support system working for you."

"That boy has disappointed me time and time again. I had such dreams for him."

Rayanne knew that was a big part of the problem. Those were her dreams. "Jeremy's got dreams of his own, and we've got to support him if his choices are reasonable."

"Taking care of a baby isn't gonna cramp your lifestyle?"

"My lifestyle changed when I returned to South Carolina," Rayanne said. "I'd be lying if I said there weren't times when I could be doing something else, but I've come to realize how precious children are. I want to provide a safe and nurturing environment for Swan. She's such a gift to us—a wonderful, delightful gift—and I want her to have a chance at a good life, and Jeremy as well. And if there's anything that I can do to help, then I sure want to. Jeremy is a man now, and we're going to have to treat him as such, give him some space."

"A man isn't a man if he can't take care of himself and his family," Lila said, a bit snooty.

"We have to crawl before we walk."

"But the air force?" Lila's disappointment returned to her face.

"This is his life, his decision, and we've got to back

away and support his choice," Rayanne said. "So what do you say?"

"What if he gets into the service and finds that he doesn't like it? Those military facilities are so regimented."

"We can't deal with a lot of what-ifs, just the reality of right now." Rayanne looked at Lila.

After some thought, throwing her hands into the air, Lila said, "Oh, what the hell."

"I don't hear a lot of conviction behind that statement."

"All right, already. If this is what Jeremy wants, and it makes him happy, then I'll support his decision. I may not be happy with it, but I will support him in this, and I won't bad-mouth him anymore." Lila laughed.

"I'm proud of you. This is a big step toward making things better between you two."

Lila looked thoughtful, but peaceful. "I suppose I could come home a little more often, look in on the baby, and give you a little help from time to time."

Rayanne couldn't believe Lila was offering to help. That was a first. Would wonders never cease? She was glad that their discussion didn't turn into a boxing match. She remembered, with sadness, the look on Lila's face when she and Jeremy had the altercation. It was a situation that could've been avoided. Rayanne grew up in a household where the Commandments, especially "Honor Thy Mother and Thy Father," were obeyed. And although she believed God was not vengeful, she did believe that one reaped what one sowed. She didn't condone all of the choices Jeremy had made, but they were his choices, and he'd be held accountable.

Lila admitted she'd blamed Jeremy for the breakup of her marriage to his father, the rocky romances she experienced with other men, and she even blamed Jeremy because she got pregnant with him before she and Perry were married.

It seemed Lila had always blamed Jeremy for something, and he was hurt terribly by it. Rayanne wished Lila and Jeremy had handled their conflicts differently early on, but Lila was willing to be supportive of her son now, and now was a good place to start.

Immediately after graduation, Jeremy volunteered for the air force. He would enlist in September, which was a step in the right direction.

20

"Hello," Rayanne called out as she entered the house through the side door. It was a quarter past ten on Saturday morning, and the house was too quiet. For that hour, it was unusual. Rayanne had gone to New York to check on her stock portfolio. She'd become wealthy from the plays she'd written, but the declining economy had caused her to re-think some of her investments. She finished her meeting there sooner than she expected, and she took the first avail-able flight back home. She picked up her car from the extended-parking section at the airport and drove home. Rayanne had missed her family very much, and she couldn't wait to see them, especially Swan.

"Where is everyone?" she murmured. John and Chris-ten were looking after Swan while Rayanne was away, and Jeremy was in New York, visiting friends before going into the air force. But where was everyone else? Had Mrs. Marshall and her mother gone shopping or something? And Josh, there was just no telling where he was.

"Hello," she called out again, walking down the hall and putting her suitcase in her room. The door to her mother's bedroom was closed, and she gently knocked before enter-ing. "Hey, Mama, how are you? Are you all right?" Rayanne greeted. Helen pulled the covers close to her throat and stared at Rayanne. Her eyes held a wild, frightened look, and she was acting like someone who was cornered by something they didn't recognize.

Rayanne moved closer to Helen. "Mama, what is it, and where is Mrs. Marshall?" She sat on the side of the bed. Helen moved away, not wanting Rayanne to touch her.

Rayanne left Helen and went into her room to check her mother's medication. Just as she had thought, her mother hadn't taken any medication in the three days that Rayanne had been gone. Mrs. Marshall always stayed at the house when Rayanne was out of town, but where was she? And why hadn't she given Helen her medication?

Rayanne went into the room where Mrs. Marshall usually slept, but neither she nor her suitcase was there. Rayanne went into the kitchen and called Mrs. Marshall at home. That was the first time Rayanne had gone out of town and left her cell phone behind, and wouldn't that be the occasion when something would happen?

Mrs. Marshall picked up on the second ring.

"Mrs. Marshall, why aren't you here with Mama? I just got back into town. Mama hasn't taken any of her meds while I was gone, and she is still in bed, looking like she's afraid of me," Rayanne said.

"I'm coming right over. I'll call you on my cell," Mrs. Marshall said, and hung up.

On the way, Mrs. Marshall called Rayanne and told her that Josh came in three days ago with some woman, telling her that her services were no longer needed. He had sent her on her way. Mrs. Marshall informed Rayanne that she returned each day to check on Helen, but she was refused entry.

"I'm sorry, dear, but that brother of yours and that woman, they took over after you left," Mrs. Marshall said.

"And I had no way of reaching you because your cell phone is on your bed."

"I'm sorry about that, and I'll deal with Josh, but right now, I'm concerned about Mama."

When Mrs. Marshall arrived, carrying a case, she entered the house and found Rayanne sitting on the side of Helen's bed. Mrs. Marshall checked Helen's temperature and blood pressure, and ordered Rayanne to prepare a light meal for her mother.

Rayanne went into the kitchen and prepared a soft scrambled egg, a single piece of toast, and a glass of milk. She returned with a tray to her mother's room. Mrs. Marshall dissolved a couple of pills in some water in a teaspoon and slowly eased the spoon into Helen's mouth. She fed her some of the eggs and toast and small sips of milk until she was satisfied that Helen had consumed enough so that the medication would not cause her to get sick.

Rayanne pulled the covers up, and Helen settled back in bed to allow the pills to work.

"Mrs. Marshall, please stay with Mama," Rayanne said. Then she said to her mother, "I'll be back in a little while, okay?" Helen stared, but she didn't respond.

Rayanne opened the door to Josh's room, where the smell of stale alcohol greeted her. She hit the switch, flooding the room with light, and found Josh and a woman asleep in bed.

"Josh," she called out.

"What? Who is it?" Josh's mind was in a fog. He and the woman had drunk excessively the night before, and neither could think clearly at that hour of the morning. "Oh shit, where'd you come from?" he said when he focused in on Rayanne's face. He scratched his head and shook the woman. "Get up, baby," he said. The woman mumbled something, turned over in bed, and pulled the covers over her head. "You gotta get up, baby," Josh said, looking sheepishly at Rayanne.

"I want you to get up," Rayanne said. "Put your clothes on, and come to the kitchen." She turned to leave, and pointing a finger at the woman, she said, "And get *that* out of here."

Rayanne went back to check on her mother. She was asleep, and Mrs. Marshall was sitting in a chair beside the bed, looking in a magazine. Rayanne went into the kitchen, where Josh sat at the table and the woman was leaving through the back door.

"Josh, what the heck are you doing?"

"What's wrong, Rayanne? We took care of Mama," he said.

"Josh, Mama hasn't had her medication in three days. It doesn't appear that she's eaten, and you sent Mrs. Marshall away. What's going on?"

"I thought I could take care of her," he said, his head drooping. "I was just trying to help."

Rayanne stared at her brother. He needed help. For years, they knew Josh had a problem, and every time they decided to get help for him, he'd straighten up enough where you really thought he'd be all right. Then, as always, he'd get into trouble again, and she told him so.

"Rayanne, I'll have a couple of drinks, but I'm not an alcoholic," Josh said.

"Josh, you drink every day."

"That's a lie," Josh growled.

"Well, every other day. What's the difference? You need help, and that's not debatable." Rayanne paused a moment. "Josh, you are allowing your drinking to kill your dreams. You always said you wanted to start your own business. What happened to that? You've got great ideas. You're creative, smart, and you're great with your hands. You have a God-given talent that you're not putting to use. Remember what Daddy always said? 'If God gives you a talent and you don't use it, He'll take it back.' Then Rayanne said, "You're grown and I can't tell you what to do, but I hope you will get it together and not let your dreams go unfulfilled." Then Rayanne chuckled. "And what was that you brought in here? I thought you were trying to get back with Beverly."

Josh laughed, running a hand over his face. "You know one woman isn't gonna hold me down."

"You old sinner," Rayanne teased.

"And you know what they say, 'Sinners never sleep.'"

"But the next time you two want to get together, do it at her place."

"I don't think so. That gal thought I owned this place."

"You don't even know her name, do you?"

"She answered when I called her baby," he said, and they chuckled.

"Why did she think you owned the house?"

"She asked why you were ordering me around in my own house. I told her you were the owner, and as she was leaving, I asked when I could see her again. Well, that lady looked at me, gave me that neck action, and told me I don't even have a house and I could kiss her black ass on credit."

Rayanne laughed and said, "That person was *no* lady."

They laughed some more.

Soon afterward, Helen and Mrs. Marshall appeared in the doorway. Helen had showered and was dressed.

"What's going on in here?" she asked, and winked at Rayanne. "Looks like I'm just in time for breakfast."

"Yes, a very late breakfast."

21

More than a year had passed since Raymond died, and less than a month since Josh had spent another six weeks on a daily basis at the rehabilitation center, when he staggered in, again, drunk. But unlike other times, he was affecting high indignation, his perspiration stank profusely, and he looked as though he'd wallowed in dirt a few times before he made it in. Josh had lost so much weight that he was beginning to look like death warmed over.

It seemed that every new season set the stage in Rayanne's life for something that was totally absorbing. Someone always wanted more, expected more, or depended more of her, and though she always thought she had untiring patience, lately she felt she'd exhausted her stock of it. Her home had become part of a machine that badly needed oil.

"I just can't get over Daddy's death. I've tried to deal with it, but it's hard," Josh said, crying again. That was the only excuse this time as the quicksand rose around him. He'd used every other excuse to explain his drinking, but he was approaching an end, and unless someone intervened, they'd be facing yet another tragedy.

"Josh, we're putting you in the New Tomorrow,"

Rayanne said, and lifted a finger to his protest. "And this is not open to discussion."

Rayanne had expected a smooth departure. She'd drive Josh to Florence, have him admitted to that center, and hopefully, when he was released this time, he would remain clean and sober. When it was time to go, Josh refused. He was out of control, and when he threatened Rayanne, she called the police. Josh was removed in handcuffs, leaving an upset Helen behind.

Maxine called later that night.

"Is Mama still angry?" she asked.

"She looks at me like she hates me, and she tells me she will never forgive me," Rayanne said.

"I'm sorry, honey. Is there anything I can do?"

"I'm okay, just worried about Mama."

"You had a tough job and you handled it," Maxine said. "Mama will come around."

"I hope." Then Rayanne changed the subject. "The boys haven't heard from Fred, huh?"

"No. I got his address from Althea and gave it to them. I so hate seeing these innocent boys get put through this crap," Maxine said, but Rayanne knew there was more going on with her than what she was saying.

The following day, Rayanne and Helen were in the den watching TV. Helen was quiet. Mrs. Marshall said she hadn't said a word all day, and when Helen went to bed that evening, she didn't even say good night.

The weeks that passed brought no change in Helen's attitude. She avoided Rayanne as much as possible, and she became depressed again. When Rayanne tried to get her involved in senior citizens programs, Helen refused, saying she didn't consider herself a senior citizen. Heck, Rayanne was thinking she felt like a senior citizen and could use some of those programs herself.

22

Labor Day was approaching, the weather was hot and sticky, and Jeremy was packing a lot of living into the weeks before his departure. Maxine took Helen and Swan to Charleston, and Rayanne was home alone when she received a call from Brenda, asking her to meet her and Hilary for lunch.

Rayanne entered the restaurant and searched until she saw Brenda and Hilary waving to her. She waved back and walked over to the table and joined them.

Each girl ordered from the salad and hot bar, got soft drinks, and returned to the table.

As they ate, everyone noticed that Brenda was unusually quiet. She was wearing large sunglasses, and when she removed them, Rayanne saw dark circles around her eyes.

"Burning the candle at both ends, are we?" Rayanne smiled.

"What?" Brenda looked at Rayanne.

"You look a little tired. Still selling those houses?" Rayanne asked.

"Yeah. I've got a prospective buyer for the house over on Forest Drive. You know the one I told you about." Brenda picked at her food.

"The one you showed last week?" Hilary asked, placing a straw in her glass and taking a sip.

"Yeah," Brenda said without enthusiasm.

"Then what's wrong? Are you on your period again, or is it PMS?" Hilary asked.

"No, I'm fine," Brenda answered, but they knew that wasn't true.

"You don't seem your usual self, Brenda. Are the children all right?" Rayanne asked, cutting off a piece of meat loaf and putting it into her mouth.

"The kids are fine. Everything's fine," Brenda said. "I'm just a little tired."

"That young man probably walked out on her." Hilary laughed. Then, unexpectedly, Brenda burst into tears. "Oh, my God." Hilary reached across the table to touch Brenda's hand.

"Brenda." Rayanne was alarmed. "What's wrong?"

"I didn't mean to upset you," Hilary said. "I was only joking."

"I'm okay." Brenda pulled some tissues from her purse and dabbed at her eyes; then she laughed. "But you hit the nail on the head. Jason and I had been dating for a while, but he's ended our relationship. I invested a lot of time with him, gave him money, bought him clothes. That son of a bitch didn't care about me. He played with my heart to get to my purse. I don't know why this shit always happens to me."

A waitress came and offered coffee.

"No. I'm wired enough as it is," Brenda said, but the others accepted. "I told Jason I wanted a commitment from him. He told me I should be happy with what we have, that he'd already brought more to my one-dimensional life than I had. Can you believe that shit?"

"You're kidding!" Hilary exclaimed.

"No, but I'm not going to waste any more time crying

over something that I can't do a damn thing about. It was good while it lasted—I've cried and now it's time to move on. Time is a precious commodity. I'll keep the good memories close to my heart and fuck the rest," Brenda said, spreading some butter on a piece of roll and popping it into her mouth. Rayanne winced at all that butter. Brenda made a face at her and laughed, knowing that look. Before long, it appeared Brenda was back to her old self.

"We are getting the adult-care facility off the ground," Hilary announced.

"How's that going, by the way?" Brenda asked.

"Real good, but so much red tape getting Social Services involved, and we're putting in twelve hours a day, except on weekends," Hilary said. "We have twenty-six residents and we're assisting them by taking them to appointments, dispensing medication, consulting with their doctors, and we keep them and their surroundings clean. This has been our dream for years, and although it is challenging, we enjoy it. Also, it is so rewarding to be able to provide a warm, loving environment for people who are not coming from such places."

"I'm sure it is," Rayanne said. "Well, Josh is still in the center in Florence. I drive over every week, but he still refuses to see me. But not only is he angry at me, Mama is so pissed-off that she can barely stand to look at me. Our relationship has deteriorated so much. To save my own sanity, I'm still trying to get myself situated to talk to high school kids about violence because it is taking over the country. So it is important to me to try to head it off and save our children."

"I heard that," Brenda said.

Hilary looked at her watch. "Well, I gotta run. I'll call you." With that, she left.

"Do you have a few minutes?" Brenda asked when she and Rayanne were alone.

"Yeah, sure," Rayanne said, looking at Brenda, who had a serious look on her face.

"I found a lump in my breast last week."

"Oh, Brenda."

"I was examining my breasts in the shower and there it was." Brenda looked at Rayanne, and then she looked away.

"Have you seen a doctor?"

"No."

"What are you waiting for?" Rayanne said in a voice that was a little above a whisper.

"I just haven't gotten around to it yet."

"Brenda, this is nothing to play with. We'll get you examined, and we'll go from there. I want you to call your doctor today, Brenda," Rayanne said, looking into her eyes. "Today."

"I will call him next week."

"Brenda, if you don't call today, I will. I mean it."

"I know," Brenda said with a little laugh. Rayanne knew now why Brenda was so upset earlier, and it had little to do with Jason.

"Sometimes there is nothing to these lumps, except they will frighten us to death until we know that nothing is wrong."

Brenda's voice cracked when she said, "Rayanne, I didn't mention this before, but I lost a sister and a cousin to breast cancer."

Rayanne didn't want to alarm Brenda, but she was alarmed herself. "That settles it. I am setting up the appointment, and I am going with you."

"That's not necessary."

"I know, but I want to, and we will lick this thing together."

Brenda smiled and brushed a tear from her left cheek.

23

Under a warm, clear October night sky, Rayanne observed the moon as it shined brightly among a scattering of twinkling stars. For a brief moment, all seemed fair and right with the world. Reality, though, has a way of raising its ugly head, forcing us to face whatever it is that's going on in our lives. She thought of Josh. He still wouldn't see her, and now he wouldn't even speak to her on the phone. She thought about the crime that had invaded their once-quiet, safe community. She remembered her mother saying on more than one occasion that something was going on in Mrs. Abigail's old house that wasn't right, but she didn't know what it was.

Rayanne thought of Brenda, grateful that her test results were negative, but she was cautioned to have regular checkups, and Brenda returned to her old fun-loving self. And Ralph? Lately her mind was in a buzz about Ralph. As she stood in the brisk breezes, memories of what they shared came back to greet her. Rayanne took a deep breath to steady her breathing. She wished the thought of Ralph didn't still have that effect on her. But how could she fight it, when the thought of him took her back to a time when she and Ralph were so much a part of each other's lives as they held each other all night, making love and listening to some of their favorite tunes?

There were times when Rayanne found her mind filled with wonder. How would her life differ, had she not moved back home? If it hadn't been Dorian, would Ralph have betrayed her with someone else, had they gotten married? Those thoughts visited Rayanne on occasions, but that was all academic now because she'd moved back to South Carolina, Ralph had slept with Dorian, and he probably would've cheated on her, had she married him. What Ralph did was unforgivable. He had not only scratched the surface of trust and loyalty of their relationship, but he'd broken it.

Rayanne also thought of Billy Peterson, how they'd make a quick stop at some out-of-the-way motel for a quick session in bed, which left her totally unfulfilled. One night after they made love, Billy asked, "When can I see you again?"

"I'll call you," Rayanne said.

"I hope one day soon we can stop meeting like this and have a real relationship. I'm crazy about you."

"We promised we wouldn't get into anything serious."

"No, you said that, not me. I'm in love with you and I want to marry you. Don't you want the same thing?"

Rayanne knew then that Billy wanted more than she could give, and she wanted more than he could offer. There was no point in him putting his life on hold. She turned him down and their relationship ended amicably. Rayanne was back to where she was when she ended her relationship with Ralph, nearly two years ago. She was alone again.

Jeremy was on standby to go to Iraq. Rayanne was getting some decorations for Swan's third birthday party on Saturday. Swan talked about her party all week, and on Saturday, sixteen little boys and girls came to the party, along with their mothers. Helen had done Swan's long sandy hair up in ponytails with pink ribbons that matched her dress and socks. Rayanne and the other mothers were in awe as Swan entertained her guests. It was fun watching her open her presents and hearing her squeals of delight at discovering the contents. She received gifts of all kinds—savings bonds, educational toys, dolls, clothes. Lila sent two dresses, and Jeremy sent a giant teddy bear from where he was stationed at. He promised that he'd be with her on her next birthday.

Swan had expressed an interest in ballet, and since three was the age requirement for dance, Rayanne assured her that she would be entering dance school that year. Swan's mother had called only a few times since Swan came to live in South Carolina, and since April had married a man from Chicago and moved there with him, she'd called Swan less frequently. April did call and wished her daughter a happy birthday on the day of the party.

"You looked like a little princess today, honey," Rayanne said when the party was over.

"Am I a beautiful princess, Aunt Rayanne?" Swan asked.

"You are even more beautiful than all the princesses in the world."

Swan walked over to Rayanne and hugged her neck. "I love you, Aunt Rayanne."

"I love you, Swan," Rayanne said, and released her.

"Thank you for my birthday dress. It's pretty."

"I'm glad you like it. Come on," Rayanne said, removing Swan's dress and leading her to the bathroom for her bath. "Did you enjoy your party?"

"Yes, I liked it a lot."

"I'm glad. Hey, guess what?" Rayanne said, changing the subject.

"What?"

"We're going to trim the Christmas tree," Rayanne said.

Swan always liked looking at the Christmas tree, but this year she would be helping to trim the tree.

"*Weee,* that'll be fun."

"You're going to be in charge of hanging bulbs on the tree, tossing icicles, hanging ornaments, and all that kind of stuff. Then, next week, we're going to ride around and look at the decorations on other homes in the neighborhood."

"I like that," Swan said excitedly.

Rayanne lifted Swan out of the tub, toweled her dry, and slipped her into a pair of pajamas. She held Swan on her lap and read one of the books the little girl had received as a birthday present. Rayanne valued the influence she had on Swan's life, teaching her and helping to mold her. Swan said her prayers and got into bed.

Helen entered the room. "I'm turning in myself," she said.

"I thought we could sit and talk awhile," Rayanne said, sitting on the side of Swan's bed, hoping to get some positive response from her mother.

"Maybe tomorrow night," she said.

"Are you feeling okay?"

"I'm fine. Just the excitement of the party is all," Helen said. She kissed Swan, waved to Rayanne, and went off to bed.

It wasn't long before Swan was asleep.

Rayanne awoke early that Sunday morning. While making breakfast, she got Swan ready for Sunday school. After the table was set, Rayanne went to her mother's room and knocked. Entering, she called out, "Morning, Mama, breakfast is ready."

Helen was usually up and either doing something around the house or getting ready for Sunday school, but she was still in bed. Rayanne walked over to the bed. Her mother was dead. The pain that hammered Rayanne's heart was overwhelming, numbing her. At first, she was too numb to cry.

* * *

Sometime that late afternoon, Rayanne walked through the backyard to the lake. As if the day wasn't unbearable enough, it began to rain. She stood as the rain pounded against the dried leaves, making them crackle. She'd lost a large chunk out of her life when she lost her father. Now she'd lost her mother, and she was devastated. She had lost too much, and could never remember feeling so alone. Was she going to lose everything she held dear in her life? She felt like an emotional cripple as she turned her eyes to the sky. *"Why?"* she screamed in a voice that was unrecognizable. As she wept, alone, clinging to a tree, she felt a pair of strong hands turning her around. Through her tears, she was surprised to see Ralph standing there. They stood facing each other for the first time, in a very long time.

"I had to come," he said, and Rayanne's body sagged against his as she cried in the cold, in the rain. She nestled in Ralph's arms.

As Rayanne stood in the comfort of Ralph's embrace, for a little while, it was as though they'd never parted. He was holding her, comforting her, and providing the strength she so desperately needed.

Rayanne was vaguely aware of the multitude of people who had come to the house, and the funeral was like an extension of her father's. As with her father, food was given to shelters, and flowers were taken to the hospital. Both parents were gone now, the two strongest links. What would they do?

Ralph returned to New York the day after the funeral, and Rayanne promised she'd keep in touch. Ivory and Dorian stayed on a few days afterward. They talked a lot, cried a lot, and they managed to laugh some, too. By the time they separated, Ivory and Dorian hoped that their personal healing had begun.

Swan was very young, but even she missed Helen. Her

confusion was obvious when she looked around the house for Helen, and did not find her. Rayanne felt she'd experienced it all as she watched her days slip into nights that were cold, lonely, and depressing. It was no wonder she'd ended up on a therapist's couch.

Rayanne entered the office of Mary Lucas, a therapist, whom she'd looked up in the phone book. Rayanne took a seat on the couch, with Mary Lucas sitting in an armchair across from her.

"So, Miss Wilson, what brings you here today?" Mary Lucas asked. Her clear blue eyes looked piercingly into Rayanne's.

Rayanne moved forward on the couch and asked, "Where do I begin?"

"Anywhere you'd like," the therapist said softly and kindly, which caused Rayanne to relax.

Rayanne pulled out a cigarette. "May I?" she asked.

"We don't normally, but I think we can make an exception this time."

Rayanne lit the cigarette, took one drag from it, and put it out with a tissue she took from the box on the coffee table, since there wasn't an ashtray around. "I don't even like these things," Rayanne said. "Dr. Lucas, can you tell me why it is that I feel guilty about everything involving everyone, you know, feeling that I have to solve the problems of the world?"

"Why don't we talk about that," the therapist said.

When the session was over, Rayanne had told her things she never thought she'd tell anyone, and although she still faced the same set of circumstances, she was feeling better, knowing there were answers and she didn't have to try to find them alone.

* * *

Rayanne sat, listening, while Swan practiced on the piano. She was making progress on the keyboard, but Rayanne wasn't meeting the same level of success with her writing. One night after putting Swan to bed and reading her a story, Rayanne sat with her laptop. At that hour, the house was quiet. Josh had been released from the center. He had not returned to the house. However, everyone told Rayanne he'd remained clean and sober, and she was so happy that he was taking care of himself.

Rayanne stared at the computer keys a moment. Suddenly words began to form in her mind, and her fingers raced across the keyboard. She'd been typing for hours when she was interrupted by the phone. Rayanne answered it.

"Whatcha doing?" Aunt Bessie asked.

"Just putting a few lines on paper," Rayanne replied.

"I wanted to check on my two favorite girls," Aunt Bessie said. "I'm glad you done started writing again." Then she said, "Stevie called last night." Rayanne wondered whether he was in trouble again. "Said he's gonna be getting some job next week, but he needed a little money to tide him over. I went on and sent him what he said he needed 'cause I don't want him coming back here. I know that's a bad thing to say 'bout your own child, but that's how I feel."

Rayanne wished she could assure Aunt Bessie that she didn't have to be afraid of Stevie. She'd been through enough at his hands and she didn't have to put up with any more of it. "Is there anything that I can do to help?" she asked.

"Don't you worry 'bout me. I'm gon' be all right. I want to tell you how much I appreciate you looking out for me."

"I wish you would move in with Swan and me, that way we can look after each other."

Aunt Bessie didn't mind visiting and spending a couple of nights on occasion, but she had no intention of giving up her own home and moving in with anyone else.

"You know how we are when we get old," Aunt Bessie said, "all set in our ways and hard to get along with."

"How would you know? You're not old, and you're definitely not hard to get along with."

Aunt Bessie chuckled. "I knew I called you for a reason. You always make me feel so good. And I can tell you're working things out since you're writing again. You sure got your mama's knack for bouncing back. What's that word? Resilience?" Aunt Bessie asked, and they laughed.

Five minutes after she hung up with Aunt Bessie, the phone rang again. It was Ralph. He wanted to visit that weekend.

"Yes," Rayanne said without thinking, and it was settled. She was glad she and Scott were friends again, but when she mentioned Ralph's prospective visit, she was met with silence. She knew Scott was thinking that she was setting herself up for more pain, because he always thought that was what Ralph's visits brought. Scott had met Ralph at the funeral, and not only did he not like him, he wasn't convinced that all of the play was out of the man.

24

Rayanne met Ralph at the Columbia Airport that Friday evening. Since her mother's death, she and Ralph had kept in touch, even though she held no hope for a future with him. He'd been supportive at a time when she needed it most.

Swan was spending the night with Marcia Raylyn, which she did regularly. They would rent movies to watch and would eat popcorn until Swan fell asleep. Swan had taken a late-afternoon nap, so when Rayanne dropped her off at Maxine's, she was full of energy and ready to stay up with the older people.

After Ralph's bag was loaded into the car, they headed to Sumter.

"You look great," he said, looking over at Rayanne.

"So do you." She returned the compliment.

"I've been thinking about you a lot, Rayanne."

Rayanne didn't respond. She was thinking about her therapy session earlier that day. She'd informed her doctor about Ralph and his impending visit.

"In order to understand and deal with what happened between Ralph and Dorian, the disintegration of your relationship with your mother, and other things you've been having trouble with, you have to understand how those things could have happened. One day you will look back, when the pain is not so bad, and you will remember good days," her therapist had said.

"You think so?" Rayanne had asked.

"I'm certain of it," the therapist said.

Rayanne stopped at a red light and waited for it to change. Ralph didn't speak again until they were flowing with the traffic. "I never stopped loving you, you know," he said.

Rayanne maneuvered the car through the Friday-evening traffic. Before long, they were out of the city and on the interstate. "What happened to us, Rayanne?" he asked.

She couldn't believe that questioned came out of his mouth. "You must know the answer to that," Rayanne said, knowing she would never forget.

Rayanne lit a cigarette and blew out a cloud of smoke.

"When did you start smoking?" Ralph was surprised.

"I hate these things," she answered, taking another draw from the cigarette.

"Then, why do you do it?"

She said, "I don't know. Why do people do the things they do?"

"You've always been against smoking, always the health advocate."

She looked quickly at him. She'd started smoking after her mother's death, and she didn't know why, because she didn't even like smoking. "I don't do this often."

Ralph looked at her a long time. He thought long and hard before he approached the subject that they'd avoided for a long time. That was the only thing that stood between them. He wanted her back in his life, and if he hoped to have a chance of her loving him again, they had to talk, try to work through the one obstacle that separated them. "Rayanne, you have to understand how this thing happened," Ralph began.

"Puhleeze."

"Don't make this harder than it already is. I want you to understand."

"Do you really think people exhibit that degree of understanding?"

"We were so much in love and I thought that love would weather any storm."

"Must we talk about this now?" Rayanne looked at him and felt a gamut of emotions welling up inside her. She didn't want to be having this conversation with Ralph, at least not while driving.

"I think we should deal with it, get past it, and get on with our lives," he said as carefully as he could.

"I'm afraid that's easier said than done."

"Are we going to waste an entire lifetime because of one stupid mistake?"

"I suspect you'd be better qualified to answer *that* question."

"Rayanne, I admitted I made a mistake, but I shouldn't have to pay for it the rest of my life. We should be able to put the past behind us and move forward. We can't avoid this any longer."

Rayanne thought for a moment. "Ralph, I thought you and I would love each other forever. I never thought something like this would happen to us."

"Neither did I."

"Really?"

"Don't act so surprised. You know I did."

"Then can you explain to me why you thought you had to do what you did?" There was complete silence. "At least, you're not denying it," she said.

"I'm not confirming anything, either," Ralph spat out.

"Then, what're you telling me?" she asked, raising her voice. "You're not saying now that you didn't sleep with Dorian."

There, she'd said it. They were having a conversation

about something that had happened long ago, but it had remained fresh in Rayanne's mind.

"It's not what you think."

"I get that you are a man, and the dog in you has its needs, but, my friend—" she said as she drove faster.

"Will you please slow this car down?" Ralph interrupted.

Realizing she was driving nearly twice the speed limit, she reduced the speed and set the cruise control at sixty miles per hour.

"Now . . . can we please talk calmly?"

Rayanne took a deep breath. "Ralph, when I left New York, and your phone calls and visits became fewer, I knew something wasn't right, but because I loved you, I didn't want to believe the worst. No woman wants to think her man is sleeping around. I'm not stupid, but I *never* thought that you would sleep with one of my best friends."

"You're projecting the worst scenario. I know what you're capable of when you let your imagination run wild."

"What was there to imagine? Let's try this scenario. What if I fuck one of your best friends? Do you think you'd ever forget it or forgive me? Hell no."

"I never meant to hurt you."

"You knew this would hurt me. Unless you thought I'd never find out. Dorian was going through a lot. She was confused, so who was going to believe her?"

"What has happened to you? You've changed."

"Yet you can't see the reason for the person I have become, can you?"

Ralph had always wondered what would ruffle her feathers, make her vulnerable. Well, there was a difference in being vulnerable and devastated, and she'd been devastated. She'd agonized over missing him, to the point of despair.

"It would make all the difference in the world if

you could forgive me. I love you, and I believe you still love me."

"That's mighty arrogant of you. You've done the unforgivable, and yet you feel you can just move back into my life and go on as though nothing has happened."

"Can you honestly say you don't love me?"

That might be true, but she was trying to move the process along. She said, "I did love you, Ralph, but that was then, and this is now. We can't turn back the clock."

"Then why am I here?" he snapped.

To his surprise, Rayanne jammed on the brakes and the vehicle skidded on the highway, leaving black marks as she pulled off onto the shoulder.

"You can go back to New York and your life there. Just say the word and your black ass will be on the way back to the airport!" she yelled. Ralph stared silently at Rayanne. "What's it going to be?" she demanded, ready to explode from frustration that had built too long.

"Let's just go on, please."

Rayanne looked at him. After a moment, she checked the traffic and pulled back onto the highway. They rode the remainder of the way in silence.

As soon as they entered the house, Rayanne called to check on Swan. She'd fallen asleep watching the second movie. Aunt Bessie called and told Rayanne that another neighbor's house had been robbed, and for the first time, Rayanne checked all windows and doors before putting dinner on the table. They were having prime rib, baked potato, salad, rolls, and peach cobbler for dessert.

After the meal, she and Ralph settled in the den in front of the TV set. They talked of Ralph being back at work, what was going on in the stock market, and his involvement with Big Brothers. "Right now, I'm just trying to hold on to my job and put some purpose back into my life," he said. "It hasn't been the same without you,

Rayanne, and this distance, you here and me there, had put such a strain on our relationship."

"It'd been difficult for me as well, but we've separate lives now, and we can never get back to what we had."

"If you continue to think like that, then we won't." He paused a moment. "I'm feeling a little out of place here, talking to you like this under these circumstances."

"You created these circumstances," Rayanne reminded him.

Rayanne realized that Ralph still had the capacity to tear her life apart, if given the chance, and she didn't want to take that chance.

"I don't think I can stand to lose anything else. It hurts too much," she said, getting up and going to the kitchen. She could feel Ralph's eyes on her, and she thought she felt goose bumps exploding over her. She returned shortly with two cups of steaming hot coffee.

Ralph picked up the remote from the table and turned off the TV. Then he faced Rayanne. "The last thing I wanted to do was hurt you. Christ's sake, Rayanne, haven't you ever made a mistake?"

"Of course, I have. I make them all the time," she snipped back.

"Don't be sarcastic." He got up, walked over to the fireplace, and looked at the pictures displayed on the mantel. Then he turned and looked at her. "Don't you believe in second chances?" he asked. "If you would just think of what we had, maybe we could get back on track."

"There isn't enough time for that."

"I ain't going nowhere. This isn't easy for me, either. It is hell when we're together like this, yet so far apart. But it's even worse when we're not together." Ralph walked back over to the couch and sat beside Rayanne. After a moment, he reached for her, but she got up, went over to her music collection, and put on a soulful CD. She sat on the floor, moving her head from side to side, with her eyes closed, enjoying the music.

Ralph took a sip from his cup. "Coffee is good," he said.

"I can heat that up for you," she said, knowing his coffee was cold by now.

"No, it's fine."

"You still like it cold, huh?"

"Old habits are sometimes hard to break." He got up, walked over, and sat on the floor beside Rayanne. He began looking through the collection. "You've got some great stuff." He smiled. "Looka here, looka here. This is my jam right here." Suddenly a frown came over his face as he held a CD in his hand. "I don't think I've heard of these people."

"It's nice. Let me play it for you." Rayanne played the song; he liked it. Before the night was over, he persuaded her to dance.

Rayanne was awakened in the morning by the telephone. Maxine was taking the kids to the carnival, and she'd have Swan home by three. After talking about the crime that had so viciously invaded their community, they agreed to discuss with their neighbors the possibility of forming a neighborhood watch group.

When their conversation was over, Rayanne said, "Let me speak to my baby." When Swan got on the phone, Rayanne said, "Good morning, sweetheart."

"Were you afraid at home last night without me?" Swan asked brightly.

"No, I wasn't afraid, but I missed you a lot."

"I missed you, too. We're going to the carnival, but if you're lonely, I'll come and stay with you."

"That's sweet, baby, but why don't you go and have a good time at the carnival. I'll see you later. Then we can read that new book I got you last night."

"You bought me a new book?" Swan sounded like she was beaming.

"Yes, *The Little Alligator.*"

"*Weee!* That's one of my favorites."

"I know, and we'll get *The Turtles* next week."

"*Yippee!*"

"Okay. Have fun now."

"Aunt Maxine wants to talk to you. I love you, Aunt Rayanne."

"And I love you, Charlotte."

"You can call me Swan. I like Swan, and I like Charlotte," Swan said. "But I don't like 'Stinkie.'"

"I don't like Stinkie, either, and your daddy needs a spanking for calling you that."

"Is Daddy going to get a spanking?" Swan said, grinning.

"Not really."

"Oooh." Swan sounded disappointed.

Rayanne chuckled. "Be good."

"I will."

"So how did last night go?" Maxine asked after taking the phone from Swan.

"You are one nosy broad," Rayanne said.

"I know, but you still didn't answer me."

"I know." Rayanne chuckled.

"He's right there beside you, huh?"

"Not in the way you think," Rayanne said, observing Ralph sleeping on the couch, where he'd spent the night. "We stopped at the bookstore, had some dinner, and we spent the evening talking and listening to music."

Maxine let out a groan. "That's it?"

"See. I told you you're nosy. Just hurry up and bring my baby home." With that, Rayanne hung up.

* * *

When Rayanne came out of the bedroom, she was wearing a blue silk blouse and a pair of blue jeans that did wonderful things for her figure. Although she'd added a few pounds, time had been kind to her. She could hold her own against any of the attractive younger women who could only hope that they would maintain their beauty when they reached her age. She looked through the house for Ralph, but he was nowhere in sight. She noticed that the hall bathroom held warm, moist air, which was evident that he'd showered and changed. She walked outside. Unable to find him, she returned to the kitchen and made breakfast.

"I wondered where you were," Rayanne said when Ralph returned.

"I was down by the lake. I didn't get a really good look when I was here the last time. It is fabulous out there," he said, sitting across the table from Rayanne. They ate breakfast.

"I spent a good part of my childhood there, when I wanted to be alone with my thoughts. My friend Scott thinks I should have a developer dig it out and plant flowers around the lake and put fish and ducks in it."

"That's an idea," he said. "You could have a few trees removed to open up that path and make the lake visible from the house. It would be beautiful, and I can't tell you what that would do for you creatively." Then he asked, "By the way, what's going on with you and Scott? And please don't tell me he's just a friend."

"Don't tell me you're jealous," Rayanne said, getting up to clear the table.

"You didn't answer my question," he said, getting up. He went over to assist Rayanne as she loaded the dishes into the dishwasher.

"Scott is a very dear friend. I don't know what I would've done without him. He's been there with me through most of my adversities—my parents' deaths, Josh's alcoholism, the problems with Jeremy, and . . ." Rayanne wouldn't allow herself to go further as she stared out the window.

"And what happened between you and me," Ralph finished for her.

Rayanne turned to face him. He'd moved up close to her and they stood only inches apart. His lips moved close to hers, she could feel his warm breath on her face, but she brushed past him. She knew if she allowed him to kiss her, just once, she'd be loving him again—just as before.

"I just bet he took full advantage of those adversities, too," Ralph said, sitting back at the table.

"Where are you going with this?" Rayanne turned and asked, her eyes matching his hard stare.

"Rayanne, I'm struggling, trying to make things right between us, and I wish you wouldn't fight me so. I love you, woman. Don't you understand? I love you," Ralph said, springing from the chair, sending it crashing to the floor. "What do you want me to do?" he asked, standing over her.

"Why don't we just take this time and try to enjoy each other's company and let the rest of it go, please," she said, getting up, her eyes becoming bright with emotion.

"How long has it been since this thing happened? I don't even know anymore, but we've never talked about what went wrong, not once," Ralph bellowed.

"Ralph, I've moved past it, and if I were you, I'd do the same thing."

"If you don't want to talk about it, fine, but why don't you sit down and shut up," Ralph said.

"Excuse me?" Rayanne said, blinking.

"You heard me," Ralph said, pointing to a chair. "Would you please come over here and sit down." She looked at him, and although she wasn't sure what it was that made her want to obey, she did. "Would you please listen? Please do that for me."

Rayanne stared at him a moment as Ralph picked up the chair he'd knocked to the floor.

"I know you're angry. You have every reason to be, but please let me say something in my own defense. It may have been easy for you to move on with your life without me, but it's not the same for me. I miss you like crazy." He stretched his hands out on the table. "Have you ever sat and thought back to what we've been through together, what we meant to each other?"

"You asked me to listen, remember?"

"Okay, okay." Ralph tried to steady his breathing. "This thing that happened between Dorian and me."

"Why don't you call it what it is," Rayanne spat out.

"No, *was,* Rayanne, *was.* That's the operative word."

"And could that be because she is now living in another country, with her husband?" Rayanne said sarcastically. "Why couldn't you have just been a friend, rather than taking advantage of her and betraying both Dorian and me?" she asked, a crease in her brow.

Ralph sighed, looking helpless. "I'm not sure where to begin."

"The beginning would be a good place to start, since you want to clear the air."

"I don't know, call it crazy," Ralph started out, "but I thought I did what I did for the right reason." He lifted a hand in protest when Rayanne was about to comment. "Please let me get through this. The first night Dorian came over, she was really messed up. She'd learned that Henry wasn't getting a divorce. He wasn't going to marry her or continue to take care of her. She'd gone through most of her earnings and she was feeling lost."

Rayanne thought Dorian had enough money to last two

lifetimes. She'd certainly made a truckload with her investments and modeling career.

"When Dorian came to me, she was a basket case. She felt that everyone had abandoned her." Ralph wanted to make sure he chose his words correctly. "I promised her I would stand by her."

"Well, something must have changed your mind," Rayanne sneered.

"That night," Ralph continued, as though she hadn't spoken, "I held her until she fell asleep. Rayanne, I, too, was vulnerable. I was lonely and missing you. I'd built my life around you, and when you came back here to live, I had no idea I'd depended on you as much as I obviously had. You leaving New York put me in a tailspin. I felt lost and abandoned. There was no real planning or discussion between us. You didn't ask me how I felt about your decision. You decided to move—you told me, and that was that."

"You and Dorian comforted each other," she said. Although she'd already heard more than she wanted since they'd started to talk, they might as well not just scratch the surface. This time, they would break it. "Go on, tell me every gory detail. Let me hear it all."

"It was getting late, so I offered her my bed for the night. She asked me to stay with her until she was asleep again. I supposed I dozed off also. Anyway, Dorian woke up during the night, and she was crying again. I tried to comfort her. Then all of a sudden, she was kissing me. It wasn't as though I was in love with her, or she with me, for that matter. You know I'm not into white chicks."

"And I suppose that makes it okay," Rayanne snapped. "As long as the women happen to be white, you can screw as many of them as you want."

"Rayanne, I'm just hoping that once you understand what happened, and have a chance to process it, maybe you'll understand how it happened."

"I wish I could understand," she said, remembering what her therapist said.

"Are you still that angry at me after all this time?" Ralph asked.

"I'm feeling something, but I don't believe it is anger. It hurts too much to stay angry, but I—" she began, but Ralph interrupted.

"No buts. If you're not mad at me anymore, that makes it easier."

"I just can't go around being angry my entire lifetime. It takes too much energy and it makes no sense being angry about something I can't do a thing about."

"Do you love me, baby?" Ralph asked softly.

"I do love you. Perhaps I always will, but I'm not in love with you. That's the difference, and we'll have to live with that difference."

Ralph stared at Rayanne a moment. "Well, if there isn't anything left between us, I don't want to beat a dead horse."

"For a time, my life was pointless and empty, with one thing happening right after the other. But there has been one constant in my life that's brought me nothing but joy." Ralph looked at Rayanne. "Swan."

"She's a wonderful little girl, but you're a vital woman, and a woman like you needs a man."

"Swan has given my life purpose." Rayanne smiled. "A word of warning—to know her is to love her. She's destined to steal your heart. She's just that special."

Rayanne continued to smile.

"She was going to commit suicide," Ralph said, and Rayanne's smile faded.

"What?"

"Dorian was going to kill herself. I'm not making excuses, but she'd become just that desperate, and I dealt with the situation the only way I knew how. Rayanne, I knew Dorian long before I met you, and I was never interested in her in that way. I don't feel good about what I did. Had the situation been different, if there were any other alternatives . . ." Ralph appeared to be struggling, and for the first time, Rayanne felt sympathy for him. She extended her hands across the table to him. He took her hands in his. "I'm sorry," he said. "I'll never do anything to disappoint you or hurt you again."

Rayanne got up from the table and was about to go to him when the door suddenly burst open and Swan rushed into Rayanne's arms. The toddler had a candy apple in one hand and a stuffed teddy bear in the other.

"Aunt Rayanne!" Swan squealed.

"Hey, you," Rayanne said. "What have we got here?"

"I won this teddy bear. It's for you."

"For me? He's fantastic. Thank you." Rayanne smiled and took the bear. "I'll take Mr. Bear under one condition."

"What?"

"That you take care of Mr. Bear for me. Deal?"

"Deal." Swan's eyes sparkled as Rayanne handed the bear back to her.

"And the candy apple is for me," Swan said, and she looked at Ralph. "But you can have it if you want it, Mr. Underwood."

"Thank you. That's very generous of you, but why don't you hold on to it for me?"

Rayanne looked at Ralph, and her smile touched her eyes.

Maxine poked her head through the door. "Hi, you two."

Rayanne and Ralph greeted her.

"I've got Marcia Raylyn and her friend waiting in the car. We're picking up a few things for the slumber party tonight. Nice seeing you again, Ralph." She winked at him and left.

"Bye, Max," Rayanne said. Then to Swan, "A slumber party, huh?"

"Yes, and I was invited," Swan informed.

"You were?" Rayanne said, putting her down.

"Yes," Swan said, "Marcia Raylyn wants me to be there. Can I go?"

"May I go?" Rayanne corrected, and said, "Yes, you may go, but first we're going to give you a nice bath and put you down for a little nap. Get up on your little stool and brush your teeth. Get the ones in the back real good, too, and I'll check them when I come in."

"I will brush them real good, because if I don't, I'll get cavities and my teeth will fall out, right?" Swan turned her face up to Rayanne.

"That's right." Rayanne took the teddy bear and candy apple from Swan's hands. "I'll put these away for you. Now scoot. I'll be there in a minute, all right?"

"Okay," Swan said, running off to the bathroom.

"She's quite a little girl," Ralph said.

"Yes, she is the best."

25

Rayanne was surprised that after she'd avoided talking with Scott when he'd called a second time that evening, he was the first person she saw when she and Ralph entered Lily's Staircase, a happening club in town. She could hear the words of their earlier conversation echoing in her brain.

"Rayanne, make a clean break from that man and get on with your life. Ralph is not the man you think he is," Scott had said.

"I will get on with my life, but with Ralph," she replied.

"What kind of life do you expect to have with a man who has screwed your best friend?"

"Scott, the man made a mistake, he's human. So if I can forgive him, what's it to you?" Rayanne said. "Ralph and I are going to work through this, and he's promised to never do anything like that again."

"And you believe him?" Scott asked, disbelieving. "You can't be that naïve."

Scott had been hurt when Rayanne told him that Ralph was the only man she'd ever loved. And if she was making a mistake by getting back with him, she'd be the one who'd suffer, not him. Love was important to her, like air and water. And Ralph was important, too. Scott wasn't happy with her decision, but he agreed to back off.

Rayanne and Ralph found a table near the center of the room. Ralph ordered a glass of tonic water for Rayanne. He enjoyed a scotch on the rocks as they listened to a jazz set.

They got up to dance as Scott approached the table.

"Scott?" Rayanne looked from him to Ralph. "You remember Ralph?"

The two men shook hands and exchanged greetings. Rayanne heard Ralph mention something to Scott about a basketball game before she excused herself to go powder her nose. The Knicks weren't playing that night, so she wasn't interested.

There wasn't much going on in the club that night. The band, mediocre at best, was on intermission, and the room was almost still. Rayanne had only been gone a few minutes, but when she returned, she could hear Scott and Ralph talking in low voices. Scott's face held a half smile that was tight and strained, and Ralph looked as though he could kill someone. It looked as though the boys had forgotten to play nice.

She walked over to the bar to speak to someone she knew. When she looked in the direction of the two men, her attention was divided. She was suddenly aware of her attraction to the strength and good looks of one man, and the sophistication, maturity, and sometimes devil-may-care attitude of the other. Her stolen glances and secret thoughts were divided as well, but for reasons she didn't understand. She felt a growing tension across her shoulders. Ralph was a man whom she hadn't had an emotional commitment with for years, and Scott was just a friend. Why, then, was she feeling the urgency to get Ralph out of the club and away from Scott?

Rayanne returned to the table, and after finishing their drinks, she and Ralph left, but not before he placed a big, juicy kiss on her lips.

When they were in the car, Rayanne asked, "What were you and Scott talking about?"

"Would you believe that son of a bitch threatened me?" Ralph said, yanking the car into gear and speeding off.

"Scott threatened you?" She knew Scott didn't like Ralph, but he had threatened him?

"Don't give me that look. You know the guy's in love with you. I've known it all along. I don't know why you don't see it."

She hadn't seen it, because there wasn't anything to see. "Scott is just a good friend. He cares about me, and thinks of me as a big sister."

"I'd never think of doing with *my* sister what Scott thinks of doing with *you*."

"You don't have a sister."

"Well, if I did, I wouldn't. The man was practically coming in his pants."

"You're being silly."

"I don't trust him, I know that."

"What exactly did Scott say to you?"

"Too much," Ralph hissed.

"Well, don't think about it. Let's just get home."

Rayanne rested her head back against the seat, not wanting to get into an argument with Ralph. Even when he sped through a red light, she didn't comment. They rode home in silence, except on occasion when Ralph mumbled something under his breath. Rayanne knew that whatever Scott had said to him had really pissed him off, and he was still simmering as a result.

When they arrived home, there was a message on her machine from Brenda. Rayanne tried to reach her, but she got her machine instead. After having coffee and more conversation, Rayanne said good night to Ralph. He went off to the bedroom across the hall from her, which she'd made up for him.

Rayanne pulled the covers up around her neck, turned her back toward the door, and closed her eyes. Unable to sleep, she turned over on her back, opened her eyes, and saw Ralph's silhouette on the threshold. He was just standing there, but she knew from past experiences that he was naked.

"What are you doing here?" she asked.

"I didn't like camping out over there by myself, while you're here in that king-sized bed alone," he replied.

"It builds character in a man when he has to do something that his heart isn't in."

"Distance has always been our problem. We can't put this relationship back together with all this distance between us." Ralph's voice was soft and sexy. "If you're here, I should be too. It's going to take both of us to rebuild what we had. We have to work together." As he spoke, he moved closer to her bed. "Right here is the place called hope. We can take this time to reflect, think about what we had, the wonderful times we've shared and how happy we made each other. Rayanne, we've always been magic together. When we made love, we shared each other's heart, soul, and mind. It's important for me to find out what we have left. I want to know what you're thinking, what you're feeling. I need to know where I stand with you, and I think we should look at this thing and decide what we're going to do about it tonight"—he paused—"or we should close the door on this forever." Rayanne didn't respond. Ralph went on. "You mean everything to me. I'm the one who fucked up. I take full responsibility, but I can't go on like this. I can't pay forever. So tell me, Rayanne, what is it going to be?" Ralph stood still. Rayanne continued to look at him, but she didn't speak. Ralph sat on the side of the bed and stared down at her.

"Ralph," Rayanne began slowly.

"Don't give me a lecture, baby," he said. "Just kiss me and let's hold each other and remember the times when we meant everything to each other." He lay next to her on the bed, and at first, he just touched her hand. Then he caressed her arm. He rose up on his elbow and kissed her gently on the lips. She didn't move away, nor did she push him away. He pushed his tongue into her mouth, hers greeted his and toyed with it. As the kiss grew passionate, she could feel the warm moistness between her legs. After all he'd put her through, he still had the power to affect her this way. "It's been a long time," he whispered when the kiss ended. "Do you still love me, baby?"

"I don't want to talk anymore tonight" was all Rayanne could say.

Ralph kissed her mouth, her eyes, her throat. His lips moved to her breasts. When his kisses returned to her cheek, he tasted the moist saltiness. "Baby, you're crying? Why are you crying?"

"I don't know, confusion maybe." She paused a moment. "Yes, I'm confused."

"But are you happy that we are at least together?"

"Yes, I'm happy. I'm so happy."

Rayanne knew that love and happiness were both fleeting. She also knew that sometimes people were happier when they had fewer choices. And when they made love that night, she gave herself to him completely, and without reservation. She wanted to trust Ralph again. She wanted to believe in him, and the promises he'd made to her, again. She wanted to belong to him again. People did different things for different reasons, and she hoped that when she'd decided never to see Ralph again, but later had changed her mind, that she had not committed some act of injustice against herself. If she did, however, she'd suffer it later, much later. At this moment, she had only one thought in mind, and that was to be happy, and happiness was a long time coming.

"I get crazy when I think what we nearly gave up, what we almost lost," Ralph said, holding Rayanne afterward. When she'd agreed to let Ralph come visit that weekend, she thought they'd spend an evening together reminiscing, but instead, they'd created yet another wonderful memory. One that would be with them forever.

The following day, Rayanne got up early, went to the cemetery, and put flowers on her parents' graves. She kneeled on the ground between the graves and talked to her parents. She told them she loved them and that everyone was fine, including Josh. She mentioned Ralph's visit, and before she left, tears rolled down her face.

"Mama, please forgive me," she said. Rayanne got up, brushed the tears from her face, and drove home.

After Swan arrived, the three of them went to the beach. They played in the water, walked along the beach, hand in hand. Ralph and Rayanne beamed into each other's eyes when they sat across the table from each other, eating hot dogs and drinking soft drinks.

When she smiled that angelic, halting smile at him, he smiled back, thinking how that smile still embraced him, like the sun on a summer day. They'd spent one of the most gloriously incredible days together. As they drove home, it was a consensus between Rayanne and Ralph that they were moving in the right direction. They were getting closer to each other's heart, which was their goal.

26

Just before the sun came up, Rayanne sat at the kitchen table, sipping from a cup of coffee. She rubbed her head to ease the headache that she felt coming on. She didn't get much sleep the night before, after returning from the Neighborhood Watch meeting. There had been more robberies and drugs than ever before in the community, and they were going to put a stop to it. They were moving the program along, a plan was under way, and Aunt Bessie was elected vice president of the program.

Soon Rayanne would leave to pick up Brenda and take her to the hospital. When Brenda had a checkup three weeks ago, the mammogram results were normal. But during a gynecological examination, tumors were found in her uterus. After numerous female problems and getting a second opinion, Brenda decided to have the operation.

Her surgery was schedule for eight-thirty that Friday morning, and Rayanne arrived at her home at six-fifteen. Brenda's mother was taking the boys to her home while Brenda recuperated. After promising Brenda's mother that she'd look after Brenda, Rayanne drove her to the hospital.

* * *

Rayanne laid down a magazine that she'd tried to read and she looked around the third-floor waiting room, where she was awaiting word from a doctor on Brenda's condition. She got up, walked to the window, and looked out. She watched the traffic moving up and down the street. Rayanne was thirsty. She wandered out into the corridor and found a water fountain. She took a drink and returned to the waiting room.

"Is there someone here regarding Brenda Robinson?" Rayanne looked up to see a doctor standing in the doorway.

"I'm here about Brenda Robinson," a man declared. He appeared to be in his late thirties, average height and build, medium brown complexion, and short black hair. He was wearing jeans and a plaid shirt. He shot up to the doctor. "I'm Cardell Robinson, her husband."

Rayanne approached the two men. "I'm Rayanne Wilson, a friend of Brenda Robinson's."

Cardell nodded to her, and then they turned their attention to the doctor.

"Mrs. Robinson is resting comfortably. We removed three tumors from her uterus." He indicated the sizes by placing his hands in a circle. "And a cyst from one of her ovaries. Her ovaries are intact," the doctor answered the question Cardell and Rayanne wanted to ask. "She came through surgery very well, and she'll be put in a room in an hour or so."

"Thank you, Doctor," both Cardell and Rayanne said.

"You're welcome," he answered. "The two of you might want to grab a bite to eat, since you have a little wait. There's a cafeteria downstairs. The food is not the best, but it's edible." The doctor smiled. Rayanne and Cardell thanked him again, and they rode the elevator down to get something to eat.

Sitting at a small table in the hospital cafeteria, Cardell said, "Our sons told me about Brenda's surgery. When I spoke with Brenda only two weeks before, she didn't mention it."

"Everything happened so quickly. It was a struggle just getting Brenda to see a doctor. She spent days trying to prepare herself and the boys," Rayanne said.

"Brenda and I have had our differences, but I care about her, and I don't know why she'd want to deal with this alone," Cardell said, and Rayanne could tell that he was a caring, sensitive man.

Later, after checking on Brenda, Rayanne left her and Cardell alone, and she drove back home. She would return later to spend the night. When she arrived home, Swan was sitting at the table, coloring. She saw Rayanne and climbed down from her chair and ran up to Rayanne.

"Aunt Rayanne, you are home."

Rayanne threw her purse on a chair, picked Swan up, and carried her to a chair, where the little girl sat on Rayanne's lap. "Did you have a good day?"

"Becky and I were partners, and we drew a picture at school today," Swan shared.

"You did?" Rayanne asked, looking into Swan's face. "What kind of picture?"

"A tree and some birds."

"I see."

"They are very pretty."

"I'm sure."

"We colored the tree brown, with green leaves, and the birds are red."

"Oh, red birds," Rayanne said. "That's nice."

"Becky wanted to make them blue, but I told her blue birds are boring."

"Why do you think that blue birds are boring?"

"Because when we colored one bird blue, it looked awful in the green leaves, but when we colored one red, it looked great," Swan said. "So we made them all red."

Rayanne laughed again.

"Why are you laughing, Aunt Rayanne?"

"I was thinking that your picture probably looks a little like a Christmas tree."

"No, Aunt Rayanne. It just looks like a tree with green leaves and red birds," Swan said, looking very serious.

"When will I get to see this picture?"

"We get to bring it home next week," Swan said, and stuck her finger into her mouth.

Rayanne pulled her finger out of her mouth, sat back in the chair, and wrapped her arms around Swan.

"I missed you today," Rayanne said.

"I missed you, too," Swan said, and hugged Rayanne's neck. When she pulled away, she asked, "Were you at the hospital with Mrs. Robinson?"

"Yes," Rayanne answered, and brushed back the unruly sandy curls that had pulled away from ponytails and dangled around her forehead. Every strand of hair was neatly in place prior to Swan having spent several hours at the day care. "She asked me to say hello to you."

"Tell her I said hello, too. Is Mrs. Robinson feeling better now?" Swan asked.

"Yes, all the bad things that were making her sick are now gone, and she is feeling so much better."

"Are you going back to the hospital today?"

"I promised Mrs. Robinson that I would come back to see her tonight." Rayanne paused a moment before saying, "Is that okay with you?"

"It's okay," Swan said, and she hugged Rayanne's neck tightly again.

"Are you sure?"

"Yes," Swan replied, still clinging to Rayanne's neck.

"Then what is it, baby? What's wrong?"

"Aunt Rayanne, I don't want you to ever get sick."

"I won't. Honey, look at me," Rayanne said, loosening the

grip the child had around her neck. "See, I'm fine. I'm very healthy. That's why it's important for us to go to the doctor and get checkups so that we don't get sick. So you don't have to worry your pretty little head about that, okay?"

With that, Swan appeared to be all right again. Then she informed Rayanne of some new games they'd played in school and the new words she'd learned.

"I write my name, this many times," Swan said, putting up ten fingers. Then she stuck her two index fingers into her mouth.

"You wrote your name," Rayanne corrected, and she removed Swan's fingers from her mouth.

"I wrote my name, and I learned how to spell wagon. That's, W-A-G-O-N, wagon, and smile. That's, S-M-I-L-E, smile."

"That's very good," Rayanne complimented. "It sounds like you had a very productive day."

"Oh," Swan said, sliding from Rayanne's lap. "My daddy wrote"—she tested the word "wrote"—"to me today." She ran off to get the mail from the table in the kitchen.

When she returned with the letter, she climbed back into Rayanne's lap. "Let's see what your daddy has to say," Rayanne said, opening the letter. She read the letter to Swan and pointed to every word in the letter, especially where Jeremy said he loved Swan.

He liked it in the air force, and although it was early in his career, he'd decided he was going to make a career of it. When Rayanne finished reading the letter, she did as she'd always done. She put it back into the envelope and gave it to Swan, who dashed off with the letter to put it with the others.

Rayanne could see Swan's excitement at knowing her father was coming home to see her soon. It was obvious that Swan loved her daddy very much, and for such a little girl, she had a lot of love inside her. She spread it around generously.

Swan was a busy little girl, learning and growing. She was singing in the choir at church, going to day care, and was taking piano lessons. She could play "Chopsticks" and she took dance lessons. Rayanne smiled, thinking of how cute Swan looked in her little leotard.

The vacuum cleaner stopped. Mrs. Marshall entered the den.

"Mrs. Marshall, how is it going?"

"Everything is fine. Your aunt Bessie called," Mrs. Marshall informed.

"Okay, thanks. I'll give her a call," Rayanne said, and Mrs. Marshall put the vacuum away. "So, young lady, what would you like to do today?" Rayanne asked Swan when she returned.

"I want to play on the swing," Swan said.

She had a full playground in her own backyard, a combination swing, rings, and slide set, trampoline, sandbox, and other playthings that converted the playground into a child's paradise.

"Sure, let me go get changed."

"May I call some of my friends?" Swan asked.

"Of course. Do you remember their phone numbers?"

Swan made a face. "Some of them."

"Okay. We'll call them when I get back," Rayanne said, and went off to her room. Suddenly there was the sound of thunder. She slipped into a pair of jeans and a blouse, and returned to the kitchen to find Swan standing at the solid glass door, staring out.

Swan turned and said very sadly, "It's raining, and none of my friends will come out to play now."

"I'm sorry, honey," Rayanne said, kneeling down beside Swan. "We can do something inside. We can watch a movie and eat some popcorn. It would be just like going to a real movie."

"But I want to go outside and play," Swan said, her eyes brimming with tears.

"I know, sweetheart, but it's raining, and if you go outside now, you'll get all wet and catch a cold. You don't want to get sick, do you?" Rayanne tried to calm Swan down.

"I don't care if I get sick," Swan said, wiping her tears away with the back of her hand.

"Why don't I read you a story," Rayanne said. "Would you like that?"

"I want to go outside and play with my friends," Swan said, and Rayanne became perplexed. She couldn't think, she was tired, and her brain wasn't working very well. She wondered what she could do to make Swan happy. Because of other commitments, she'd not spent as much time with Swan as she would've liked, and she felt guilty. Swan deserved much more than she'd gotten lately, and Rayanne would do something about it.

Rayanne went into her bedroom, and when she returned, Swan was still standing at the door, staring out, her tiny face pressed against the glass. Rayanne kneeled beside her again and ran her hand across Swan's back. Swan looked at her, eyes moist with tears, then looked outside again.

After a short while, the doorbell rang. Mrs. Marshall answered it, and instantly the patter of little feet raced across the kitchen floor. One neighbor brought over her own twin girls and another little girl, and they all squealed with delight at seeing each other. The girls brought their dolls, several of their favorite cartoons, and Swan provided the refreshments that Rayanne served.

27

Rayanne arrived at the hospital that evening. She ran into Brenda's mother and her sons as they were leaving. Rayanne sat with Brenda as Brenda drifted in and out of sleep. She awoke during the night, laughing. When Rayanne asked what was so funny, Brenda explained that many years ago, one of her sisters had the same surgery. When she told her sons the reason for the surgery, her youngest son said he hoped he'd never have to have any tumors removed from his uterus. Rayanne chuckled softly as Brenda drifted off to sleep again.

Cardell came in shortly afterward. A nurse checked Brenda's vitals and changed the bag of fluid that was connected to Brenda's hand. When Cardell insisted he'd be spending the night, Rayanne took the cue and left, but she agreed to spend the remainder of the night at Brenda's apartment, rather than driving back to Sumter. Rayanne felt a warm tingling feeling when she saw the look Brenda and Cardell shared as she left the room.

After another night with very little sleep, Rayanne woke early to a morning that was gloomy. It was going to be one of those days, because her day got worse. The doorbell rang, and when she answered it, the young man who stood there identified himself as Jason. Rayanne was surprised to see him there, and wondered at the reason for his visit.

"I'd like to see Brenda," Jason Davis said.

"I'm sorry, but she's not available right now," Rayanne replied.

"Why don't you let Brenda be the judge of that," he said, looking confident.

"I'm sorry, what did you say your name was?" she asked, pretending not to remember his name just to bring him down off his high horse.

"Jason," he responded, and she could tell he was a little put out. He looked as though he couldn't believe any female could forget his name.

"Jason, why don't you call her in a few days," Rayanne said, wanting to be rid of him.

"Why don't you march your fine behind in there and tell her I'm here."

Does he understand English? Rayanne wondered. "We're going around in circles here. Now listen to me good. Brenda is not available, so why don't you give her a call in a couple of days."

"Who are you? Her maid?" Jason said, forcing his way into the apartment. "Brenda," he called out, heading toward her bedroom.

Brenda had shared with Rayanne and Hilary the intimate early-morning rendezvous that she and Jason had shared, but Rayanne thought that was over. If that was the case, then why was Jason there, demanding to see Brenda?

"Brenda is not here," Rayanne called after Jason.

When he returned, he asked, "Where is she?"

"She's away for a few days."

"Where?" He stared into Rayanne's eyes.

"If Brenda wanted you to know where she was going, I believe she would've told you."

"When will she be back?"

"In a few days."

"Then I'll be back." Jason flashed Rayanne a smile.

"You do that," Rayanne mumbled, going toward the door, hoping Jason would follow.

He did, but he said, "You got a problem with me?"

"No, I don't *got* a problem with you," Rayanne said sarcastically. She wondered why Jason wanted to see Brenda now. Why the urgency? It had been several weeks since Brenda had seen him, and her disappointment was evident at not seeing him before going into the hospital.

Rayanne eyed Jason suspiciously and he noticed it.

"Why are you looking at me that way?"

"Just leave, please." Rayanne stood, waiting for Jason to leave. When he didn't, she said, "Brenda is a sweet girl, and you could have treated her better, you know. She acts tough, but she has her fears, just like the rest of us. She's looking for an emotional investment, and I believe she thought she'd found that in you." Rayanne knew because of Brenda's insecurities, she liked having a man around, but it was clear when the going got tough, Jason got lost.

"I bet you're not afraid of anything."

"Excuse me?"

"I like a woman who isn't afraid of anything, and you're a beauty, too. That's a real turn-on."

"And, you're disgusting."

"Aah, and sometimes beauty is the beast," he said, giving Rayanne a sexy stare. When he saw that his stare was matched with a look of disgust, he jammed his hands into his pockets. "I've gotta get going. Let Brenda know I stopped by."

Jason faced Rayanne and she could see, physically, why Brenda might be attracted to him. He was handsome and had a great body, but he was as selfish as hell. When they reached the door, Jason turned to Rayanne.

"Look, I don't know what you think I did that makes you

despise me so, but you might be wrong about me. Maybe you're not giving me enough credit."

"Maybe you're expecting too much credit."

Brenda deserved so much better than what he was offering. She was really good to Jason because she cared about him, and Rayanne told him so. "Some of you men don't seem to realize that a woman's love is a privilege, and not your right," Rayanne scolded.

"Brenda knows how I feel about her," he began. But did he ever tell her? Rayanne wondered.

"Women want to be told and shown how her man feels about her. Women don't want to have to guess at it. I just know that when she needed you, you weren't there, and it hurt her a lot."

"Maybe I should've opened up more to her."

"Perhaps you should have."

"I'm not good at this love thing. I care about her, she's good people, but beyond that, I don't know. I mean, she's got kids almost as old as I am."

"What difference does that make? I'm certain you knew all that before you got involved with her."

"Yes, I did, and like I said, Brenda is good people." Jason considered a moment before asking, "Do you think she still cares for me?"

"I'm the wrong person to ask," Rayanne replied, and looked toward the door.

"I think I came here today for all the right reasons, you know," he said.

Rayanne was silent. Her immediate thought was that he showed up this morning for a quick tumble between the sheets and to hit Brenda up for as much money as he could get. Jason talked a really good game. Rayanne remembered Brenda saying that some months back. She'd said that Jason could be a real sweet-talker, a conniving liar, and he ran games on women all the time.

"I think I can make it up to her," Jason was saying. "I know I can make her understand how I feel. I'm the best thing that she's ever had. She's told me as much."

"You certainly don't oversell yourself," Rayanne said sarcastically.

"I do like Brenda, but I just got tired of her demands," Jason said, apparently looking for sympathy.

"You had a real conclusive way of showing how tired you were," Rayanne murmured, thinking everything was fine until Jason thought Brenda had some life-threatening problem. Rayanne felt she'd already said more than she should have, but what she really wanted to say was that he shouldn't cause a problem for Brenda if he didn't have the cure. Instead, she said, "I'll let Brenda know you were here."

"You do that," he said. Then he was gone.

Rayanne stood with her back against the door and shook her head. The only thing that she could say about Jason was what a ball-less wonder he was.

28

At daybreak, on a cool South Carolina morning, Rayanne got up and sat on the side of her bed. Sometimes, she thought, the world passed right by her window, leaving her behind, but from her front porch, she was always able to put things in its right perspective. It was at those times that she was truly at peace. She and Ralph were together again, were spending more time together, and she was happier than she'd been in the two years since they'd been back together.

They talked often by phone, went on a cruise to Mexico, and they did countless other things. On one of Ralph's visits to South Carolina, he brought with him a four-carat diamond ring. They were officially engaged. And although the wedding date hadn't been set, they knew that nothing would stop them from walking down the aisle together this time.

Her life had almost returned to perfection once again. There was only one thing that haunted her daily, and it was that her mother had died and hadn't forgiven her or said she understood why Rayanne had Josh admitted to the rehab center. Rayanne was hurt about the disagreements she and her mother had only days before her death.

Leading up to Swan's birthday party, Helen had fussed until she'd fallen into an exhausted sleep, trying to persuade

Rayanne to bring Josh home from Florence. Helen was aware that although Rayanne tried to see Josh, and he continued to refuse her visits, she'd kept in touch with the doctors and was aware of his condition at all times. Josh was getting the help he needed, but he was not even close to being well enough to come home. After such nights, Helen would wake the mornings afterward as though nothing had happened.

As Rayanne wished she could beg her mother's forgiveness, and knowing it wasn't possible, she asked God's forgiveness.

Brenda recovered from surgery and had returned to work. She was selling houses, dating every chance she got, and still maxing out her credit cards like there was no tomorrow, but there was no talk of Jason or Cardell. Rayanne didn't know whether Jason had told Brenda of their conversation; Rayanne knew she hadn't. Even though they were very busy, they found time to get together for dinner, an evening out, or they enjoyed a card game in one of their homes.

Swan was five years old on Friday, and on Saturday, Rayanne invited family and friends over for the celebration. The party was set up in the huge indoor playroom that had been added for Swan, which extended off from the den. While the kids enjoyed the party, Rayanne tried a speech she had been working on out on the adults present, and she received constructive criticism, but they thought she'd done a good job.

After everyone had left, and Rayanne had listened while Swan read an alphabet book she received, they climbed into bed and talked about the party. Later, Swan said her prayers, ending with, "And God bless my daddy, my mom, my grandma Lila, and Great-Grandma Helen and Great-Granddad Raymond, who are in heaven with You, and, God, please bless the rest of my family and friends especially my friend, Becky and my great-aunt Rayanne. Amen."

"Amen." Rayanne tucked Swan in, kissed her, and left the room, leaving the door slightly open.

Rayanne called Ralph and filled him in on the party, the reaction she'd gotten to her speech, and the fact that he was sorely missed.

"I'm sorry I couldn't be there. Give that little lady my love and let her know I'm bringing her a present when I come," Ralph said.

"I will."

"So you got good feedback on your speech."

"Yes, good reviews, if you can call it that. They were kind."

"Honey, you've got a great mind and you're a wonderful writer, so I'm sure the speech is great."

"Lately, my writing has been anything but great, but I am happy with the way the speech is progressing. Oh, by the way, the lake is completed, but it was quite a trick keeping Swan away while the work was being done."

"I'll bet it was," Ralph said. "The questions must have gone on forever."

"Yes." Rayanne chuckled softly and mimicked Swan, "Aunt Rayanne, what's that noise? Aunt Rayanne, what's this? Aunt Rayanne, what's that?"

Rayanne and Ralph laughed.

Rayanne had hired a land developer to come in and remove some of the trees so that the lake was in full view from the back of the house. She gave instructions that the dogwood, the magnolia trees, and some of the pine trees remain on the property. Rayanne planted an assortment of flowers—azaleas, mums, zinnias, in an array of colors, as her mother had done—that would create bursts of colors all year. She'd added a deck off the den and a concrete patio that connected to Swan's new playroom. A grill was built and grass ran the length from the patio to the lake. The backyard was fenced in temporarily, as a safety precaution for Swan, because she loved the lake, and Rayanne didn't want Swan to wander off there alone.

A window seat with compartments underneath were installed in Swan's room for her dolls, books, and all of the other things that she could put away and have easy access to.

"So what is my baby up to tonight?" Ralph questioned.

"Just missing my baby."

They talked about their wedding; they'd even narrowed it down to a season. The only problem was that Ralph wanted to continue to live in New York for a while after the wedding, and Rayanne didn't want to leave South Carolina again. This was home for her, and she wanted to keep it that way. They loved each other and knew they'd work something out. With love, they would prevail.

After talking for a half hour, and before they hung up, Ralph said he was going to turn in early. He was tired and he'd call her in the morning. When she hung up, she was happy, and Ralph was happy. All her friends were happy, too.

Ivory called, sending birthday wishes to Swan. She told Rayanne that Dorian was glad she was able to forgive Ralph and forget, and was moving on with her life.

The sound of the doorbell interrupted Rayanne's thoughts. She opened the door. Scott stood there, looking handsome, as always.

"Where's the birthday girl?" he asked as Rayanne stood back and allowed him to enter.

"She was asleep by the time her head hit the pillow. She told me to thank you for the present. She loves it, and she saved some birthday cake and ice cream for you," Rayanne said over her shoulder as Scott followed her into the kitchen.

"She did?" Scott smiled.

"Yes. You want some punch?"

"Yeah, I'll get it." He poured for himself.

They went to the den. Rayanne took a pillow from the couch and tossed it on the floor, where she lay.

"How's Donnie?" she asked when Scott was settled.

"He's fine. It's his mother who I'm worried about." Scott sipped from his glass.

"You want to talk about it?"

"It's just plain stupid some of the things women do, and that's putting it mildly."

"What's going on?"

"Same old thing, telling me I'm not Donnie's father, which is nothing new, but it still pissed me off. Frannie asked me to come over tonight. She wanted to talk. But when I got there, some guy was there who she said was Donnie's father, and I'm a friend."

"What did you do?"

"I got the hell out of there as fast as I could. I've got to admit, they could be father and son because there is a re-semblance."

"Why have you not had a paternity test done? This way you'll know."

"Who am I kidding? I suspected that Donnie wasn't mine even before Frannie started telling me."

"But you hung in, anyway. That shows your character, Scott. You are a good man."

"Yeah, yeah, yeah." He got up and walked toward the

door to the hall. "What about a game of backgammon or Scrabble? You decide and we'll play when I get back."

"Scrabble," Rayanne said quickly, "but first we'll have some cake and ice cream."

"Sounds good to me, and watch me beat the pants off you."

"Promises, promises," she said, flirting with him.

Scott was a whiz at the game and had beaten Rayanne many times, but when he saw that devious look on her face, he smiled, shook his head, and walked down the hall to Swan's bedroom. He looked in on her, something he'd done since they met. Scott walked over to the bed, lifted Swan's arm, and put it under the covers; then he kissed her on her forehead.

"Happy Birthday, sweetheart," he whispered. "I love you."

He returned to the den, where Rayanne had set cake and ice cream on the coffee table. He picked up his saucer and spooned some into his mouth.

"She's a wonderful little girl," Scott said.

"You get no fight from me," Rayanne agreed, pushing ice cream into her mouth.

When they finished, Rayanne returned the saucers to the kitchen. Scott set up the board and waited for Rayanne to return.

"Ralph and I decided to get married this spring," she announced just as Scott sat on the floor, facing her. He was silent. "Did you hear me?" Rayanne asked, looking at him.

"Yeah."

"Well, what do you say?"

"Sounds like you done already made up your mind. What do you want me to say?"

"I want you to say that you're happy for me, for us, and that you want the best for Ralph and me. Scott, you're one of my best friends, and I know you want me to be happy.

Well, Ralph and I are very happy, and I'd like to know that we have your blessings."

Scott wanted Rayanne to be happy, but how could he tell her that he could see it happening all over again? He remembered how Ralph had hurt her before. He was a self-centered bastard who, Scott thought, put his own interests ahead of hers. That son of a bitch had left her devastated before, and Scott couldn't imagine any man doing something like that to a woman like Rayanne.

"Baby, I just don't want you to get hurt. Everything you've said about that guy, I committed to memory, and every time you mention his name, I replay it in my mind. I just don't know if he's the man for you."

"I love him, Scott, and I hope you understand."

"I can, if you can. If you're sure you can live with what you know about him, then there's nothing I can do."

"I think you're hurting because of what happened between you and Frannie tonight. I'm sorry, but don't punish me. I care about Ralph, and when you care about someone, you take some things on trust. Scott, you're important to me. I want you in my life, but you and Ralph have got to find a way to coexist."

"Even if he isn't the type who commits totally to one woman?" Scott asked, then said, "He's just not built that way."

With hurt in her eyes, Rayanne said, "Stop it, Scott. Stop it right now. How can you say that? You don't even know Ralph."

"It doesn't take much to see through him. You could, if you opened your eyes."

Rayanne didn't reply. She twisted the large diamond ring on her finger as she looked at Scott.

"I don't mean to be giving you a hard time, and you know I want you to be happy," Scott said honestly.

"I want to hear you say it like you mean it."

"All right, already. If Ralph is the man you want, and he makes you happy, then you have my blessing."

Rayanne looked searchingly into his eyes. "Do you really mean that?"

"Yeah. If he does it for you, then I wish you two the best."

Rayanne smiled and leaned across the board and kissed Scott on his cheek. They resumed their game, and Scott said, "I won't ever do that again."

"Do what?" Rayanne looked up from the board with a puzzled expression, but she returned her eyes to the board. She was on the verge of beating him in this game and she didn't want to lose her concentration.

"Hurt you," he said. Rayanne looked into his eyes and held them as he said, "That's a promise."

As Scott observed Rayanne from across the board, he thought about how Ralph had hurt and disappointed Rayanne in the past. He thought of the times when she'd needed him and Ralph wasn't there for her, and now Ralph wasn't willing to give up New York to be with Rayanne once they were married. And who knew what else? Yet, Rayanne had forgiven him for it all. How forgiving can she be? he wondered. What was it going to take for her to see the guy for what he really was?

The final score for each game was 500 points or so, and Rayanne was winning once more. Scott had been a bit pre-occupied, and after her fourth straight win, Rayanne didn't want to play again.

"You are no longer a challenge," she teased.

Rayanne lay back on the floor with her head propped up on the pillow. Scott lay on the floor alongside her. He whispered, "It's going to be all right."

Rayanne's next move was unexpected. It took Scott completely by surprise. She rolled over into his arms, kissed him full on his lips, and then she fell asleep. Scott lay there for some time, his thoughts racing.

As Scott observed Rayanne asleep in his arms, he had an overwhelming desire to remove the hairpins from her hair and let it fall loose around her shoulders or spread out on the pillow. He was definitely a hair man, and she definitely had a beautiful head of hair. However, he really didn't care whether Rayanne had hair or not, because she was the woman he'd fallen in love with.

Scott had fallen in love with Rayanne on that rainy day when they had the accident. Actually, even before that day, because he'd seen her long hair before. Although he'd not believed in love at first sight, it had definitely happened to him.

He'd actually caused the accident. That morning, Scott saw Rayanne on the highway and he noticed her reading from her notes. He maneuvered his vehicle until he'd gotten in front of her. When the light changed from red to green, he moved several yards and stopped suddenly, causing Rayanne to run her car into his. Yes, he'd caused the accident, and yes, he'd fallen in love with her.

At two o'clock that morning, Scott covered Rayanne with a blanket and let himself out. Rayanne awoke before daybreak. She picked up the blanket and pillow and put them away before she checked on Swan and went to bed. Within a week, Ralph would be there, she thought excitedly. She sat up in bed, lifted the phone, and dialed Ralph's number. He'd wanted to get a good night's sleep, and by that time, she felt that he had.

The sun was beginning to come up, and the phone rang three times before the sultry, unfamiliar voice answered. "Hello?"

"I'm sorry, wrong number," Rayanne said, and quickly hung up. She dialed Ralph's number, and again, the same voice answered. "Is this Ralph Underwood's residence?"

Rayanne asked, thinking she couldn't have dialed the wrong number twice.

"Yes, it is," that voice answered.

"May I speak with Mr. Underwood, please?" Rayanne said, her palms becoming wet and clammy as she got out of bed, gripping the phone tightly to her ear.

"I'm sorry, but he's not available right now. May I leave him a message?" the woman offered.

"Who are you, and w-where is Ralph?" Rayanne stuttered, trying to keep her voice calm.

"I'm Mandy, and Ralph went for a run," she answered.

"Mandy, who are you and why are you at Ralph's?"

"I'm a friend of his, but I expect him shortly. May I take a message, please?"

Rayanne struggled to control the hysteria that was mounting inside her. "No, that won't be necessary," she said, and hung up.

Rayanne was shaking all over, and all she wanted to do was scream, run, then scream some more, but she felt frozen. When she was able to get her legs to move, she turned and sat on the side of the bed, motionless, not knowing what to do next.

Rayanne didn't know how long she sat there, or when she began to move around. She just knew that most of the day found her in a daze, numb, and she couldn't help wondering what had she done that caused her to suffer as she had. Either she'd done something that was wrong or she hadn't done something, which was equally wrong. How long would she continue to pay?

She collected herself and called Ivory. At the sound of Ivory's voice, she burst into tears. Rayanne shared her new disappointment with Ivory, who offered as much sympathy as she could. Ivory called Ralph the worst son of a bitch they'd had the misfortune of knowing. They hung up, and Rayanne didn't share that unfortunate situation with anyone else. She didn't know what to do, how she was going to put her life back together. She did know that there was no way that Ralph would be able to talk his way out of what he'd gotten himself into this time. She'd never be able to trust this man again.

29

Early on Wednesday evening, the doorbell rang. Ralph was standing at her door. He'd flown in, rented a car, and drove to Rayanne's house. Shortly afterward, Swan announced she wanted to go to bed. Rayanne told Swan a story while giving her a bubble bath, and just before Swan drifted off to sleep, she drowsily asked Rayanne to say good night to Uncle Scott.

"What about Mr. Underwood?" Rayanne asked.

"You can say good night to him, too," Swan said, but gone was the smile that lit up her face when she'd left the message for Scott.

It was strange how children's insights into humans and their behavior were sometimes better than adults'. Swan was pleasant enough with Ralph, but not in the way she was with Scott. She had established her own relationship with him. During the years, Rayanne and Scott spent a lot of time with Swan and Donnie, taking them on many outings. They were like a family.

Rayanne went back to the den to find Ralph standing in front of the fireplace, both hands buried in his pockets. He stared at the flames that licked out and ate the logs that sat on the hearth, sending sparks up the chimney.

"Why are you here, Ralph?"

"Do you even have to ask?"

"Maybe I'm just stupid," she began, "but you and I were planning a wedding, a wedding that was to take place a few months from now. We made a vow to each other that we wanted the same things, that we would be faithful to each other and live our lives as a unit. Well, forgive me, but I thought when we made that commitment, we meant it. I did. I didn't take it to mean that there would be any outsiders interfering in what we shared."

"Why are you using the past tense? If you've already decided that we have no future together, then I have to wonder what I am doing here as well."

Is he crazy, or does he think that I am? Rayanne almost said it out loud. Instead, she said, "Why don't you just say what you came here to say, and then I want you gone."

"Just let me explain, please," he begged. "Just hear me out."

She lifted her hands into the air and sat on the couch. "Go on, say what's on your mind, but I think you should know that it will take nothing short of a miracle to save us this time."

Ralph didn't like the tone of finality, the conclusiveness of her statement, and he became angry. "I believe in miracles," he said.

They went through an intense relationship, but an indiscretion had ended their romance before. They'd managed to put it back together, so it was natural that emotions ran high, now that the relationship was threatened again.

"Rayanne, you and I belong together. There's no one who knows you better than I. I know your passion, what gives you joy." He lifted a hand to quiet Rayanne's intended protest. Then he began to pace the floor. He either stared at his feet or at the ceiling, but he didn't look at her. "Rayanne, I love you more than anything, and you know that." Then Ralph turned to face her. He did love her, and wanted to spend the rest of his life with her. "You're the consummate romantic," he picked up again. "And you don't want anything less in a partner. You want everything in perfect order, no flexibility. I'm not saying there's anything wrong with that, but who wants to be set in the old ways, like old concrete? The only thing I find wrong with that is sometimes that way of thinking is not realistic. Baby, what happened in New York hasn't diminished the way I feel about you. If anything, I love you more. You know how good we are for each other—we're good together," Ralph said, kneeling on the floor, near Rayanne. "You're a creator. You get to make things the way you want them. You like being in control, but that doesn't always work. We have to live life as it comes to us. There are bumps in everyone's life, and we're no exception. That doesn't mean if I do something or say something that you wouldn't do or say, that I don't love you. Because if you believe that, you couldn't be further from the truth." Ralph got up, walked to the window, and stared out into the darkness. He turned and looked at Rayanne. "The woman who answered the phone doesn't mean anything to me, absolutely nothing. Everyone who knows me knows my heart belongs to you. Baby, it took both of us to start this relationship, and it should take both of us to end it. I know this isn't what we want. I love you, Rayanne," he said, again kneeling in front of her, searching her eyes.

He was like an actor on a stage, Rayanne thought. "Are you finished?" she asked. ·

"I've just got one more thing to say. I was never once unfaithful to you while you were living in New York. Doesn't that tell you something?" Ralph asked, then whispered, "Baby, neither of us would be happy without the other. You know that."

Rayanne looked at Ralph and she studied the face that she'd loved for nearly two decades. For the first time since she'd known Ralph, he looked tired, defeated. As she continued to look at him, he laid both hands on her thighs and awaited her reply. She lifted his hands and stood up. She walked over to the window and peered out, not looking at anything in particular. She gave thought to all that Ralph had said, and even more to what she was about to say, because once said, she didn't want to have to take the words back or repeat them. Rayanne knew that Ralph loved her. There was never a question about that, but he loved her in his own way, and that was the problem. She wanted him to love her unconditionally, the way she loved him.

Rayanne turned to face Ralph. He was still kneeling on the floor in a half-turned position.

"I just realized tonight, after all this time, that you don't know me. You really don't know me at all, and we can argue about that until morning, but all we'd be doing is running into brick walls all over the place. If you think I would be interested in the kind of relationship you just described, then you must think I'm a complete idiot. I'm through being hurt by you. It is obvious you and I don't want the same things. So if the kind of relationship you want is the kind that I find between your words, then, by all means, I want you to have it. You deserve to have what you want, but it's not for me. Ralph, I've done a lot of thinking about us, but it was our conversation tonight that has had the biggest effect on me. I really don't know you as well as I thought I did. You've done things I never thought you'd do, and what do I do? I let you right back into my life, and the reason was because I loved you. And because I did, I put you up high on a pedestal," she said, lifting her hands. "The problem, Ralph, is that you couldn't handle it. You got dizzy from the height." Rayanne paused. Ralph got up, sat on the couch, and clasped his hands together. "You're right about some things, though," she continued. "Yes, I love creating. I create characters. I breathe life into them, and I do control them in that respect. I like having a little control—who doesn't? I don't think there's anything wrong with that, but, obviously, you do. Those characters I create don't cause pain. They live the life that I give them. They don't have the luxury of living like regular people, who have the option of making their own choices or decisions. And yes, you and I were good together, darn good, but we weren't necessarily good for each other. You've hurt and disappointed me too often." She paused again. "You said you never cheated on me when we were together in New York." Ralph blinked, looking at her. "Well, let's give the man a hand." Rayanne clapped her hands several times. "So what you're telling me is that if we went ahead with our plans to get married, you'd be faithful to me *as long as I'm there with you,* but the minute my back is turned, you'd have some hoochie keeping my place warm until I came back?"

"No, Rayanne, it's not like that," Ralph said, shifting nervously on the sofa.

"Seems that way to me."

Ralph breathed deeply, his head bending low now, almost between his legs. Then he got up and went over to face her. "Rayanne, if you love me, you won't throw this away." Rayanne tried to move away, but Ralph put out both hands and stopped her. "Know what I wish?" he said.

"Yes. You wish I was stupid enough to take you back again."

"I wish things were the way they were twenty years ago." He let his hands slide down to her slender waist.

Rayanne was a levelheaded, strong-willed girl, and although her body still tingled at his touch, she knew there was only one option left open to her. She had to stand her ground. She had to end this, once and for all. She removed his hands from her waist, but she continued to hold on to them.

"I'm not going to do this anymore. It's over." She looked at Ralph sadly. "For what it's worth, I didn't cheat on you, either. I never even thought about it. You said it will take both of us to end this relationship. Well, I don't think so, especially since it was *you* who couldn't seem to keep your pants on."

Ralph heard the words, all of them, but he didn't give up. "You never forgave me for what happened between Dorian and me, did you?" he said, and the question surprised her.

"If I didn't, you and I wouldn't be back at this crossroads again."

"Rayanne, what I did was no different from what men have been doing for centuries. It didn't mean a thing. It's just something men do. It's not rocket science. It's just a man's thing. It was just something to do. You're the woman that I want and need. Can we give it one more try?"

Rayanne smiled sadly at him, and before she spoke, he knew her answer. There was something different about her demeanor. He knew it was over. "Sometimes there's pain that we can work through, and then there is the kind of pain that never goes away. Thanks to you, I've experienced both."

"I'm sorry," Ralph said, and his voice cracked. "I'm truly sorry."

"I know," Rayanne said in a whisper.

"Where do we go from here?"

"We'll go on with our lives."

"I don't know what I'm going to do without you, baby."

"I'm sure you'll be just fine."

"What about you?"

"I'll be okay."

"I'm really sorry I caused you so much pain. Please believe that," he said sadly.

"I do, and you're going to be okay also."

Ralph didn't answer. He picked up his coat from where he'd draped it across the back of the couch. Rayanne reached into her sweater pocket and removed the ring he'd given her only a short while ago. She handed it to him. He was about to protest, but she forced it into his hand and closed his fingers around it. When she released his hand, Ralph opened his hand and looked at the ring. He looked at her, and then he put the ring into his pocket.

"I'm sorry," he whispered, and he left.

When the door closed behind him, Rayanne stood at the door and cried. Her body shook as deep, racking sobs escaped, erupting like a volcano. She was sorry, too. Sorry about everything. She'd loved Ralph deeply and had lost him, but she was grateful that she had a new insight into the man with whom she'd planned to spend the rest of her life. It was simply a coincidence of timing that had brought their relationship to this point. If she hadn't had an overwhelming desire to talk with Ralph that Sunday morning, she might never have gotten to know the real man. She would've married him, and shared him and his love.

Circumstances and time bring on changes, changes that people don't always understand, but maybe folks are not supposed to. She continued to cry. She was closing the door on a relationship and opening the door to her future. Her tears weren't because Ralph didn't love her the way she'd loved him, and her tears weren't because she'd lost him and would be forced to face the future without him. She cried because something inside her felt sorry for Ralph. Sorry that he might never be able to commit to anyone or be happy and have the quality of life that everyone deserved.

Rayanne stood at the door and watched as Ralph walked to where he'd parked his car. She wiped her eyes clear of the tears, while others replaced them. She watched him until he got into the car, drove off, and disappeared into the darkness. She would go through the bumps and bruises of losing him again, but at least this time, she knew it would be the last time. When they were in love, it was like a fire burning out of control. Rayanne had done things with Ralph that she'd never done before, and might never do again. He'd taught her many things. In essence, he'd educated her taste buds to the many spices of life. He'd taught her to laugh, to cry, to forgive, and to forget, but he didn't teach her how to erase the pain of a broken heart. She'd have to do that on her own. That chapter of her life was over, it was gone forever. She would finally turn the page and close that book. Tomorrow she would begin a whole new chapter in a whole new book.

30

Rayanne submerged herself in her work during the weeks that followed. However, there had been such a void in her life after Ralph that for a while she couldn't find any real satisfaction in anything she did.

As time passed, though, she polished the speech that she was going to give at another high school in a couple of weeks, and she wrote several chapters for a new book. She'd written a number of plays with enormous success, and she had written several that didn't go anywhere. Then she decided to write a book, which would be more truth than fiction, chronicling stages of her own life and involving Swan. She would probably entitle it, *My Little Girl.*

Rayanne's work at the adult facility was rewarding. She enjoyed communicating with the elderly, reading to some of them, giving flowers or a birthday card to another, or just sitting and listening to them. It was gratifying, witnessing their joy because someone had remembered them. Rayanne had even increased the time she spent counseling teenage girls as well. She was busy, but her personal life was taking a serious beating.

One night, when Rayanne had lived with the pain long enough alone, she decided to share her feelings. She called

Brenda and Hilary and they drove to Rayanne's house. After she told her story, Hilary said, "I can't say I know how you feel, never experiencing something like that, but I can certainly sympathize with you, because I imagine it must hurt like crazy."

"I can't believe that son of a bitch got caught with his pants down again. I sure hope you got up close and personal with his ass," Brenda said.

"He should be taken out and shot," Hilary scorned.

"What did Scott say? Bet he's glad you are on your own," Brenda said.

"I haven't told him," Rayanne replied.

"Why not?" Brenda spat out.

"I haven't talked about it much," Rayanne said. "Aunt Bessie, she didn't seem surprised."

"Smart woman, that Aunt Bessie," Brenda said.

"I still say he should be taken out and shot," Hilary repeated.

"Why haven't you mentioned this to Scott and let him help you through this, instead of handling it alone?" Brenda asked.

Rayanne knew she hadn't told Scott because she didn't want to hear him say, "I told you so."

"Well?" Brenda questioned.

"I don't know. I just didn't." Rayanne went into the kitchen and returned with three cups of coffee.

"What have you been doing for yourself?" Brenda asked as Rayanne set the tray on the coffee table.

"I've been keeping busy," Rayanne replied.

"Is there anything we can do?" Brenda asked.

"Yes," Hilary said. "You want to do something? Go out and tie one on?"

"You know, most of the time, I'm in so much pain, but I'm all right today. I don't know how long it will last, because some days I think the pain is gone and something will happen, or I'll hear a song that'll remind me of Ralph, and the pain will come back as fresh as it ever was," Rayanne said, blinking back tears.

"I'm so sorry," Hilary said.

"Don't you dare fall apart over that nigga. He ain't worth it. You've got so much going for you. I almost pity that fool, because he has no idea what he's lost," Brenda said. "Stupid fuck."

"I agree, Rayanne," Hilary said. "You've got to go on with your life."

"Life is filled with hurt and disappointments, but you really have to leave them in the past. I know you will," Brenda said, and winked.

"We love you, Rayanne, and we just want you to feel better," Hilary said.

"I do, and I'm lucky to have friends like you," Rayanne said, looking from Hilary to Brenda. "Okay, enough about me. Talking with you guys has made me feel so much better, and I want to thank you." She looked at Brenda. "Now, tell us, how are things with you and Cardell?"

Brenda smiled and looked off into space.

31

Rayanne pulled the sheets from the bed and was putting on a fresh set when the phone rang that Saturday morning. She picked it up, but before she could answer, Maxine said, "Rayanne?"

"Yes, Maxine. What's wrong?"

"I've got a problem. I found a condom in my car."

"Well, don't panic. There's probably a logical reason for the condom being there. They do give them out in health education classes, you know."

"A used condom!" Maxine screeched. "It was a used condom, Rayanne."

Rayanne knew that someone in that house had a lot of explaining to do. "What do you make of that?"

"Someone was screwing in my car, and I'm gonna find out who. Either my husband or my fourteen-year-old daughter has been fucking in my car. And right now, I don't know which is worse," Maxine said, but Rayanne was certain there was no question as to which was worse. Since whoever left the condom had the good sense to use one, Maxine had better hope that it was her daughter, and not her husband. Rayanne didn't condone someone Marcia

Raylyn's age having sex, but the situation would be much worse if Marcus was the guilty party.

"What are you going to do?"

Rayanne knew Maxine was angry, but that emotion seemed overshadowed by hurt, perhaps fear.

"Rayanne, I can't go through another divorce. I'm in love with Marcus, and I thought he loved me."

"Maxine, don't go jumping to conclusions. Marcus does love you, you know that."

"You think my baby is having sex?" Maxine was grabbing any straw she could.

Rayanne couldn't imagine that either of them used that condom and left it there, but when Maxine explained that in the past three weeks, Bobby had been riding with other members of his track team, and hadn't driven the car, that gave Rayanne good reason to be concerned. And if she had her way, it certainly would've been Bobby.

"I could handle this a lot better if it had been Bobby," Maxine said. Then after a shaky laugh, she said, "God, did I say that?"

"I know you didn't mean that, Maxine. You are human, and it's only natural that you'd look for the safest solution to this, and as I said, there's some logical explanation for this whole situation, I'm sure."

"I just want this whole nightmarish situation to go away."

"Do you want me to come over?"

"No. I'm all right. I just needed to talk. Look, I'm gonna have myself a beer and get myself together. Then I'm gonna get some answers."

"Maxine, please try to get some answers *before* you go accusing anyone," Rayanne pleaded.

When they hung up, Rayanne sat on the foot of the bed, scratching her head with both hands.

"Are you all right, Aunt Rayanne?" Swan asked, standing in the doorway.

Rayanne looked at Swan. She knew that whatever else might be wrong in her life, it certainly wasn't Swan. She was the brightest spot in Rayanne's existence. She was sweet, uncomplicated, beautiful Swan.

"My little girl," Rayanne said. "Come here, you."

Swan rushed over, and Rayanne lifted her up on her lap. "You have a headache?" Swan asked, holding Rayanne's face between her tiny palms.

"No, I'm fine."

"You were holding your head, like this," Swan said, mimicking Rayanne. "So I thought you had a headache."

"No, honey, I was just thinking about something."

"I'm glad you don't have a headache. Donnie's mommy gets headaches a lot," Swan said, and Rayanne looked at her. "Donnie said his mommy yells at him, and then her head hurts, and she makes him go to his room. I don't think Donnie's mommy is very nice."

"I'm sorry to hear that." Rayanne ran her hand over Swan's head and listened as Swan told her about times when they picked up Donnie, how his mother never smiled. And that once, she even gave Donnie a slap on his bottom and told him he'd better be good.

"What makes people mean, Aunt Rayanne?" Swan asked, looking up into her face.

"That's a tough question." Rayanne pondered how she could answer that question so a five-year-old would understand. "But there are lots of reasons why people sometimes act that way. They could be unhappy about something that has happened to them, or they could be angry at one person and yell at another for no reason, which isn't fair. And sometimes some people just like to make a fuss, but I think that most people really don't want to be mean. Sometimes it just happens." Rayanne tried to explain, and then she said, "I'm hungry. What about you?"

"Yes."

"What would you like for breakfast?"

"Let me see. . . ." Swan pretended to think, when she knew exactly what she wanted right down to the kind of syrup she would smother her French toast with. It was her favorite breakfast food. "I'd like some French toast, eggs, and sausage"—she paused, her eyes twinkling— "and chocolate milk."

"You've had this planned all along, haven't you?" Rayanne asked, and Swan giggled. Rayanne hugged Swan once more, kissed the top of her head, and answered her unasked question. "And yes, you may help me make breakfast." Swan smiled and Rayanne lifted her from her lap to the floor. Rayanne got up from the bed and said, "Let's get ready for that special breakfast."

32

"That son of a bitch did what?" Scott raged when Rayanne finally told him that she'd ended her relationship with Ralph, and why. "Why didn't you tell me about this?"

"Because it was embarrassing."

"You don't have to be embarrassed about anything with me. Don't you know that by now?" Rayanne knew Scott was angry at Ralph, maybe even a little at her, but he exploded when she told him that Ralph had called earlier that day. "Hasn't he done enough?"

Rayanne could tell that his adrenaline level was unparallel to what it was at any other time that she'd known him. "Scott, calm down. Do you see why I didn't want to tell you this?" she asked. "I'm dealing with it."

"This man is crazy as hell." He gave a short laugh and looked around the room.

The two large pictures of Ralph that sat on the sofa table in the living room and the mantel in the den had not been taken down. Scott looked at the picture with a question in his eyes when he turned them on Rayanne. She simply lifted her shoulders. She hadn't taken the pictures down because she'd wanted to avoid the questions she knew would come, once she did. She got up from the couch and silently gathered the pictures and put them into a drawer of a lamp table. "I'd like to take 'em and burn 'em and put my foot in his—" Scott's statement was interrupted.

"It doesn't matter anymore. Ralph is out of my life, so can we just forget him?"

"He'd better not show his face around here no more. If he does, he's gonna have to deal with me." Scott came back and sat beside Rayanne. "Are things between you and Romeo really over now?"

"It is over."

"Probably not for him, though. He needs to be told once and for all to leave you alone. He's done enough damage. You told me time and time again that you didn't want me involved in whatever was going on between you and Ralph, and up to now, I have stayed out of it, but that's over. I'm not gonna stand by and watch him hurt you again. I care too damn much," Scott said.

Every time she thought she'd put Ralph behind, he'd call and open up the wounds again. But she'd already seen Ralph and had put closure on their relationship.

"That guy just doesn't get it. He had the best woman in the world and he didn't know how to treat her. He's a damn fool." He turned, and when he saw the look on Rayanne's face, he said, simmering down, "Okay, okay, what are we gonna do?"

Rayanne couldn't have appreciated him more than at that moment, and she became weak with that realization. Scott was angry, and he'd said a lot, but he didn't say, "I told you so."

"Would you just hold me for a minute, please, because I am feeling really vulnerable right now?" Rayanne asked.

Scott complied and she stood with her face against his chest. "Thank you. I needed that," she said, and tried to move away, but he held her and they looked at each other. He put his arms around her again, and just as she knew her own name, she also knew that everything was going to be all right.

When Scott left that night, he knew Rayanne had given the ring back to Ralph. It was finally over.

Rayanne invited Scott out to dinner one evening, and when they returned home, he told her that he and Frannie weren't together anymore, but he continued to see and support Donnie. She admired so many things about Scott, and as she turned to tell him so, she found him staring at her. "What?" she said, raising her eyebrows.

"Loneliness is a two-way street, you know, and neither of us has to be lonely. I think both of us have suffered enough. We deserve to be happy. I know how you feel. You don't want to take a chance, afraid you'll get hurt again. Well, I've been there. I'm scared, too, but I'm so willing to take that chance, with you. I'd like to make you and Swan my priority. I think we'd be good together. I can be whatever you want in a man. I care just that much," he said. "I just want to be here for you for as long as you want."

Rayanne leaned away from him and looked at him for a long time. Then she got up from the couch, picked up a pillow, tossed it to the floor, and lay on it. Scott got up from the couch and slowly walked over to where she lay on the floor. He lay beside her, encircled her in his arms, and held her. He whispered, "I'll always be here for you." That was the last thing he said to her that night.

Rayanne awoke the following morning to the aroma of coffee and bacon. She rubbed the sleep from her eyes with the back of her hand, threw back the blanket that Scott had covered her with, and said, "Gosh, what time is it?"

It was six-thirty and he was leaving to get to work, he'd told her.

"Scott, about last night," she began, getting up from the

floor and folding the blanket. She returned the pillow to the couch, but Scott interrupted.

"There's only one thing I want you and me to remember about last night. I meant everything that I said."

"How did I get so lucky to have a friend like you in my life?" she asked.

"You musta been born that way." Scott walked up to her, kissed her on her forehead, and left.

33

The night Scott and Rayanne finally made love was one of the most spontaneous things that she'd ever done. It just happened. She arrived home that afternoon from work and she and Swan ate a dinner that Mrs. Marshall prepared. Mrs. Marshall and Swan planned to go through the flower seeds that evening, because Swan and Rayanne would plant them in Swan's little garden soon. Rayanne was going to the movies. She had just stepped out of the shower and the phone rang. It was Scott. "What's up?" she asked.

"Nothing much. What's going on with you?"

Rayanne and Scott had seen each other regularly after that night of his confession, but they never mentioned that conversation. She'd liked Scott, but it was a brotherly thing, a younger brotherly thing, if she'd had a younger brother.

"Not much. I'm going to a movie," she said. "Come and go with me."

"Sounds good. Want me to pick you up?"

"Why don't I meet you there."

They met at the theater for the seven o'clock show. Rayanne arrived at five to seven, and there were other late-comers in line ahead of her. When she reached the window and was about to purchase the tickets, Scott called out to her from inside the theater, waving a pair of tickets in his hand. She joined him, and they sat in the seats he'd held for them. The movie was filled to its capacity.

While the coming attractions and the advertisements of what was available at the concession stand were previewing, Rayanne took the opportunity to look around in the theater and saw what appeared to be parents with their children. *Now,* she thought, *this is what this country needs more of.* It was wonderful seeing so many parents taking part in their kids' development. The movie was packed with entertainment, humor, family life—things that motivated. When it was over, Rayanne found that not only was she more in love with Denzel Washington than ever, and moved by his portrayal of Malcolm X, she'd changed her mind about the man and she promised she'd read every piece of information she could find in order to learn more about who Malcolm X was. The movie wasn't a white movie or a black movie. It wasn't even a racist kind of movie. It was a people movie. For years, she'd had this misconception about the man. She had grown up in ignorance, listening to what she'd heard, rather than finding the truth and forming her own opinion, rather than holding ones that were formed for her.

After the movie, Rayanne followed Scott to his house. He popped in a CD; she kicked off her shoes and curled up onto the couch. Scott returned with a soft drink for Rayanne and something stronger for himself. He sat on the other end of the couch from her. She'd noticed that Scott was a little distracted, and when did he start drinking alcoholic beverages?

"Is everything all right?" she asked.

"Everything's fine. Why?" he asked.

"You seem distracted. I'm here. Sure you don't want to talk about it?"

"I'm just a little tired," he said, and when he looked at her, she knew it was more than that. "I lost the bid for that apartment complex and I'm a little bummed out about it."

"Oh, baby, I'm sorry," Rayanne said, sliding closer to him. "But there will be other contracts." She got up. "Why don't you let me give you a neck rub. That usually makes you feel better." She began to massage his shoulders. When his body began to relax, she said, "Now tell Rayanne what's bothering you. I have known you to lose bids before and they have never affected you this way." When he tried to come up with another excuse, she said, joining him on the couch again, "Talk to me. I'm here for you, and if you say so, I won't go anywhere until you're feeling better." She smiled in her usual teasing manner. She had stolen his words and was using them on him.

Scott turned his head, glanced at her, and they laughed. He got up and she watched him go into the kitchen and return with a fresh drink. He sat back on the couch.

"I don't want to sound like an old mother hen, but for someone who doesn't drink, that's your second one in a matter of minutes."

He stared at her a moment, got up from the couch, and kneeled on the floor in front of her. He looked up into her eyes, as though he wanted to say something. He changed his mind, shook his head, and sat on the floor with his back against Rayanne's knees. She placed her soda on the coffee table, and she resumed the massage. She massaged his neck and shoulders. Then her fingers moved to his face, and she massaged his temples, allowing her fingers to play along the side of his face. She ran her fingers through his beard, and Scott moved his head from side to side, enjoying the massage and the music. She massaged his throat; then her fingers traced his mustache.

She began to hum along with the record, engrossed in the music herself. As Scott turned his head slightly, her right thumb brushed against his lips. He caught her thumb in the corner of his mouth, and Rayanne's eyes popped open when Scott began to suck gently on it. It felt good, real good, so good, in fact, that Rayanne closed her eyes. When she realized what was happening, three of her fingers were in Scott's mouth. She tried to pull her fingers free, but he held her hand and he used his tongue to circle her fingers.

Rayanne's pulse raced as Scott sucked and nibbled on her fingers. In one swift movement, Scott got up from the floor, lifted her from the couch, and began kissing her. He kissed her slowly and softly, at first; then the kisses became deeper. He kissed her again and again, but what surprised her more was that she responded. Scott didn't kiss her like she was a big sister; he didn't kiss her like she was just a friend; he kissed her like the woman that she was.

When their bodies drew apart, Rayanne thought, how long had it been since she was kissed like that? Had she ever been kissed like that? It felt so good. Scott kissed her forehead, her eyes, then her lips, again. He raised his head and his gaze searched hers. When he bent his head to kiss her again, her tongue darted into his mouth before their lips touched.

"Rayanne, I love you," he whispered, and kissed her again. When the kiss ended, he said, "I've always loved you."

She looked into his eyes, and for the first time, she didn't know what to say. Something was getting out of hand, and she had to put a stop to it. She backed away from him.

"Scott, I think I'd better go."

"Why?" He looked into her eyes and repeated the question. "Why, Rayanne? Don't you know how I feel about you? I love you. I always have."

"I'm sorry," she said, shaking her head. "I'll call you tomorrow."

Rayanne turned and left, with Scott staring after her.

* * *

When she arrived home, Mrs. Marshall was returning to her room with a glass of milk.

"Is everything all right?" Rayanne whispered.

"Everything's fine," Mrs. Marshall whispered back. "I just looked in on the baby and she's sound asleep."

"Thanks, Mrs. Marshall. I'm going to look in on her, and then I'm going to bed myself. It's been a long day. Good night now."

"Good night, Rayanne," Mrs. Marshall said.

Rayanne checked on Swan; then she called Ivory and shared the events of the evening with her. Ivory asked, "Girl, you mean to tell me you didn't get none of that?"

"Ivory, didn't I just tell you what happened?"

"You the fool," Ivory said, and they laughed. Then she asked, "Have you heard from Dorian?"

Rayanne didn't answer the question. Instead, she asked, "Is she all right?"

"Yeah, she's fine." After a moment, Ivory said, "She misses you, Rayanne. I know, I know. This is between you and Dorian, and I'm butting out. Are you all right, honey?"

"Yeah. I just wanted to hear your voice."

When they hung up, Rayanne took off her clothes and got into bed and tried to go to sleep, but sleep was the furthest thing from her mind. She played and replayed the evening. Why was she holding Scott at bay? She'd been with men her own age and some who were older, but where did it get her? Besides, who was she fooling? She didn't know how the situation would go with Scott or how long it would last, but she knew that no one in her past had ever made her feel the way he had. No one had ever touched her heart, as he'd done. No one. And although she didn't know where it would lead, she owed it to herself, and to him, to see, because not only had Scott fallen in love with her, suddenly Rayanne was aware that she'd fallen in love with him, too. With that realization, she got out of bed, got dressed, and told Mrs. Marshall that she was going back out.

It was drizzling when she left her house. By the time she arrived at Scott's house, the drizzle was a downpour. As she ran to the porch, lightning zigzagged across the sky. The loud clap of thunder that followed made her race across the yard and up the steps. She was soaked by the time she reached the door. Just as she reached out to press the doorbell, the door opened suddenly. Scott stood there, devouring her with his hungry gaze. She rushed into his waiting arms. As they clung to each other in the doorway, kissing passionately, the rain slammed down from heaven. The kiss ended, they drew apart, and she asked, meeting his gaze, "Am I that predictable?"

"I wish," he said, not believing that she was in his arms again. He stood back and allowed her to enter as she looked questioningly at him. "I called your house to see whether you made it home safely, and Mrs. Marshall told me you had, but that you were on your way back over here."

She wondered how Mrs. Marshall knew where she was going. Then she remembered Mrs. Marshall saying on numerous occasions, "That young man cares about you, young lady, and more than you think." Rayanne had told her they were just friends, but Mrs. Marshall's eyes always held a twinkle, as if she knew something no one else did.

"Let me get you outta those wet clothes," Scott said.

After she'd changed into one of his shirts, she sat at the table across from him and sipped the hot tea he had made for her.

She looked at him for a long time. "What do you want?" she asked. When he didn't answer, she asked again, "What do you want, Scott?"

"I want you to be happy," he replied.

"My happiness is my responsibility. It's up to me to

make me happy. I want to know what it is that you want for yourself."

"I want you in my life, and I want that for the rest of my life. I want *us*," Scott said, and he was certain that that was exactly what he wanted. Anything less just wouldn't do. "You're on my mind all the time. I love you. What else can I say?"

"What about Frannie?"

"I told you about that. I'll be there for Donnie. As far as me and Frannie, that's history," he replied, and it was without emotion or regret.

"Scott, I'm carrying around a lot of emotional baggage. It goes with me daily, and I don't want to mess up your life."

"Some wise man once said, 'Whatever problems one might have, all one needs to do is meet them, greet them, and defeat them.'"

"Life really isn't quite that simple."

"It can be," Scott replied, and he knew that everyone had their own cross to bear, but he also knew that together they could find a solution to any problem they might face. "Rayanne, I just want to give you all my love, that's all. I'm offering you a contract for love. All you gotta do is accept it."

"Quite the poet tonight, aren't you?" she said.

Scott may have added a little humor to lighten the conversation, but he meant every word. "I've never felt about anyone the way I feel about you, and I want to protect you. If I could pull you inside me and shield you from pain, I would. I feel that deeply for you."

"Oh, Scott" was all Rayanne could say. It was becoming difficult to speak, difficult to breathe, as her feeling for Scott took possession of her.

He got up and walked around the table to where she sat. She lifted her glowing eyes to him, and there was no mistake. Her love was there, shining for him to see. She wanted him to see, to know that she loved him as much as he loved her. Scott pulled Rayanne to her feet. He stood behind her, held her close to his chest, and gently explored her neck with his lips. She turned to face him. She pushed his T-shirt up until it exposed his bare chest and she kissed it. She opened the buttons on her shirt, revealing her breasts. A deep moan escaped Scott's lips when he caught sight of them. Rayanne moved closer to him, allowing her naked breasts to strike his chest. This time, she initiated the kiss, and when she did, the lights suddenly went out. Although they knew it was because of the storm, which was hammering outside, Scott said as they withdrew, "Hey, do that again." They laughed, and Rayanne placed a finger to his lips. She didn't want to make light of what was happening between them, because they were experiencing a storm of their own.

"I want you to make love to me, Scott," she whispered. "Make love to me now."

He looked into her eyes. Then he kissed her. He swept her up into his arms and carried her to his bedroom. He whispered against her ear, "I want you to believe in me and my love for you."

As Scott laid Rayanne on his bed, she was too overwhelmed to say the words that she felt in her heart. She could only think how she felt. She did believe in him and his love. She knew he loved her. He slipped on a condomn and when he filled her with his hardness, she felt as though she was seeing her life pass right before her eyes. Rayanne had never experienced anything so passionate, so intense. It was like pouring wine into a glass that'd been empty for a long time, like stepping into paradise. They really turned the century out, giving each other pleasure—deep satisfying pleasure.

"Whose baby are you?" he whispered as their bodies moved together harmoniously. "Whose baby are you?"

Rayanne opened her eyes slightly. "I'm your baby, Scott. I'm your baby."

"You are my baby, aren't you?" he asked, plunging deeper and deeper into her.

"Yes," she whispered, dizzy with desire for him. "I'm your baby. You're my Scott, and I love you."

Scott fulfilled every desire Rayanne had ever fantasized about. She was caught in a web of passion that she welcomed as it possessed her mind, her body, and caused her spirits to soar. Afterward, they held each other as they communicated with their hearts. As she observed him later, Rayanne realized that Scott never did tell her what was bothering him earlier. However, as he lay sleeping, the look on his face told her that he was better able to handle whatever it was, because they'd handle it together. From that moment, Rayanne saw Scott differently. For the first time, she saw him, not as a younger man, but as a man, and he was the man she loved.

34

"What's on your mind, pretty lady?" Scott said as he and Rayanne lay in bed together.

"I was thinking about you," she answered.

"Really?" Scott asked, a smile curling his lips. "What were you thinking about me?"

"I was thinking that with all that has happened in my life—the pain, the loneliness—all the time you were right here." She still couldn't believe all that was happening between them.

"And just think what you've been missing all this time," he said, looking at her body, which was still lean, long, and curvy. She was right out of a dream, he thought as he pulled her to him. "Do you know when I first knew I was really in love with you?"

"No."

"Remember the night when you called and told me you'd killed a squirrel?" He snickered.

"Of course, I remember, and it's not funny," she said, and nudged him in the ribs. Rayanne remembered the day she hit that squirrel. She nearly lost control of her car, trying to avoid it. "I can still hear that little creature hitting under the car."

"Poor baby." He hugged her closer to him. "I knew if you could get that worked up over hitting a squirrel, you must have the best heart." Scott stared at her a moment. "Do something for me."

"Okay."

"Let your hair down."

She smiled. "Why don't you?" she said, sitting up in bed.

Scott slowly removed the pins from her hair, and thick, wavy locks fell down her back. He ran his fingers through the mass of long brown hair.

"I really love your hair. I told you I'm a hair freak, didn't I?"

"Once or twice," she smiled.

When they made love again, they felt they'd settled on an ocean of paradise. Sometime later, Rayanne rose up in bed and Scott asked, "Where are you going?"

"I need to be getting home."

"Why so soon? Tomorrow isn't a workday, and Swan is fine," Scott said, sitting up in bed also. He was right, Rayanne thought, Swan was fine. Mrs. Marshall was very capable of taking care of her. It was a messy night, she'd already been soaked, and Scott didn't want her going back out in that kind of weather. Rayanne lay back and they listened as the rain splashed against the windows.

"I want to be home when she wakes up," Rayanne said.

"Who's gonna be here for me when I wake up?" he teased.

"Scott."

"I was joking," he said. "Well, maybe I wasn't joking. I'd love to wake up every morning with you, and knowing that Swan was in the next room would be the best thing I could ever ask God for. If you stay here with me tonight and let me take care of you, I'll make sure that you're safe at home when Swan wakes up in the morning."

When Rayanne settled back in bed, she could never

remember feeling more safe and loved. And Scott was true to his words. He got up early, made coffee, and woke Rayanne.

The house was quiet when Rayanne arrived. She slipped into her room and into her own bed. As she lay there, she thought about her mother and Josh. If only her mother had understood that all she wanted to do was save Josh. Well, Helen hadn't, and because there was no way that she could now, Rayanne felt guilty and would live with it the rest of her life.

Rayanne dozed off to sleep, but sometime later, there was a knock at her door and Swan came in. "Come here, you," Rayanne said, throwing back the covers. Swan ran and jumped into bed with her. "What are you doing out of bed so early?"

"I wanted to see you and play with my toys," Swan said.

"Is there something special you want to do today?" Rayanne asked, toying with Swan's hair.

"Can we go out to breakfast?"

"Sure, but we'd better let Mrs. Marshall know before she makes breakfast or she'll be mad at us. We don't want to make her mad at us, do we?" Rayanne touched Swan's nose.

"Oooh no." Swan pushed back the covers and jumped out of bed. "I'll tell Mrs. Marshall we're going out for breakfast."

"Mrs. Marshall may want to come with us."

"Okay." Swan rushed out but returned moments later and climbed back into bed. "Mrs. Marshall said she'll go out to breakfast with us."

"Okay."

"May we invite Uncle Scott to have breakfast with us, too?"

"If you want to."

Swan made the call and informed Rayanne that Scott would join them for breakfast, and that he'd drive over later and pick them up.

"You like Uncle Scott, don't you," Rayanne asked when Swan was settled back in bed.

"Yes."

"I bet he'd like to know how fond you are of him."

"He already knows."

"He does?"

"Yes. Want to know how?" Swan asked. Rayanne lifted her eyebrows. "Because I told him."

"You two are keeping secrets from me, huh?" Rayanne teased.

"Yes. Uncle Scott is my friend," Swan said, nestling closely to Rayanne as they listened to the rain. "I love you, Aunt Rayanne."

"I know, baby. I love you, too," Rayanne said, holding Swan in her arms, and it wasn't long before she heard the soft sound of a child sleeping. Looking down into the face of that sweet, innocent child, Rayanne vowed that she'd do her best to keep her as safe and happy as she was then. Another sound could be heard, the sound of a siren wailing somewhere in the distance, which Rayanne noticed was happening more frequently. She wondered who had gotten shot, or stabbed, or killed, now.

35

"Aunt Rayanne, are we still going to the supermarket?" Swan asked.

Rayanne was sitting at the kitchen table, reading a card from Lila. She'd already read the card twice, laid it on the table, and picked it up again. Lila hadn't been home since Helen died, and now she was canceling another trip home and wanted to know what color dress and shoes Swan would like. She rarely offered the child a bond or anything like that. It wasn't that Swan needed money, but Swan was Lila's only grandchild, and Lila hardly ever offered.

"Since when have you been so interested in going to the grocery store?" Rayanne asked.

"I'm interested now," Swan answered. "So when are we going?"

"In a while. I'm reading this card from your grandmother, and then I'm going to make a shopping list. After that, we can go."

"You read my grandmother's card already. Why are you reading it again?"

"Good question." Rayanne returned the card to the envelope and laid it on the table. She listed several items on a pad and looked up at the clock. When she glanced over at Swan, she was standing at the table, impatiently watching Rayanne. "I'm almost finished," Rayanne said.

Swan continued to look anxiously at Rayanne, and she looked questioningly at Swan.

"Nothing," Swan said to the unspoken question.

Rayanne returned her attention to her list and added other items. Swan sat and waited. She clasped and unclasped her hands, until Rayanne said, "Okay, we can go now."

"Weeee!"

"You really don't have to go, if you don't want to," Rayanne teased, knowing that wild horses couldn't keep Swan from going to the grocery store now, only she'd never had any interest in going before.

Swan made a face when Rayanne insisted that she wear a sweater, but she readily obeyed after Rayanne told her she wouldn't be going to the store if she didn't wear one. Rayanne gave a little laugh as Swan ran off to get her sweater. When she returned, Rayanne was pulling her own sweater around her shoulders. They left the house, and Rayanne lifted Swan into the car seat in her Volvo station wagon.

"Aunt Rayanne, do I have to ride in this seat?"

"Yes, you do," Rayanne said as she strapped her in and closed the door. She got into the car, fastened her own seat belt, and started the car.

"Why, Aunt Rayanne?"

"Why? What?" Rayanne asked, putting the car in reverse.

"Why do I have to ride in this seat? This is a baby seat."

"Swan, you are a baby," Rayanne said, backing the car out of the driveway. After checking the traffic, she headed for the store.

"I thought I was a young lady."

"In a way, you are," Rayanne said, and looked in both

directions before she crossed the intersection, merged, and began to move with the other traffic.

"Then why do I have to ride in this baby seat?"

"Honey, because it's the law, like a rule. You know how we have rules at home. Well, it's sort of the same thing. Laws and rules are to be obeyed, and when we don't, we can get into trouble. And if we do get into trouble, we have to pay to get out, and we won't have any money left to buy toys or books or pretty dresses."

"It is a rule like we have at home, where I can't put anything in the VCR except a VCR tape, because if I put something else in the VCR and it gets broken, I can't watch my tapes, right?"

"That's right."

"So I have to ride in this baby seat until I'm six, and if I don't, we will break the rule and we'll be punished, right?"

"Right again. See how smart you are," Rayanne said, smiling. They rode along several minutes in silence. Then Rayanne suggested they play a game, which delighted Swan. "Let me see," Rayanne began. "Which red fruit hangs on trees?"

"Apples."

"Okay, let's try another. How many letters are there in the alphabet?"

"Twenty-six," Swan said, and she began to recite them.

"Very good. Now, this is a tough one. Which fruit grows on trees in Florida and is the same color as its name?"

"That's easy, Aunt Rayanne. That's an orange."

"Very good. Let's try a few more. What is the name of Dick and Jane's pet?"

"Which pet?" Swan asked.

"Dick and Jane's pet," Rayanne repeated.

"Which pet? Dick and Jane have two pets, a dog and a cat. Which one do you mean?"

Rayanne suppressed a snicker. "Okay, their dog."

"Their dog's name is Spot, and their cat's name is Puff."

"That's great," Rayanne complimented. "You're learning so much."

When the car was parked and they entered the grocery store, Rayanne pulled out a shopping cart. "Do you want to ride in the cart?" Rayanne asked, reaching for Swan as she always did.

"No. I want to help you do the shopping," she said, walking a little ahead of the cart.

"Okay. Anything in particular you want?"

"Yes, but I'll let you know when we get to it," Swan said as they moved up and down the aisles. When they arrived at the shelf where the canned meats were, Swan began examining the shelves, something she'd never done before, except when looking for cereal and cookies. When she saw the Vienna sausages, she became very excited. She picked up two cans and handed them to Rayanne. She gave Rayanne four additional cans. "Aunt Rayanne, will you make lunch for me tomorrow?" Swan asked, looking up into Rayanne's face.

"You want to take lunch from home tomorrow?" Rayanne was surprised.

"Yes."

"You don't like the lunches at school anymore?"

"I do, but I'd like you to pack some of those little worms for me tomorrow."

"What?"

"Becky brought these little worms for lunch yesterday, and I liked them," Swan said. "Aunt Rayanne, why are you laughing?"

"I was just thinking about something." Rayanne snickered. Now she understood why Swan wanted to come to the store, as well as not wanting to ride in the cart as she always had. "But, honey, these are Vienna sausages," Rayanne explained with a can in her hand.

"Vienna sausages?" Swan said, puzzled. "Becky said they are little worms."

"I know, but they are Vienna sausages, and I will pack some for you tomorrow."

"Ooooh, yummy," Swan replied.

Rayanne returned the container to the cart, and Swan walked down the aisles, content with her selected items. Rayanne snickered as she shopped. Later, when Rayanne saw a friend and shared the story about the little worms, laughter ensued.

Driving home, Rayanne looked at Swan through the rearview mirror and saw a pleased look on her face. Rayanne laughed to the point that tears rolled down her face.

"Aunt Rayanne, are you crying?"

"No, sweetheart. I'm not crying."

"You have tears on your face."

"Something must've gotten into my eyes."

"Do your eyes hurt?"

"It's fine now," Rayanne said. "We're going to stop by the bookstore for a minute. Have you decided which book you want?"

"I'm not sure," Swan said thoughtfully. "I have two books in mind."

"Decision, decision," Rayanne teased.

"The Oak Trees That Talk, the Summer series," Swan decided.

"Is that the book about the mother tree being upset over losing her baby leaves?"

"Yes."

"Okay. What was the other book?"

"The Frog and the Shoe."

"That's a popular book, too. You know what I think? Why don't we get both books?"

"I thought I could get only one book a week," Swan said. "I won't get a book next week."

"We will get those two books this week and let next week take care of itself, okay?"

"Oooh weee! Which book are you getting?"

"I'm getting a book called *Secrets*."

"Secrets?"

"It's a book about a young girl who went searching for the truth about her family."

"Does she have trees?"

"I imagine she does, but I'm going to keep the book and give it to you when you're old enough to read it. Deal?"

"Deal."

Little worms, Rayanne thought, and laughed again.

"Do you have plans this Friday?" Rayanne asked.

"No, Becky is going to visit her grandmother, and Marcia Raylyn is spending the night with one of her friends."

"Why don't we get a couple of movies, pop some popcorn, and spend an evening in front of the TV set?"

Swan beamed. "It'll be like going to the movies."

"That's right."

Rayanne thought of the comical things Swan said or did without knowing how funny she was. Like the time when she was just about three and she was helping Rayanne wash the car; both of the car doors were open. Swan took the cloth from the bucket, and as she turned to the car, she hit her head and screamed, dropping the cloth to the ground as Rayanne rushed to her and took her inside. Later, Swan told Rayanne she was fine, but she wanted to go back outside and tell the car to shut up. There was another time when Rayanne was giving Swan a bath and noticed Swan staring at herself in the full-length mirror that hung in the bathroom. Rayanne asked what she was looking at. Swan said she was looking at her little butt up front and a large butt in back. Rayanne also remembered the night when she and Swan were sitting on the front porch and Swan was pointing a finger toward the stars she was counting, when she said, "You'd better come on down before you fall."

Swan had grown a lot since that time, but she still said the funniest things.

That night Rayanne entered Swan's bedroom and found her sitting on the window seat in pajamas, playing with her dolls.

"You're still up?"

"I was waiting for you to read my books to me." Swan set her dolls in their proper places and picked up a book before jumping onto the bed.

"I thought you were going to read your own book tonight," Rayanne teased.

"Aunt Rayanne, you know I can't read that well," Swan said.

Rayanne was teaching Swan to read and she was making progress, but there were still words Swan didn't understand or couldn't pronounce. She'd begun memorizing her books, and if you didn't know better, you would think she could actually read because she would call out words and turn the pages at the appropriate time. Swan could now color without going outside the lines, and her enunciation and pronunciation were distinct and clear.

When Rayanne finished reading the book, Swan said her prayers and was tucked in for the night.

Rayanne said good night to Swan and left the room to answer the ringing phone. It was Maxine. Marcia Raylyn told her that on the evening before Maxine found the condom, she'd gone to dance class and one of her friends had asked to put her books in the car. Sometime later her friend confessed that she and her boyfriend had had sex in the car, and Marcia Raylyn was certain it was her friend who'd left the condom behind. Maxine sounded happy, and Rayanne understood. She showered and went to bed early with her book.

36

Rayanne awoke with a start in almost total darkness, and for a split second, she was unsure where she was. She'd gone into Swan's room the night before because Swan had had a nightmare, and Rayanne wanted to be with her until she felt safe and was asleep again. As it turned out, Rayanne had fallen asleep as well.

Early that morning, the doorbell rang. It was Josh. Rayanne hadn't seen him in weeks and she'd missed him. She smiled and was about to embrace him, but he pushed past her and went toward his old room. Josh had found a small place and he'd come for some more of his things. Josh was still angry at Rayanne. She understood his anger and could live with that, but she hoped that he understood why she had him committed, because he was alive and she hoped he'd continue to do well. Before Josh left, he told Rayanne he'd get the rest of his things later. He turned away from her and left the house with the tails of his topcoat flapping wildly.

Rayanne ran into Brenda at the fitness club. Rayanne hadn't worked out in a while, just an occasional walk to the lake. After climbing into her leotard, she entered the exercise room and took a place on the floor next to Brenda.

"What's up, girl?" Rayanne said, falling into the routine.

"I didn't know you came here," Brenda said, stretching and sweating.

"I just started a little while ago. It's time I took better care of myself," Rayanne said, beginning to work up a sweat herself from the vigorous routine.

"Well, you certainly are serious about it," Brenda said, and laughed, trying to keep up the pace. She noticed that Rayanne hadn't missed a single beat since she fell into the routine.

"When we're through here, I'm gonna get a big cone of ice cream." They giggled as Rayanne fell back on the floor. She recovered soon and they continued the routine.

Outside, after the class was over, with towels draped around their necks, Rayanne talked Brenda into getting the largest cone of yogurt.

"I showed a house to some people today," Brenda said, taking a lick from the yogurt cone.

"Oh yeah?" Rayanne said.

"A nice couple. He's an engineering instructor and she's a doctor in pediatrics."

"Where is the house?" Rayanne asked as they walked to their cars.

"WildeWood."

"Does it look promising?"

"Umm-hmm. Mr. Redmond said they'll contact me in a couple of days, but his wife whispered to me saying that house was hers." Brenda's eyes twinkled. "You feel me, girl?"

"I feel you, girlfriend. Well, good luck," Rayanne said, licking her yogurt. "How are the boys?"

"They are great, bringing in good grades, keeping out of trouble, and even Cardell and I are relating better than ever," Brenda said as they approached Brenda's Jaguar. After they talked a few more minutes, they embraced and drove away.

37

"You're screwing him, aren't you?" Brenda said one evening when the three girls met at the Township to see a play that they'd purchased tickets for more than a month ago.

"Shut your mouth!" Rayanne laughed, looking around, hoping no one had heard them.

"Shit, you're glowing," Brenda said.

"What is she talking about now?" Hilary asked.

Rayanne lifted her shoulders and pretended not to know what Brenda was talking about.

"Rayanne is screwing that young buck's eyeballs out of his head." Then she said to Rayanne, "Aren't you?"

"I don't know what you are talking about," Rayanne said.

"You're holding out on us because you look like a peach, and it's not from the exercising, either," Brenda said.

"Rayanne, you do look great. A woman usually looks her absolute best when she's in love or when she's pregnant," Hilary said.

"Which is it? Are you fucking, or are you pregnant?" Brenda asked.

"I'm not pregnant, ladies," Rayanne declared.

"Then you're fucking?" Brenda gave Rayanne a sly smile.

"She's in love," Hilary said.

Rayanne paused a moment; then she admitted, "Yes, I'm in love."

"Hold on, let's take a moment. I knew something was going on." Brenda smiled, looking at Rayanne. "And it is Scott, isn't it?" Brenda asked. Rayanne nodded affirmatively.

"You go, girl," Hilary said.

"Scott is great. He is exciting, caring, and listen to this. The man plays with my hair. I love a man playing with my hair. Girls, Scott is everything that Ralph isn't."

"I'm feeling you," Brenda said.

"Ralph who?" Hilary teased, and they laughed, because Hilary rarely joked about anything.

"But listen to this," Brenda began. "Hilary has become a new woman. She's taken that stick out of her butt and is letting Ben eat that cat," Brenda said, and they fell out, laughing.

"Scareda you," Rayanne said to Hilary, giving Brenda five.

Hilary's attitude had changed, along with her appearance. She'd cut her hair in a very becoming style, and her clothes were more fashionable. She began wearing contacts, resulting in her looking ten years younger while adding a dimension to her face that the unattractive horn-rimmed glasses concealed for years.

"So how's it going with Scott?" Brenda asked.

"Great," Rayanne replied. "He does everything he can to make each day important for me. The man has taught me how to love freely and how to trust again, and that is huge. Scott is the man I'd like to spend the rest of my life with," Rayanne said with certainty.

Brenda reached out and gave Rayanne five. "I'm definitely feeling you, girlfriend," she said.

"When did this happen?" Hilary asked.

"Kind of recent," Rayanne said, feeling warm inside at the thought of Scott.

"Tell us about it, every nasty, slutty detail," Brenda said, and Rayanne obliged, beginning with the night when they'd first made love. She knew that what she felt for Scott was real, because what she had felt for anyone else was like a shadow on the wall in comparison to what she felt for Scott.

"Why didn't you tell us? You're not ashamed of being in love with a younger man, are you?" Brenda asked.

"No, I'm not ashamed of the relationship with Scott, but I do value discretion," Rayanne teased.

"To hell with discretion. We're your friends. Besides, any man who makes you as happy as you obviously are should be paraded around like a king," Brenda said.

"You got that right," Hilary agreed.

"Listen to Hilary," Rayanne said to Brenda. "She's become a totally different person—the way she looks, the way she dresses. The girl has got it going on."

"I want to hear more about Scott," Hilary said.

"There isn't much more to tell. We're very much in love, and we're going to see where it takes us." Rayanne smiled.

"Scott's a great guy," Brenda said. "And he is *foine*!"

"He's a hunk," Hilary put in.

Brenda and Rayanne laughed, because in the past, Hilary would not have voiced that opinion. Now, though, she openly agreed with Brenda's assessment of Scott.

"I'm certainly glad that the age thing doesn't bother you anymore," Brenda said.

The line moved about a yard closer to the auditorium. Rayanne smiled at how happy she was that she'd had the good sense to realize that age was just a number, as Scott had said. It didn't spell "man," and it didn't mean a thing as long as the people involved loved each other, took care of each other, and made each other happy. There was so much violence and unhappiness going on in the world, Rayanne thought, that it simply didn't make any sense for people to make each other more miserable than they already were.

Rayanne remembered talking to Scott, not long ago, about the myth concerning younger men and older women. "Which myth is that?" Scott had asked. "You mean the one about easy sex, without commitment, or the one about having an older woman take care of the guy?"

"It's not a myth, Scott. It's a fact. Besides, ten years from now, what will you want with a woman who is nine years older than you?" Rayanne asked, and she was never happier than when he replied, "The same thing I want with her now."

The line had moved, not more than a few yards the first twenty minutes, but then it began to crawl like a snake with a purpose. The patrons entered the auditorium and found their seats. Brenda was seated between the girls. She made a face and said, "Nobody asked me what's going on in my life."

Hilary and Rayanne laughed. Rayanne said, "Feeling left out, are we?" They laughed some more.

"Damn right." Brenda pouted.

"What's going on with you, Brenda?" Rayanne teased.

"Oh, nothing much." Brenda giggled. "Same ole, same ole."

"Oh, heck no. I know you've got something to say," Hilary said.

"That's right. So tell us. What are you up to, woman?" Rayanne asked.

Brenda looked at each of them, paused, then said, "There's one little thing I could share with my best friends."

"You sold another house," Hilary said happily. "This woman is going to be a millionaire."

"No. It's better than that," Brenda said.

"What?" Rayanne asked.

"Better than selling expensive houses and getting fat commissions?" Hilary asked.

"Well, more exciting, then," Brenda replied. "Cardell and I are back together."

"You're lying." Rayanne jumped from her seat.

"Yeah, she is lying." Hilary was standing, looking at Brenda also.

"We've been together two weeks now, and Cardell is more considerate and loving than he's ever been. The boys are ecstatic having their daddy back home."

"You two have become secret keepers. What's up with that?" Hilary smiled.

"Are y'all mad?" Brenda asked.

"I should be, but I'm not," Hilary said.

"I haven't seen you guys, and I wanted us to be together when I told you. Y'all sure you ain't mad at me?" Brenda joked.

"No, Brenda!" Rayanne laughed.

"I wouldn't give a damn if you were mad. Hell, you'd get over it." Brenda laughed again.

"Girls, we all have got some really great things going on in our lives right now," Rayanne said, and they embraced each other. There was a combination of laughter and tears while other patrons looked on. "Let's get out of here," Rayanne said, brushing the tears from her face. "This calls for a celebration."

"It certainly does, but what about the play?" Hilary asked.

"We can see it another time. It'll be here another week. Besides, it's not one of mine," Rayanne joked.

"And we'll have to stand in that long-ass line again." Brenda wrinkled up her face.

"So what?" Rayanne said.

"Yeah, so what?" Brenda said.

"Yeah, *sooo whaaat,*" Hilary said, and laughter followed as they left the auditorium.

When they were out on the street, the women gave their tickets to the first three people they met. They climbed into Rayanne's station wagon and rode to the Olive Garden, one of their favorite restaurants.

While on the way, Brenda said, "Maya Angelou is coming to town next month."

"I saw her only once, and she was dynamite," Rayanne said.

"I've seen her several times. The lady has inspired me for years," Brenda said.

"So, are we going?" Hilary asked.

"Of course, we are going," Rayanne replied.

"It'll be great." Brenda eyed the scenery as they rode down the street. "Girls, my priorities certainly have changed. I see things differently now. Remember when I used to charge everything?"

"Who could forget that?" Rayanne laughed.

"Well, back then, I wanted everything, and I charged it. There was a time when I thought I'd owe Jesus Christ, and God would hold a second mortgage. God has answered my prayers and given me insight into other things. I have my husband back, my kids are happy, and I'm selling houses like a madwoman. My life is good and I'm grateful," Brenda said.

"You deserve it all, Brenda," Rayanne said.

"She certainly does," Hilary agreed. "Rayanne, what about your next speaking engagement?"

"I'm speaking at another high school day after tomorrow," Rayanne replied. "I hope I can make some impression on them."

"Just give it your best shot. You will reach them. Hell, if you make a difference in one person's life, then you would've done your part. But you'll do fine. You've got that gift. You reached Jason. Six months too late"—she laughed—"but you reached him nonetheless."

Rayanne laughed. Brenda had seen Jason only once since he and Rayanne had had that little talk, but she'd made it clear that she had no interest in him, and that if he didn't want to tangle with her husband, he'd better stay away. Jason never returned after that.

"You'll be a smash," Hilary said.

Rayanne didn't say anything. When she wrote the speech, she'd put a lot of thought into it. The words had come straight from her heart. She didn't sugarcoat it—she was being honest.

"We shall see whether I'm a smash or whether I crash and burn. We shall see," Rayanne said.

Rayanne found a spot in the restaurant parking lot. They got out and walked toward the restaurant with their arms around one another.

"Yeah, girlfriend, you're going to be a smash," Brenda said.

"And you are the eternal optimist," Rayanne said.

"That's true, too," Brenda said. "If Cardell can change, and Hilary lets her old man go to the 'Y,' then anything is possible."

"Shut up!" Hilary giggled.

"And I thought you had faith in my abilities," Rayanne said.

"I do," Brenda said. "All I'm saying is that when you walk your ass up on that stage, make eye contact with them little bitches and drive-by shooters. Get their attention, let your hair down, girlfriend, and go for it. You'll have them eating right out of your hands," Brenda said.

"Goodness gracious." was all Rayanne could say.

38

Spring was a time for new hopes and new beginnings. The birds communicated as they twittered in the trees and darted off in pairs. Rayanne stood on the front porch and looked up at the sky. She thanked God for His many blessings. In less than two hours, she'd stand before an audience of almost two thousand students and faculty members and speak to them on issues that would affect some of them for the rest of their lives. She'd be relating directly to individuals on topics that some of them might find offensive, perhaps condescending; while others might view it as absurd and totally ridiculous. Hopefully, some would identify with the message and find some answers.

Rayanne was dressed in a navy linen suit with a gold pin in the shape of a four-leaf clover on one lapel. Her mother had given her that pin on her twenty-first birthday. She wore a white silk blouse, a single strand of white pearls, with matching earrings, and navy pumps and bag.

She entered the auditorium. It was quite noisy. She brought a large shopping bag with her, which she placed on the floor by the chair where she sat.

After a moment, the principal walked up to the podium and said, "May I have your attention, please?"

The students immediately became quiet, and he introduced the speaker. He mentioned that Rayanne had been one of the youngest playwrights in New York, that she'd acted in some of her own creations, and he stated some of her other accomplishments. When he was finished, Rayanne was met with a warm ovation as she walked on shaky legs to the podium. She'd only done this a couple of times, and it still made her a little nervous.

She looked out at her audience, took a deep breath, and said, "Good morning, ladies and gentlemen. How are you this morning?" Different responses came from the crowd. "First I'd like to invite each of you to take a ribbon from this bag." Rayanne passed the bag along to each person who sat on the stage beside her, and several students were invited to take the bag and assist in passing out the ribbons to the audience. "You will notice that the ribbons are yellow. Yellow means friendship, and in friendship, there is love. And if we can love one another, we can heal our state, our nation, our world. I want you to hold on to your ribbon, and if or when you feel inspired, I'd like you to pin it on yourself. If there isn't anything that is said here today that moves you to want to bond with others and try to make your space a better place, then you can just discard your ribbon. If you feel a sense of unity and want to make a difference, please put on a ribbon and wear it proudly."

Before she began her speech, some of the students began pinning on ribbons.

"I'd like to speak with you this morning, young ladies and gentlemen, on issues that are of great concern to me. Issues that require solutions. I don't proclaim to have the answers to the world's problems that we are facing on a daily basis, but together we can talk about some of the things we can do to try to combat these problems and make the world a little better. And I think a little better is something, don't you?"

The audience responded, "Yes."

"Let's talk about violence, crime. I think a part of the crime wave that we are experiencing is related to drugs and the economy. One of the things I feel strongly about is education, because education does help equip us for better jobs, and better jobs mean more income, and more income can keep us from the path of selling and using drugs. Therefore, education is very important. There aren't that many good jobs out there, but when employers look for new employees, they are going to be looking at the applications of the best qualified persons." She paused, making eye contact with the crowd. "Some of the crime is because folks just can't find decent jobs, or jobs, period. So if there is a man out there who is unemployed and he has a family, not in every case, but in a lot of cases, that man is going to feel his world is coming apart. He has to take care of his family. He gets depressed. He takes his last couple of dollars and he gets that fix that will relieve his pain temporarily. It's going to make him feel as free as a bird, but what he doesn't know is that with that first hit, he just compounded his problem. In addition to not having a job or money to support his family, he now has a habit to support, and that habit becomes his mistress. You know what they say about mistresses. If you can't afford one, don't go out and get one.

"Anyway, he now has a mistress, and he has to support it. He goes out and he robs someone. He may get caught and go to jail, or he may hurt someone, or someone may hurt him in the process, and where is he? There are a number of reasons why an individual may turn to drugs, but there are as many reasons why that individual shouldn't. I am not going to give you the pros—let's try some of the cons. Well, maybe some of both. We look for this utopia, this ecstasy of passion, if you will, but what we really get is the agony of pain, defeat. Drugs give us some false sense of security. Drugs destroy what would have been an otherwise good mind. Perhaps a brilliant mind. It distorts our thought processes. Drugs rip at the very fabric of our society. I tell you this. Drugs are equal opportunity employers, if you get my drift. You may be riding around in a BMW, a new BMW at that, but do you have a house? Do you have any legitimate investments, a bank account with more than a hundred dollars in it, in your own name? Probably not. We are sometimes caught up into selling drugs because it is perceived as being glamorous, exciting, attractive. And this is an area where I believe scriptwriters, producers, and directors should take some responsibility. For them, it's the money. We sometimes get involved in that kind of activity to do so on a small scale, but let me tell you, ladies and gentlemen, what may begin as a minor situation can mushroom into something major, and get out of control. Dealing or using drugs is trouble.

"Another thing we have to remember about involvement in drugs is that we are the ones who take the risks. We take chances from the time we take possession of the drugs until we pay the man. We go out and take risks selling the drugs, not knowing if we will have to kill someone to get the money for the man, or be killed. And the worst part, I think, is that we sell that stuff to each other, and for someone else. We don't even get the big share of the profit for all the chances that we take. We live in fear daily, worrying about who is after us, who is going to take over for us if we go to jail or are killed. Is it worth it? We take all of the risks and live like trapped animals, and we don't even get the big payoff. We don't bring the stuff here. How are we going to get the drugs into this country? Do we have planes to fly it in or boats to float it in? No, but we are willing to risk everything to sell and make someone else rich and powerful, while we just go out and get taken out, killed, in some dark alley, alone, trying to make a score.

"I have visited schools and penal institutions filled with kids, such as yourselves, and adults, who were arrested on drug charges. Some of them used very creative methods to conceal the drugs. Some used Goody's Powder packages. They stuffed it into ballpoint pens and ink pens. They carved out pages in their books, et cetera, but that didn't keep them from getting caught. They got caught, my friends. What I am saying is some of those minds could be used in more positive ways. To use those minds that way was a complete waste. Minds like that can inspire all kinds of wonderful ideas, and I don't have to tell you how angry it makes me to see those minds sitting idle in a jail cell. Another thing that gets to me is that drugs are sold to kids, to pregnant women, and to anyone who is willing to buy them. There is something about drugs that is so sinister, and when they are brought into the schools, we have to impress upon each other to just say no.

"There was a time when kids got into fights in school, there would be a little hair pulling and a little face scratching, but not now. Now we are getting security guards and metal detectors in our schools, because along with the drugs, there are weapons. Kids are being shot, cut, maimed, and those are the lucky ones, because it gets worse. Many of them get killed. Those young lives are over. Don't destroy your sisters and brothers. If there ever comes a time when you have a gun and you want to take someone else's life, think. Take the time to think about what you are doing. Don't pull the trigger. Fifteen, twenty years from today, that person who that knife or gun is trained on could be your son or your daughter. They could be the recipient of that knife blade or that bullet. The best thing to do, young men and young ladies, is to stay away from that kind of behavior, and start preparing yourselves now for a better way of life. Prepare yourselves so that if there is a job out there, be the best qualified, and if there is no job, get the education to be able to help create jobs. All it takes to start is a little money and a good mind, good business sense, and you can make it. And you can help the before you and the after you to make it. You have to think and prepare yourselves. I know peer pressure is hell, pardon me, please, but it makes me so angry when I see what is going on around me. I know peer pressure is tough, and I know the way sometimes looks dark and dreary, but we can make it, ladies and gentlemen. We can, because we have got to. If we become drug dealers or get involved in some other illegal trade, what are we going to tell our children, our families? We certainly can't tell them that. We want to be proud of our accomplishments. We want our families and our friends to be proud of our accomplishments. Who are we going to tell that we are a drug dealer, a pimp, a prostitute, a gambler, a robber, a crook? The thing we want to do is enhance our lives and those of others. Each of us was given a life and a good head. We must live that life, not gamble it away. Life is not a game. It is real and it can be productive, worthwhile. If we choose to live our lives as one of those 'good'"—Rayanne used her fingers to make quotation marks—"professions that I have just named, there is no one who is going to be proud of us. It is important to look to the future and what lies ahead.

"I have heard many times that we didn't ask to come here, we didn't ask to be born, and we don't owe anyone anything. Well, of course, we didn't ask to be born, but we do owe. We owe our parents for bringing us here, and we owe our forefathers. They brought us into a world that can be beautiful, if we help to make it so. Yes, we owe, ladies and gentlemen. We owe a lot. We owe our ancestors for the painstaking ways in which they helped in molding our lives. They taught us so much. Always to put our best foot forward. They taught us not to be afraid of failure, because sometimes it is through failure that we learn and discover new ways of succeeding. They impressed upon us to look to each day for something good to build on, to find something special and different, as well as look to the future with promise and possibility. We owe them. They taught us first to believe in ourselves and to work through obstacles and not overlook them. We learned to believe that we can be whatever we want to be, because we are filled with potential. They instilled in us the knowledge that it is all right to get discouraged, but never to give up. They taught us that the simplest pleasures are often the most rewarding. Yes, we owe them. They nurtured us to know always that they love and understand us, as well as let us know that they will always be there for us, even when sometimes we feel alone. They are with us, even if in spirit only. Through their wisdom, we are at a point where we can respect our weaknesses and compliment our strengths. Their teachings have motivated us to not allow life to slip through our fingers, without affecting some change. They gave us examples to live by and dreams to realize, for we know that without dreams, hope, goals, and desires, it is to be without purpose.

"Let's center our attention to some of the movies that we see. While I think everything has a purpose, I think that some of the movies we see influence us in such a negative way. We see the drugs, the guns, the killings, and the tough guys. Everybody wants to be top man. That whole scene is glamorized to the point that we try to emulate the characters we see on the screen. We want to be the warrior—this violence, and that violence, is being passed down to our children. Drugs and killings shouldn't be glamorized. We cannot glorify these acts of violence. The suicide rate has increased due to mental stress. Then there is the fear that we have to deal with, and, ladies and gentlemen, fear transforms into rage and aggression.

"Poverty areas are particularly vulnerable to television violence. Violence is disturbing and dangerous. There was a time when we could leave our homes without locking our doors. We didn't even have to lock them at night, but we can't do that anymore, can we?

"And you, young ladies, remember to try to maintain your identities. Keep in control of your own minds and bodies. Don't let anyone dictate what you should do or where you should go. Let those decisions be made by you, and only you. What I am getting at is teenage pregnancy. We can get pregnant when we have absolutely nothing else to do. Besides, why would you want to sit at home raising babies, when you are babies yourselves, and miss out on all that life has to offer? You let these little boys know that you are smart and you have no intention of being taken in by anyone. There are some girls who are pregnant, some already have a baby or babies. There is no disgrace in that. I have always thought that if a girl gets pregnant, it is the good girl who follows through and has the baby. But if you are not pregnant and don't already have a baby, *don't*. At least don't do it right now. There is plenty of time for that. There are answers to some of today's problems, and we know what we have got to do. We have got to stay in school, get a good education, advance our learning, enlarge our educational level, and build our positive attributes. Education broadens us as people. It opens our minds to new experiences and challenges, and it prepares us to face the future. And your future will look so bright, you will need to wear sunglasses." Rayanne looked around, and she could see some of the students giving each other five. "We are living in times of such rapid change, and we sometimes lose control. Remember, our past does not have to be our future. We can have wonderful, happy lives. Happiness is a choice, and it is life. Our lives depend on where we put our attention. Yes, I have been fortunate. I have had some wonderful things come into my life. I have been blessed. I have had some success, but it didn't come without a lot of hard work. I have had rejections, yeses and nos. I worked on changing the nos into yeses.

"There are tragedies out there. Try to learn to turn them into miracles. As strange as it may seem, miracles do grow out of tragedies. We have got to find enough strength from within to determine our own worth, because, ladies and gentlemen, we owe. Take that little point of view and add it to your own repertoire, and you will make a quantum leap into whatever kind of future you choose for yourself.

"There is the topic of gangs. Gangbanging is another area of disturbance. Don't you wonder why gangs even exist? That is so dumb. Why would an intelligent person want to belong to a gang? You don't need anyone like that controlling your life, telling you what to do. There is no need for gangs. All that comes out of gangs is more violence—cruel, horrible deaths. As gang members, we are killing each other. Don't you see that? Gangs are a dead-end street. I see most gangs as kids who are confused. They don't know who to listen to anymore because the information given out is so contradictory. Don't destroy one another.

"I'd like you to do something for me, please. Will each of you turn to the person on either side of you and tell them that you love him or her? Very good," she said when that was done. Now, think about yourselves and your fellow man. Think about life, peace, joy, happiness, and love—love for one another. We have to stop the violence and start to love. Those of you who have children, we have to tell them each and every day that we love them.

"Goals. Think about your goals, your dreams, think about your future. Always have a plan for yourself, because if you don't, then someone will have one for you. In each of us, no matter how far down it is, we have love inside of us, and that's the key that brings all of the good things out of us, and brings us all together as one people. We have to love ourselves, love each other, and we have to teach that love to others."

Rayanne noticed many of the students pinning on their ribbons and she smiled. "We have got to have love in our own hearts before we can begin to have any hope.

Remember we can accomplish anything in life that we want. You know why? Because we are all winners. There are no losers here. You are the best that this world is ever going to find. Be proud of your own self-worth, because it is valuable. We are going to make our mark. We are going to affect change. We are going to be focused. We are going to be motivated and in the right direction. We are going to heal this country, because this is our country, and this space belongs to us. We are going to take care of each other. We are going to exercise our knowledge of the three R's, which are . . . ?" she asked, and the students responded, "Reading, 'riting, and 'rithmetic." Then she said, "And we are going to add and practice an additional three R's and they are restraint, responsibility and respect. We are going to stay in school, and not just to make something out of ourselves, because we already are something pretty special, but we are going to improve on who we already are. We have an important legacy to pass on, a legacy to preserve our youth, and we aren't through owing yet. We owe the children who have come into this world after us. We owe them a future, ladies and gentlemen. They deserve it. They deserve a future . . . and so do we. We have got to stop the violence and start to love. Are there any questions?"

39

"That jackass is coming here again," Maxine said, angrily pacing around in Rayanne's den. "I'm sick of his shit. I don't care about what he's done to me, but I will be damned if I'll have him hurting my children."

Rayanne was quietly sitting on the couch, packing her suitcases, because she and Swan were spending a few days in New York. She knew Maxine well enough to know that she needed to vent as much as possible.

"And you know he's got that silly-ass schoolgirl who he calls his wife hooked on all those lies. All I know is that she'd better wake up, take her head out of his ass, and grow up. I should've busted a cap in his ass when he was here before. He doesn't know who he's fooling with, does he?" Maxine asked. Huh-uh, Rayanne thought, but she didn't say a word. "But I'm gonna get his black ass this time. I hope he isn't so naïve as to think that he won't have the bitter with the sweet. You know what I'm saying." Uh-huh, Rayanne thought, but she still didn't comment. "You just wait. I'm gonna get him good."

When Rayanne thought Maxine had wound down some, she asked, "What are you gonna do?"

"I haven't decided yet, but he'll be sorry," she said, and Rayanne knew she meant it.

"When is he coming back here?" Rayanne asked.

"A week from Sunday," Maxine answered.

After a while, Rayanne decided to change the subject to get Maxine's mind off Fred.

"Thank you for taking my place at the Neighborhood Watch meeting tomorrow night."

"No problem," Maxine said. "Besides, it's not even necessary with Aunt Bessie there. She's a one-woman army."

Rayanne had to agree, because although Aunt Bessie was old, she was feisty, and the only person whom she would let get over on her was her son.

"What time is your flight?" Maxine asked.

"Four-ten this afternoon." Rayanne had finished her new book and had decided to fly it to New York. She wanted to see her friends, and this was a perfect time to do it.

"Marcia Raylyn would have gone with you, but because she just started that challenge program at the university, she'll have to pass this time. Maybe next time," Maxine said.

"Sure, there'll be lots of trips," Rayanne said, but she was still concerned about the situation between her sister and Fred.

"Don't worry about me. I'm okay. Just pissed-off."

"And don't you let this situation get the best of you. Fred isn't worth it," Rayanne said, placing the last two items into the suitcase.

"You'll be seeing everyone?"

"I'm not sure," Rayanne said, knowing Maxine meant Dorian, since she'd told Maxine that Dorian and her family would also be visiting New York at the same time.

Maxine believed that was why Rayanne had picked that time to make the trip. "Do what you feel is best," she said.

Rayanne and Dorian hadn't worked out their differences to become friends again, but Rayanne was no longer angry at her. Her only regret was that she hadn't put Ralph out of her life way back when, and left it that way. It would have saved a lot of hurt.

"Did you get the travel toys for Swan?" Maxine asked, interrupting Rayanne's thoughts.

"Yes. I've packed them in the carry-on bag."

"Do you plan to see Ralph?"

Rayanne looked up from the suitcase that she'd just closed. "No. I wish Ralph well, but I got no business with that man."

Maxine shrugged her shoulders and asked, "Where is Swan?"

"She's napping. I'm going to get her up in a few minutes."

"You two have a good trip, and thanks for listening, sis," Maxine said, and left.

Rayanne would never forget the way Swan's eyes lit up at seeing New York at night. She was fascinated by the lights, the people, the traffic, everything. She was in complete awe.

Rayanne took Swan with her to Greg's office when she dropped off her manuscript. Swan was a hit with his entire staff. Rayanne and Swan had dinner with Ivory and her family, and before they left, to return home, they went to visit Maggie, but they didn't see Dorian that trip.

In Swan's fascination with New York, she whispered to Rayanne in the plane, on their way home, that she liked New York very much, but she liked South Carolina better. After dinner their first evening back home, Rayanne remembered how much she enjoyed seeing her old friends again, but also how much she missed Scott. Her first telephone call when she returned was to him. He wasn't there, she left a message.

Rayanne was humming as she drove to the grocery store, and just as she was pulling out of the parking lot, she saw Scott's truck parked on the street. She waited for the light to change; then she drove around and parked beside his truck and waited for him. She didn't have to wait long, and he wasn't alone. He was walking with Donnie and a tall, attractive woman who had to be Donnie's mother. The threesome walked to the truck, got in together, and Scott drove away.

For years, Rayanne had listened to Scott tell her how unhappy he'd been with Frannie, what a vindictive person she was. Well, the cozy little scene she'd just witnessed was far from the picture he'd painted. They looked like a happy family, and the effect it had on Rayanne was like a knife blade in her heart. What was it about her that made men lie and deceive her? Would she ever be happy? She wasn't sure what to expect from Scott, but she never thought he would hurt her so.

Rayanne wished Ralph hadn't called her earlier. They'd said things they shouldn't have. She was angrier than she'd been in a long time, and he ended the conversation by saying, "All men lie and cheat."

When Scott called that evening, Rayanne was angry to the point where she didn't ask any questions, but she accused Scott of lying and cheating. She told him she knew now that he'd never ended his relationship with Frannie. She also told him she should never have gotten involved with him.

Scott had always had a hot temper. When she attacked him, he said, "You have to remember I had a life before I met you." She was devastated.

Aunt Bessie answered her phone on the first ring. Rayanne poured Swan a glass of milk and set it on the table. She told Aunt Bessie about her trip.

"Sounds like y'all had a good time."

"We did," Rayanne said, but not liking the sound of her aunt's voice.

"Stevie's back," Aunt Bessie blurted out. "He went after

me again, but I managed to get into my room and lock the door."

"Where is Stevie?"

"He's somewhere in there, sleeping off that old poison he's putting in his body."

"You stay where you are, and I'll be there soon."

Rayanne hung up. She called the bus station and drove Swan over to John's house. She filled John in about Stevie on the way to Aunt Bessie's house. Rayanne used her key to get in, flipping on lights as they went along. A chair was turned over and lay on the kitchen floor. Rayanne was frightened.

"Aunt Bessie," Rayanne called out. "Aunt Bessie," she called again, but there was no answer.

"Stevie," John called out. "Stevie, where are you?" There was no answer, and they proceeded toward Aunt Bessie's bedroom.

Rayanne tapped lightly on the door. "Aunt Bessie, it's me, Rayanne." The door opened slowly, and Aunt Bessie appeared shaken, with dried blood under her nose. Rayanne was shocked by her aunt's appearance. She took Aunt Bessie by her hand and led her to the bathroom, but not before she heard John swear under his breath.

"Look how he done tear up the place," Aunt Bessie said. "He comes in here, takes what he wants, and he leaves again."

"Aunt Bessie, where is Stevie?" John asked through clenched teeth.

"I reckon he's in here somewhere, 'cause he had too much of that old poison in his body to go too far."

John walked away from them to search the house, shaking his head.

"Let me take a look at you." Rayanne dampened a towel and gently wiped the blood from her aunt's nose. Aunt Bessie explained that Stevie didn't actually hit her, although he tried. She got the bruises on her face when she was running away from him and ran into a door. Rayanne led Aunt Bessie into the kitchen.

"There ain't no telling what he woulda done if he'd caught up with me," Aunt Bessie said, and assured Rayanne that she didn't hurt anywhere else.

Rayanne told her she'd called the bus station, and if she agreed, they'd have Stevie on a bus to New York that night. "You just tell me what you want," Rayanne said.

"I want him outta here, and I don't want him to come back until he knows how to behave." At that moment, Aunt Bessie didn't care where Stevie went or what he did. She just didn't want him to do it in her house. Rayanne was infuriated about what her aunt was going through. She shouldn't have to give up on her only son, her only child.

"We'll get him out of here. Don't you worry," Rayanne assured her, and they were joined by John nearly dragging Stevie into the kitchen. He rammed him into a chair and stood over him with his fingers rolled into two huge fists. Rayanne sensed that John had punched Stevie a few times.

Rayanne and John took Stevie and his small suitcase to the bus station. She left them in the car, went inside, and purchased a ticket with her credit card. Stevie was leaving South Carolina tonight, no matter what it took.

"Your next bus departs for New York at eleven-thirty, right?" Rayanne asked the ticket agent.

"The next bus out of here for New York is twelve-thirty," he replied.

"When I called earlier, I was told eleven-thirty."

"I'm afraid you must've misunderstood me. We haven't had a bus leave here for New York at eleven-thirty for some time now."

Rayanne checked her watch. She didn't want to have to sit there two hours to make sure Stevie got on the bus, and she didn't want to take him back home. She just wanted him gone.

"Ma'am, do you want the ticket?" the agent asked, and Rayanne looked at her watch again. There were several people in line waiting to purchase tickets behind Rayanne. "Are you making the trip, ma'am?" he asked, looking annoyed.

"No, sir. My cousin is, but he doesn't want to," Rayanne said. "Sir, will he be able to cash the ticket in?"

Rayanne was relieved when the ticket agent replied, "If you charge the ticket on a credit card, he can't cash it in with me, but he can sell it to the next passenger who walks through the door for what price he was willing to accept. It just depends how badly he wants the money, or how badly he wants to stay here. Now, if you wanted to cash it in, you would be subjected to a small penalty, but there would be no other problem."

"I see," Rayanne said. She walked over to the bus schedule, studied it, then went back to the line.

"Is there some reason why you think your cousin might not get on that bus?" the ticket agent asked when the line had advanced and she stood before the agent again.

"He's just that kind of person. One way to New York, please," Rayanne said. "He's my cousin, but he's not very nice. His mother wants him gone, and so do I."

The elderly agent handed her the ticket and her credit card.

Just as she was about to walk away from the counter, the agent said, "Young lady, the next bus pulls out of here in an hour and twenty-five minutes. You give me that ticket." Rayanne obeyed, but she was puzzled. "Your name is Rayanne Wilson?"

"Yes, sir." Rayanne looked at him, still puzzled.

"Your telephone number, Miss Wilson?" he asked, and she provided. "Where is the passenger?"

"He's outside in the car." She looked over her shoulders, nodding her head in the direction of her parked car, where John and Stevie awaited her.

"Leave him here and go on home," the ticket agent said. "I'll hold on to the ticket and put him on that bus myself."

"Would you do that, sir?" Rayanne was grateful as she handed him the ticket.

"Yes, ma'am. You go on, and I'll take care of this."

"You're a godsend, sir. Thank you very much."

Rayanne returned to the car, tapped on the rear window, where Stevie sat slumped in the backseat, and motioned for him to put down the window. He obeyed, and she placed her elbows in the window and looked at him.

"Stevie, the next bus for New York leaves in a little more than an hour, and I want you on it. You've hurt your mother enough, and if you ever come back here and do something like this again, I'll have you arrested—cousin or not. You can believe that won't happen before I see to it that you get your behind whipped, and we'll see how you like it. Am I making myself clear?" Rayanne posed.

"Stevie, just get out of the car, and wait for the bus inside," John said, standing next to Rayanne. Stevie was about to protest. "Get your shit and get out." John jerked open the back door to the car.

"What's wrong with everybody?" Stevie asked, looking from Rayanne to John, but he dragged himself out of the car and staggered toward the station. John and Rayanne drove off after Stevie was inside, and they went back to Aunt Bessie's house. She was reading her Bible when Rayanne entered. It took a little persuasion, but she was able to talk Aunt Bessie into spending the remainder of the night with her and Swan.

Rayanne was pressing a dress for Swan for church when the phone rang. Was it Scott? she wondered.

"Miss Rayanne Wilson?" the voice asked when she answered the phone.

"This is she," Rayanne replied.

"Miss Wilson, this is Mr. Barkley down at the bus depot. I just wanted to let you know that the package is on the way," he said.

"Thank you, Mr. Barkley. Thank you very much," Rayanne said.

Aunt Bessie was sitting at the table, having a cup of coffee and eyeing Rayanne nervously.

"Stevie is on his way back to New York," Rayanne said, "and you're not going to be having any trouble out of him anytime soon."

Aunt Bessie sighed. She thanked Rayanne and whispered a prayer.

40

In Rayanne's memory, although less than one year had passed since she ended her relationship with Ralph, it seemed like such a long time ago. She knew she owed the majority of this revelation to Scott. He'd been there for her all the time. She remembered the night she fell in love with him and all the wonderful times they spent together. Rayanne had trusted Scott completely, and he'd shown nothing but unconditional love and understanding for her until now. But why? she wondered.

It'd been almost two weeks since Rayanne last spoke with Scott. That conversation was fresh in her mind. After not hearing from him, she realized her imagination had begun to run wild. Was Scott involved with Frannie again or someone else? Had his and Frannie's relationship never ended? After seeing Scott with Donnie and Frannie, she'd called him. Not only was she rude, her statements were laced with accusations, and she didn't give Scott an opportunity to explain. Scott had been so taken aback by her tone and her distrust that he didn't bother to explain or offer an apology.

At around one o'clock in the morning, the phone rang. "Hello?"

"How are you, baby?" he said in a whisper.

"I'm fine, Scott," Rayanne said stiffly; however, relief poured through her at the sound of his voice.

"Baby, I've missed you so much." There was a slight pause. "I know I broke a promise to you," Scott whispered.

Rayanne was almost delirious, unsure whether that state of mind was because of lack of sleep or sheer happiness at the sound of Scott's voice—more than likely, the latter.

"I told you that I'd never hurt you or do anything to have to say I'm sorry. Well, I am sorry. I didn't handle our conversation very well when we spoke, but you caught me at a bad time."

"Obviously, I did."

"There was a really bad misunderstanding."

"Where are you, Scott, and why are you whispering?"

"I don't know. I just know I miss you and I want to see you." Scott paused. "Baby, can I see you right now?"

"Scott, it's late."

"Does that really matter? I could be there in just a minute. Look out your window."

Rayanne had experienced so many emotions since she and Scott last spoke, but all she felt now was love and desperate longing, and the tingling between her legs intensified as she looked out through the blinds. Her body began to moisten with anticipation, just from seeing Scott sitting in his truck parked in her driveway.

Rayanne opened the door and allowed Scott to enter. All the anger and disappointment and betrayal she was feeling quickly disappeared, and were replaced by happiness upon seeing him.

The two of them stood motionless, facing each other. Scott looked exhausted, as though he were carrying the weight of the world around on his shoulders, but he looked good. When Scott moved closer, Rayanne lifted her hands against his cheek. Then she moved closer to him and kissed him on his lips. No explanation was necessary. There wasn't a need for words. The unspoken words they felt in their hearts were enough. Scott pulled Rayanne gently to him. She allowed her tongue to trace his lips, then probed deeply into his mouth, searching out his own hungrily. The kiss lasted a long time, and when it ended, they whispered how much they loved each other, missed each other, needed each other.

Rayanne felt faint as her heart raced out of control.

"I love you, baby," Scott whispered, his voice hoarse.

Rayanne was dazed with the love that flowed through her. Scott withdrew and pulled her behind him.

"Come," he said. "We need to talk."

She followed him into the kitchen, where he sat at the kitchen table.

"The day you saw Donnie and Frannie with me was the day we'd returned from Georgia. We'd gotten the results of the DNA test. I'm not Donnie's father. He'd overheard us arguing and he took some medication his mom had around the house. The little fellow nearly died. Richland transferred him to a hospital in Georgia. It was touch and go for a while, but he pulled through. I never left his side while he was in the hospital. Anyway, I made Donnie promise never to do anything like that again." Scott sighed deeply. "I told him I love him, and he'll always be my son."

"Scott, I'm so sorry," she said across the table from him. "Is Donnie all right?"

"He's doing better. Frannie's just gotta watch out for him, and, Rayanne, don't blame yourself for anything that happened. You had every reason to act the way you did. I didn't talk to you about anything, I just tripped."

"I'm just glad that everything is all right now."

They were silent for a moment. "You should get some rest, honey," Rayanne said, and touched his hands.

"I'm good. I just needed to see you."

Rayanne allowed a deep sigh to escape before saying, "I'm glad you're here."

"That brings me to one of the main reasons why I came tonight," Scott said, but she didn't care what the reason was. She was just glad that he was there. "I love you, Rayanne, and I want us to get married. Will you please marry me?"

Rayanne looked into the eyes of the man she loved. "Yes, Scott, I will marry you."

Scott got up from the table and walked around to where Rayanne was sitting. He reached for her hand, took it, and pulled her to her feet.

"You've made me a very happy man," he said, and kissed her.

Rayanne had such a feeling of belonging. Scott sat and pulled her into his lap and he ran his nose along the side of her face and neck. "I heard about your speech."

"You did?" she said, relaxing against his chest.

"Sure did. Some of the guys on the site have kids who go to that school, and the way I heard it, my baby knocked the socks right off their feet." Scott was beaming.

She hoped she was able to reach some of the students. She informed Scott that since that time, she'd received invitations to speak at other schools, even on the elementary level. She was most interested in that grade-school forum, because she felt that was where it would be most effective. "That is where the real education begins."

"You're trying to make a difference, and I'm so proud of you. That was a mean challenge you laid on them, though. You're a gutsy lady."

"Honey, I was scared to death, walking into that auditorium and looking at those faces. God knows, I didn't know what to expect. I just had to try. There's such a need in this country for us to save our children. They're our future. Without them, we have no future."

Snuggling in Scott's lap, Rayanne thought of the yellow ribbons that she took with her when she made her speech. As she left the building, she'd noticed some ribbons had been discarded to the floor in the auditorium, but it was nothing in comparison to the number of ribbons that the students wore proudly as they went about their daily activities.

"I think it's great that there're people like you who are willing to dedicate that kind of time to these kids. They're really fortunate. When I was a kid and even a young adult, I did things that you wouldn't believe," Scott said reflectively. "If I did those things now, I'd be in jail or, worse, dead."

Rayanne was reminded that Scott had turned his life around. He'd told her things about himself, but she loved the man he'd become.

Scott squeezed her hands. "You care and that's what we need more of."

"Caring goes a long way. If the parents and the communities took an active role in the kids' lives, it would go a long way toward fixing this country and, ultimately, healing it. If enough parents don't take part in their children's lives, the communities aren't going to, either. Parents have to do their part and not depend so much on the teachers and the police. More often than not, when the police become involved, it's sometimes too late. It's going to take a combined effort. We've all got to help if we want a world decent enough to bring up our children." Rayanne paused. "Mama and Daddy taught us to believe that our world was safe, but it is no longer that way," Rayanne said sadly.

"It can be safe again, but it's like you said, people are gonna have to get involved."

"You'd think that the government would put its money to better use. They stick big bucks in the wrong places, like the prisons, for instance. They are making the prisons larger and more livable, which seems to attract people. If they would put those prisoners to work and took away some of their privileges, we possibly would see a difference. Some of these criminals wouldn't be so eager to be criminals. Also, if they came up with programs for kids after school, something that would keep them off the streets, that would help. It would be a start. They should try some preventive measures for a change," she said. "If we can reach, prevent, or rehabilitate as little as one at a time, that would go a long way."

"I hear ya."

"It's funny how things change. I suppose it has a lot to do with putting our priorities in order. I remember someone once asked me, if I had two wishes, what would they be?"

"What did you say?"

"I said, with good health and happiness of family and friends being first and foremost, that I wanted the love of my man and a hit play. Something like that. I got the hit play, a number of them, actually, but if I were asked that question now, I would answer it differently."

"How would you answer?"

"Well," she said thoughtfully, "health and happiness are still at the top of my list, and the next would be a healing of the entire world. I just wish this could be a good place to live again."

"My baby, the world's advocate," Scott said affectionately.

After some time, they heard a dog barking somewhere, a wake-up call to a new day. He asked, "Are we going to make the announcement in church tomorrow?"

"Announcement?" she asked.

"How quickly they forget," he teased.

"Are you talking about our engagement?"

"Yes, that little thing." Scott smiled.

"That wonderful thing."

"Are we going to make the announcement tomorrow?" he repeated.

Later today, she thought, because it is already Sunday morning.

41

After services, Maxine approached Rayanne and Scott, who were standing on the concrete steps of the church, being congratulated on their engagement.

"Congratulations, you two," Maxine said.

"Thanks, sis," Rayanne said, and they embraced.

Maxine then hugged Scott. "You make my little sister happy, you hear."

"You can count on it," Scott said, releasing her. "I love Rayanne very much."

"I know you do, and I'm glad you guys found each other," Maxine said. "Be happy, you two." Then, as an afterthought, she said, "That hypocrite gave a good message again today, but I've got something for him."

Maxine's smile didn't come near her eyes before she walked away, got into her car, where her family was waiting for her, and waved to Rayanne and Scott as Marcus drove them away. Rayanne didn't know what that something was that Maxine had for Fred, but she knew he'd get it, and it wouldn't be pretty.

It didn't take long for Rayanne to find out what Maxine had in mind for Fred, because the following day, he was arrested for failure to pay support. It appeared that he and Irene were preparing to return to Florida, when two police cars pulled up in front of his mother's house. Fred was taken away in handcuffs, leaving a bewildered Irene staring at the car as it disappeared down the street.

"Well, Irene," Maxine said after relaying the story to Ray-anne, "welcome to the real world."

Maxine had visited Fred at the jail. She told the guard she was there to see her husband, Fred Duncan, and was shown to the window partition where Fred was already in his seat, waiting. He looked up as Maxine approached him and his jaw dropped. She was the last person he expected to see, or wanted to see.

Maxine sat in the chair across the partition from Fred. She picked up the phone and motioned for him to do the same, since he appeared too stunned to do so on his own. He picked up the phone and placed it to his ear.

"Hello, Fred," Maxine said, trying to sound casual.

"What are you doing here?" Fred asked.

"I suppose you were expecting Irene."

"She is my wife."

"For now, she is."

"What is that supposed to mean?"

"Just that I was your wife once, but now, there is a new Mrs. Fred Duncan in town. I wonder how long it will be before you get tired of her and run off with some younger woman, like you did to me and your children."

"Do you have any idea what you've done?" Fred sneered. "Do you? You've ruined me. Do you realize what this will do to my career, my marriage, my life?"

Maxine looked at Fred. "What I've done? What about what you've done?" she asked, matching his sneer as her eyes squinted to just cracks in her face. "Do you think I give a damn about you, your marriage, or your fucking career? No, hell no, damn it."

"I can't believe you put the white man on me," Fred said, disbelief dripping from his voice. "I can't believe you did that."

"Fred, putting the white man on you was the least of what I had planned for your black ass. Bruce and Bobby are your children. You're their father. It was you and I who brought them into this world, and you and I are responsible for them until they can assume that responsibility themselves. What if I walked away from them? You seem to think I was so wrong by putting the white man"—she made a face—"on you. If I was so wrong, then so be it, because I don't give a damn. I put the man on your black ass, and I'd do it again, just like that." Maxine snapped her fingers.

"Good-bye, Maxine," Fred said, and was about to hang up the phone.

Maxine motioned for him to put the phone back to his ear. When Fred didn't do as she asked, she said, "Don't you dare hang up on me. I will tear this freaking place up if you do. Let's see how the reporters will treat that."

He stared at her. There was something about the cold look she gave him that made him obey.

"It's a damn shame that I would have to go to anyone, let alone the white man, to get you to take care of your own black kids. Fred, I told you a long time ago that you can fuck me over all you want, but don't fuck with my children. I'd rather eat shit and die than see them hurt." Maxine turned her eyes to the ceiling. "This wasn't necessary. I tried to arrange for you to see the children, spend a little time with them, and make them happy. I didn't think that was asking too much. Your boys ask about you often. They love you, for some reason. I don't know why. You were so high and mighty, involved in your own life, that you wouldn't even give those great kids the time of day. Well, you gave me no choice—

now you will give more than that to the state." Maxine smiled ruefully. Then she said quietly, "I'm married to a wonderful man, and I can't tell you how happy he makes me. I'm only saying that to say this is not a vendetta against you for what you did to me, because you leaving was the best thing you could've done for me. My husband does things for me that you just couldn't begin to understand. I'm in love with him. I didn't want to hurt you. I wouldn't think of intruding in your life, had it not been for the kids, and I believe you know that, but I will not allow you to mistreat them. I will not," she said, and he knew she meant it.

"If it's a matter of money, Bruce is almost eighteen, and—" he began, but Maxine interrupted.

"I don't give a damn if he's one day away from his eighteenth birthday. I don't give a damn if he only collects from you one day, just as long as he does. You see, it's not so much the money as it is the damn principle. You have to stop thinking only of yourself. You may not know it, but you're not the only one who is important." Maxine looked at Fred. "Let me share this with you. Bobby will be going to college when he graduates high school, and that will be a four- to five-year period, so you might want to think about that." Maxine watched as Fred began to process the information he'd just received. When she was sure he understood what she meant, she said, "Now, you have a nice day, ya hear." Maxine hung up the phone, got up, and walked away, with Fred left holding the phone and staring after her.

Maxine exited the building and was walking toward her car, feeling the warm sun on her face, when she saw a familiar face approaching her.

"Good morning," Irene Duncan said to her.

"Morning, Mrs. Duncan," Maxine said, taking the limp hand Irene extended. "I was just visiting the reverend. He's all yours, now." Maxine released Irene's hand and walked away with a look of bliss on her face. Her next stop would be at a record shop. She was going to pick up a CD for her sons by a rap group called Wu-Tang Clan that the country was going crazy over. The song had something to do with protecting your neck, which Bruce and Bobby were raving about. Too bad Fred didn't know how to protect his neck, Maxine thought as she got into her car and drove away.

42

"Mama and I talked the night before she died," Josh said as Rayanne filled his cup with coffee. Josh had said he was in the neighborhood and had just stopped by. Rayanne hoped it was more. She hoped he still cared about her and missed her as much as she did him and was ready to put the past behind them.

"You were in Florence when Mama died," Rayanne said. "Did you call her?"

"I got out." Josh looked down and toyed with the handle on his cup.

"You got out?"

"I'd gotten to know one of the nurses at the center pretty well. We talked a lot. I explained that Mama was sick and that I had a bad feeling about her all day. I needed to see Mama and I promised I wouldn't drink or do anything stupid. She believed me and helped me get out. I hitched a ride here." Josh looked up at Rayanne. When she didn't respond, he said, "Mama and I had a long talk."

"Mama never said a word."

"I wanted to make sure that you didn't know. It would've just given you something else to worry or feel guilty about." Josh sighed.

"What did the two of you talk about?"

"We just talked. Like I said, I'd been having some really strange vibes about Mama, and I just had to see her." He sipped from his cup. "You know, when John came to the center and told me Mama had died, I was hurt, devastated, but I wasn't surprised, because I felt something was going to happen."

Rayanne sat back in her chair, and it was her time to sigh. "When will the pain stop? When will the pain just go away?"

For a while, they sat in complete silence; then Rayanne looked at Josh. She studied his face. The tired lines were gone and so were the bloodshot eyes that had been so much a part of his life the last few years. Josh had turned into a submissive individual after he started drinking, and submissiveness had become a way of life for him, but there was something different now. Out of genuine concern, Rayanne wondered what Josh was doing with his life.

"What am I doing with my life?" Josh stated, reading her mind again. "That is what you were thinking, right? I know I've made a mess of my life, and I made my family's lives miserable as well. I lied, broke promises, used Mama to do things I wanted to do—whether they were good or bad. I've been whining and pissing and moaning most of my adult life, and I had to put an end to that. I had to put all that silly-ass shit behind me. I've gotten the treatment I needed, I go to my AA meetings, and I haven't touched a drink since I left the center. I'm gonna make it this time." Rayanne and Josh had always been close, so much so that each knew what the other was thinking without a word being spoken. They'd been more than siblings, they were friends. But along the way, their friendship had gone sour. As she looked at her brother, it was with a newfound respect. Respect for the man her brother once was and had become again. "I want to try my hands at something close to my heart," Josh was saying.

"I've always wanted to build furniture, and who knows? I may be able to sell a few pieces."

"I'm gonna need some new furniture," Rayanne joked, but she reflected on the table and chairs Josh had made for her dolls when they were kids. When Rayanne and Josh laughed, each knew that they were having the same thought.

"The furniture wasn't bad, either."

"Not bad at all, but Daddy had a time keeping his good lumber out of your way," Rayanne said, and they laughed some more. It felt good. It was good.

"I talked with my partner last week, and he and I are gonna put some pieces together and see what we can do with them. I'm not gonna push. I'm gonna take my time and I'm not gonna get discouraged if something doesn't work out. I don't expect miracles overnight. This is gonna be a gradual process, but I'm gonna give it my best shot."

"That's all you have to do, Josh," Rayanne said. She was so glad to have her brother back. "Josh, I'm so proud of you. I just wish Mama could be here to see you this way. She would be so happy."

"Mama knew," Josh said. "When I came home to visit, Mama and I talked, as we hadn't done in years. It was great. Mothers are something else. Remember how she always knew everything about us? She knew us better than we knew ourselves. She told me she knew I was gonna kick that habit. She had so much faith in me." Josh suddenly looked very sad. "Rayanne, Mama was no good after Daddy died. She was just a shell of a person, just wasting away. I honestly believe that Mama lived until she knew things were gonna be all right with her children, me in particular."

Rayanne got up and put her coffee cup in the sink and looked out the window. "There are so many things I wish I could change."

"Like what?"

"The unpleasant things that happened between you and me. You're my brother, and I love you. You and I were so close, but we got to the point where we barely spoke to each other. I regret that so much. We're family," she said, and turned to face Josh. "You know what else I regret?"

"What?"

"I regret that Mama didn't see us together like this and that I'd not been able to make things right between her and me. She was so angry and never forgave me for taking you to the center in Florence. That's my biggest regret. I wish she could've understood."

"She did," Josh said softly.

Rayanne waved a hand. "You don't have to say that for my benefit. I'll just have to live with the fact that Mama went to her grave hating me."

"Mama forgave you," Josh said.

"Josh, you don't know how things were between us before Mama died, but I understand. How was she supposed to feel when someone she loved was being taken away?"

"Mama did understand," Josh said, and Rayanne felt good just knowing that he cared enough to try to make her feel better. "It's the truth. She told me."

"What are you talking about?" she asked, walking over to the table, where Josh was sitting. "What did Mama say?"

"Mama became realistic there at the end. She told me she knew you had to do what you did, that you didn't have a choice. She said you did it out of love for me, that I would've died otherwise." Rayanne sat across the table from Josh and listened. "Mama understood, and she made me promise to forgive you, although I would have, anyway"— he gave a little laugh—"after I blew off some steam. I know now that it was the liquor that had me so out of control, not wanting to accept responsibility for my own actions, and it was my fault. Mama told me that she wanted to say to you so many times how sorry she was about how she'd treated you, but she was too ashamed. She was going to pray for strength and ask you to forgive her."

When Josh looked up, Rayanne thought he was going to cry. "Oh, Josh." She reached across the table and took his hands into her own.

"Will you forgive me, sis?" Josh said. "I'm so sorry about everything. It took losing both of our parents and a stay in a detox ward to make me see the light."

"It's all right, Josh. I know it's gonna be all right."

When Maxine called that night, and Rayanne shared her revelations, Maxine was glad that maybe her sister could get on with her life now. Maxine, also, had some news to share. It seemed Irene had learned the truth about Fred, but because she loved him and believed in his love for her, she'd stayed with him. She felt that with the kind of love the two of them shared, nothing could get in the way of their happiness. Irene believed she could help Fred become a better person, and who knew? Perhaps she could. Rayanne had never put much stock in the old adage that a leopard never changes his spots. The important thing was that Irene knew the truth about her husband, and she loved him and wanted to save their marriage, in spite of what she knew. She was equipped with the knowledge that Fred was no saint, and if she could live with that knowledge, then she could deal with the situation as she saw fit.

Rayanne had just turned off the TV set. The telethon had just ended, South Carolina raised over $50,000, and the overall total for the United States was over $81 million. It was wonderful seeing people come together for such a worthy cause, in the name of love and commitment in ensuring an education for children. The performances were great, so much so that Rayanne almost gave some of them standing ovations from where she sat in her den.

The hour was late, the house was quiet as a tomb, and Rayanne was experiencing some difficulty in concentrating on the exam papers that required grading for the following day. She picked up a copy of a magazine, leafed through the book, and read some of the articles, some of which brought hope and peace and love to the readers. Rayanne found enormous satisfaction from the articles, but when she read the "In the Spirit" column by Susan Taylor, she found so much that enhanced her life.

Josh had left long ago, and Rayanne would've forgiven him if there was something to forgive him for. There wasn't, but she did thank him repeatedly for what he'd given to her. It was like having freedom put back into her life. He'd given her peace of mind and made her feel whole. With that, she knew there wouldn't be a need to continue to see her therapist.

She looked at the letters she'd just read. There were twenty-five or thirty. They were letters Dorian had written to her during the years, none of which she'd read before. The most recent letter stated that Dorian was pregnant.

"Bet that will put some weight on those bones." Rayanne giggled.

She picked up the test papers again; then she laid them back on the couch and put her hands up to her face.

"Mama forgave me?" she whispered incredulously. "Mama forgave me," she said the words out loud that time. She wanted to hear the words. She needed to hear the words. She'd felt guilty for so long because of not being able to reconcile her differences with her mother before Helen died. She'd felt guilty about having had Josh committed to the rehabilitation center, guilty because of the way her father had died, and that guilt had weighed heavily on her. She'd never be able to fill the void left in her by the loss of her parents. That kind of loss, one almost never completely recovered from. She'd suffered enormously, and she knew she'd never be the same, but she'd be able to put the guilt to rest. Knowing her mother forgave her made it a little easier, and she thanked God.

Rayanne walked over to the telephone, lifted it up, and a smile touched the corners of her lips. She dialed 0, and when the operator answered, Rayanne said, "I'd like to place an overseas call to France."

43

Greg's telephone call was a welcome surprise. Rayanne had contacted everyone about her engagement to Scott. She hadn't talked with Greg, but she'd sent him a note and had followed it up with a message for him to call, and he did.

"How are you, Greg?"

"Can't say I'm as good as you," Greg said. "So you're going to tie the knot?"

"Yeah. It really feels right. I love Scott very much."

"I'm happy for you, doll. I never thought the other guy was good enough for you, anyway. You're one of my favorite people and I'm glad you've moved on."

"You never said a word."

"You're a smart girl, and I knew sooner or later you'd figure it out for yourself. Your mother, the sweet lady that she was, didn't raise no fools."

"Yes, Mama was sweet. She was everything that was good, everything that a mother could be, and she could never be replaced, but you're giving me too much credit, because I almost didn't."

"The important thing is that you did."

"Have I ever told you how important you are to me?"

"Only about a dozen times or so." Greg chuckled.

"Well, I'm telling you again. You're the best. So how is that wonderful wife of yours?"

"Cinnamon is fine, sends her regards."

"You two are coming to my wedding?"

"Of course. My wife loves weddings. Weddings make her happy, and I love keeping her happy."

"Cinnamon is always happy, and why wouldn't she be? She's got a man who simply adores her, has given her two wonderful kids."

"It's more than that. Cinnamon is still spending my money by the truckloads, and that's what is uppermost on the list of things that make her happy. But, you know, money in general makes you women happy."

"Among other things." Rayanne chuckled. "Ivory and Dorian will be coming in to help me plan the wedding. We'll have a nice visit. It'll be like old times. Oh, did I tell you? Ivory is pregnant again, and Dorian is expecting her first."

"Get outta here."

"Ivory has had the ultrasound and it's a boy. She and Desmond are really looking forward to the new addition. Dorian and her Frenchman want to be surprised."

"That's great. You're happy, too, aren't you?" Greg said. "You sound wonderful."

"I'm wonderfully happy."

"This is some shindig you're having."

"It's only money," Rayanne said, smiling.

"Women. But speaking of money"—he chuckled softly— "I tried to reach you yesterday. I wanted to tell you that the fish are biting for your new book."

"You're lying," she said, surprised and elated at the same time.

"Yeah, *My Little Girl* has got them jumping. My phone's ringing off the hook."

"Wow. That's great."

"Is that all you've got to say? I remember years ago

when this was the kind of news you wanted to hear more than anything."

"It's wonderful news, and I hope I don't sound ungrateful, Greg, because I'm extremely happy, just surprised."

"I don't know why. You're a great writer."

"I just hadn't been able to put anything decent together in a long time. That's why this seems so unreal."

"You've had a lot going on in your life. It's understandable that you've had a slow period, but it looks as though things are back on track and we're in business again."

"I love you, Greg," Rayanne said affectionately.

"I know you do," he replied. "We'll be talking soon, and I'll see you at your wedding."

When Rayanne hung up, she jumped up and squealed with delight. She turned to leave the kitchen; then she saw Swan standing in the doorway, her coloring book and crayon in her hands.

"Are you all right, Aunt Rayanne?" Swan asked.

Rayanne walked over and kneeled in front of her. "Yes, darling, I'm fine. Finally, my little girl, everything is fine."

Swan wrapped her arms around Rayanne's neck and squeezed. "I love you, Aunt Rayanne."

"And I love you, Swan. I love you very much."

44

One evening, in Scott's bed, Rayanne snuggled up closely to him. She thought of the call she'd received from Greg several days ago. Scott was working on a job out of town and she'd been so involved with the center that she hadn't had an opportunity to share the news about the book with him yet. They'd just watched a video, and when she heard the song "Hero," Rayanne thought of Josh. He'd gotten his life back and was doing the things he wanted to do. Beverly had taken up with another man, and although Josh didn't like it, he'd accepted it and was moving forward. He was handling his business, and to Rayanne, Josh was a hero, even if he was a hero only to her.

"Who are all those guys?" Scott asked when he tuned in to a hip-hop program on TV.

"That's Wu-Tang Clan," she said.

"Oh, that's the Wu-Tang Clan. I heard Masta Killa has Southern roots."

"That what Bobby and Bruce said. They're always talking about that group, and Brenda's sons, Chris and Devin, buy everything that has Wu-Tang's name on it."

When the video was over, Scott turned off the TV.

"It took Swan a while to get to sleep tonight," he said. "Is she all right?"

"She's excited about us getting married, but Mrs. Marshall did say she had a long nap this afternoon. Swan asked me to say good night to you."

"How did she know you were coming to see me tonight?"

"Because she's a smart little girl."

"She's a terrific kid. It's gonna be so nice when we can be together, without either of us having to get up and go home."

"I know," Rayanne said. She lifted her left hand and smiled admiringly at the ring on her finger.

Scott took her hand and looked at the ring also. "You like it?" he asked.

"I love it."

"I'm glad." He brushed her hair away from her face. "Did you have a good day?"

"I had a great day. Christen called earlier. She thinks she's pregnant. I hope she is. She and John have been trying so long."

"That's why John has been walking around with his chest sticking out." Scott chuckled.

"She'll know next week after her appointment."

"Children certainly do complete families," Scott said, and he turned Rayanne's face so that they faced each other. "How do you feel about children?"

"I love children. You know that."

"I'd like us to have another little girl, just like Swan, and maybe a boy or two."

"A boy or two? My goodness. You must think you've got a young woman here beside you," she teased.

"Baby, you're as young as you feel. How young do you feel?" Scott teased back.

"Oh, about sixteen."

Looking down at Rayanne's pretty, glowing face, Scott said, "We're gonna be together for a very long time. Can you think on those terms?"

"I can think as far as"—she looked adoringly at him—"forever. Is that long enough?"

"Sounds perfect to me." He held her closely a moment before releasing her to say, "Honey, I know planning a wedding is women's doings, but I'd like to make one suggestion."

"Sure."

"I'd like Swan to be a part of our wedding. I don't care which part she plays—well, except the bride, 'cause I already got the perfect person for that part—but I'd like her to be in our wedding and be a part of our lives in every way," he said. Rayanne blinked, feeling so much happiness at that moment that she could hardly breathe. "What do you think?"

"Sweetheart, that's wonderful," she said, and when they kissed, she wanted to swallow his lips.

"Happy?" he asked when the kiss ended.

"Yes, baby," she said. "Scott, there are some things that I haven't had a chance to talk with you about."

"Baby, we've got all the time in the world."

45

That summer proved to be one of the happiest in Rayanne's life. She and Scott had been married nearly two months, and she was still sending out thank-you cards for the wedding gifts they had received. Ivory and Dorian had met Hilary and Brenda when they came for the wedding. They shared some of the same interests and it was agreed that they all would keep in touch. Surely, they would meet again in South Carolina or New York, or the rendezvous could even happen in France, where Dorian lived. These friendships meant that much. These were friendships the ladies wanted to preserve.

That Saturday morning, Scott had gone out with his softball team. Sitting on the front porch, Rayanne had just licked the last envelope and sealed it when Swan stuck her head out the door.

"Aunt Rayanne, are you busy?" she asked, squinting against the brightness of the sun.

"Not anymore," Rayanne said, stacking up the envelopes. "What's up?"

"I want to talk to you," Swan said.

"Then why don't you come over here and sit beside me," Rayanne said, and waited for Swan to walk over and climb into her lap. "I said, sit beside me, not in my lap," she teased. "So what's going on in that pretty little head of yours?"

"A couple of things, actually."

"Actually, huh? I see." Rayanne was impressed by her little girl's word usage. "And they are?"

"When Auntie Christen has her baby, she's going to be my cousin?"

"Yes."

"Do you think she'll like me?"

"Of course, the baby will like you, but what makes you think the baby is going to be a girl? The baby could just as well be a little boy, you know."

"I suppose that's true," Swan said, a thoughtful expression on her little face. "But I hope the baby is a girl."

"Why? Wouldn't you like a little boy cousin just as much?"

"Yes."

"Are you sure?" Rayanne said, holding Swan closely.

"Yes, but I've got something else to tell you."

"Okay, tell me."

"I've decided on a name for the cat that you and Uncle Scott got me."

Scott and Rayanne bought Swan a cat. She loved animals, and the day she got the cat, she took over caring for it, except for the litter pan—that she wouldn't touch—and she treated that cat as though it were a baby.

"You have?"

"Yes."

"That's great. What name did you decide on?"

"Actually, I liked the name you suggested more than any of the names Becky or I thought of."

"Well, don't keep me in suspense." Rayanne gently tapped Swan on the nose with the tip of her finger. "What name did you decide on?"

"Sapphire," Swan said with pride. "I've decided to call her Sapphire. I think it's cool."

Rayanne looked out across the front yard. It was a beautiful day, a perfect day from were she sat on her front porch, and she thanked God for His many blessings. She thought of John and Christen and how happy they were about having an addition to their family. They'd wanted a baby for so long, and just when it seemed they'd given up, or at least had stopped talking about it, Christen became pregnant, and the thought caused Rayanne to smile. She almost laughed out loud, thinking of the morning sickness that plagued John daily.

Maxine and Marcus were as happy as they could be. Bruce and Bobby were doing well in college, and Marcia Raylyn had graduated high school with honors that spring and she, too, would be heading to college that fall.

Rayanne remembered the phone call she got from Lila that morning. She'd been made vice president in the advertising agency where she worked and she was thrilled. It took different things to make people happy, and Rayanne hoped that Lila would always be as happy as she was then. Lila still hadn't found the man of her dreams, but she was happy. When you think about it, that was the important thing.

Ivory and Desmond had toyed with the idea of moving to the south, perhaps Atlanta, nothing definite, but they were thinking about it.

Dorian and her family were doing well in France, where she owned a modeling agency, and her name was often in the fashion magazines. She and Rayanne spoke often.

Rayanne thought of her conversation with Scott that morning before he left for softball practice. Some of the proceeds from her book would go toward funding a center for disadvantaged people. She had a meeting scheduled with some city and county officials and other concerned citizens about situations going on in their cities, as well as across the country, and they wanted to make a difference. The center for the disadvantaged would assist teenagers in earning money to further their education—kids who didn't have any other legitimate resources to do so. Those involved would perform community services, assist in day care centers, and do odd jobs as a way of helping them better themselves.

Rayanne also thought of how much safer her own neighborhood had become. After they formed the Neighborhood Watch, things were better. They had gotten rid of the drug dealer who had moved into Abigail's house, and, amazingly enough, it was a group of women who'd resolved that issue. The women caught the dealer going into his house one night. They tied his hands together, ripped his pants from his body, and it was Aunt Bessie who pointed the barrel of her shotgun into the crack of his behind.

"Will someone make this old woman take that gun out of my ass!" the drug dealer yelled. Not only did Aunt Bessie not remove the point of the gun from where she had it aimed, she cocked it. "Lady, please don't shoot me, please," he pleaded.

Aunt Bessie said, "If you ain't outta that house and this neighborhood within twenty-four hours, we're coming back here, and I can promise you, the next time I won't hesitate to pull the trigger."

Needless to say, the house was empty the next day, and a new FOR SALE sign was posted in the yard soon afterward. A number of women participated, and as the saying goes, there is power in numbers, especially if it is a number of fed-up women. Those women had taken back their neighborhood, and they intended to keep it safe for themselves and their children. Scott had laughed at Aunt Bessie's feistiness when Rayanne revealed to him that Aunt Bessie was a regular Calamity Jane, with that shotgun in her hands.

Rayanne and Scott's conversation the prior night was the

one that prompted her to stop taking her birth control pills. It seemed everyone was having a baby. Despite being in her early forties, who knows? Perhaps they would be announcing another little addition to their family soon. Scott had said to Rayanne that when she got pregnant, he knew her parents, especially her mother, would be smiling down at her from heaven.

Rayanne looked at Swan, sitting in her lap, so peaceful, so happy. She smiled and breathed in the sweet, fresh air. She gave off a little sigh, a happy sigh, as slight breezes drifted across the porch, hinting the air with the aroma from the flowers in the yard. Rayanne hugged Swan close and thought how fortunate she was to be surrounded by such wonderful people. Family and friends were important to Rayanne; they always were, and always would be. She felt like a whole person again. She turned her eyes to the sky and silently thanked God for everything He'd put into her life—her past, her present, and what His plan was for her future.

Rayanne thought how frantic Ivory had been about getting involved with a younger man. Rayanne had also had that same concern, but things were working out very well. She knew that was only because in each situation, there was a lot of love and respect, and as Scott had always said, "Age ain't nothing but a number." Rayanne still believed it.

Rayanne walked barefoot with Swan across the yard and stood in the flower bed in Swan's little garden, feeling the soil between her toes.

"What do you think, Aunt Rayanne?" Swan asked, looking up into Rayanne's face, interrupting her thoughts. "What do you think of calling our kitty, Sapphire?"

Rayanne looked down at Swan and saw in her tiny face peacefulness and tranquility. Exactly the way she felt life should be. After eight years of shouldering the responsibility for her family, and feeling the guilt for their assorted problems, she was finally able to release those burdens and enjoy the freedom of getting on with her own life. It was her time to revel in her happiness, in life and love. Looking forward, she knew that everything was going to be all right.

"I think it's cool, too, Swan," she said. "I think Sapphire is a really cool name."